Dear
Isaac Newton,

You're
Ruining
My Life

Dear Isaac Newton,

You're Ruining My Life

Rachel Hruza

Sky Pony Press
New York

First Edition

This is a work of fiction. Names, characters, places, and incidents are from the author's imagination and used fictitiously.

Sky Pony Press books may be purchased in bulk at special discounts for sales promotion, corporate gifts, fund-raising, or educational purposes. Special editions can also be created to specifications. For details, contact the Special Sales Department, Sky Pony Press, 307 West 36th Street, 11th Floor, New York, NY 10018 or info@skyhorsepublishing.com.

Sky Pony® is a registered trademark of Skyhorse Publishing, Inc.®, a Delaware corporation.

www.skyponypress.com

10 9 8 7 6 5 4 3 2 1

Library of Congress Cataloging-in-Publication Data is available on file.

Cover design by Sammy Yuen

Print ISBN: 978-1-5107-2526-3
Ebook ISBN: 978-1-5107-2528-7

Printed in the United States of America

To every scoli out there,
but especially to the original Scoli Squad:

Mom
Grandma
Sarah
Honorary Members: Dad and John

Thanks for always having my back.
—R.

CHAPTER 1
Gravitational Pull

I hate Isaac Newton. The moment that apple fell from the tree and he thought up gravity was the moment my body was doomed.

Let me back up. I have scoliosis, a sideways curvature of the spine. When people hear the word "scoliosis," they either cringe (because they don't know what it is, or they think it is something they can catch) or laugh (because they're heartless, maniacal jerks). I used to think of Quasimodo, the hunchback in Victor Hugo's story, whenever I heard it. Now, I automatically cower when I hear it, hoping no one associates it with me. I detest saying it, but I hate it even more when other people do.

For most people, scoliosis is something that develops due to genetics, or at least that's what my doctor says about the type I have. But scoliosis doesn't run in my family, so I have no one obvious to point a finger at. Instead, I blame what feels like the most probable cause: gravity, the force pulling everything (my spine included) toward the earth. And whose fault is gravity? Isaac Newton's. Granted, the poor guy didn't *invent* gravity—it had already existed long before a name was given to it—but I like to have someone to blame for my present predicament.

And that present predicament is even worse than just having scoliosis: I found out this summer that I had to start wearing a brace for it. A *brace*.

There are various kinds of braces depending on curvature and necessity, but I ended up with a Boston brace because my curve was low enough. Boston braces are made of white plastic and lined with a thin "cushion," though I use that word liberally. Fastened with Velcro straps, the brace hugs the body, pushing against the curve to keep it from shifting further, and it can be concealed under clothing.

At least Newton and his gravity were considerate enough for *that*.

But even with the brace worn under my clothes, I was still afraid of what people would think and say about me. Pretending people wouldn't say things behind my back (literally) made me angry, and knowing they'd be staring and whispering made my belly boil with a rage and fear I couldn't handle. I kept thinking about my best friend, Megan, and whether she'd want to be associated with a girl who had to be strapped into a plastic container every morning. What kind of clothes would I even wear? Megan and I loved to shop together; maybe she wouldn't want to shop with me anymore.

I also couldn't stop my mind from picturing one boy's perfect face: Brendan Matthews, fellow seventh-grader, beauteous maximus. For over a year, I'd had a major crush on him. And I'd just been preparing myself to talk to him this year.

Last year he was in my math class, and I hoped he would be again. I had dreams that we'd be table partners and we'd fall in love over quadratic equations and polynomials. He'd plot points onto graph paper so they formed a heart, and then he'd give the heart to me so everyone would know we were meant to be together.

But with a huge piece of plastic wrapped around me, how could I lean close to him as he whispered ratios and proportions equal to his desire for me?

I couldn't. And Brendan definitely wouldn't want to whisper to a plastic-cased, seventh-grade nobody.

Perhaps the worst thing to think about was that the doctor said it was impossible to cure my scoliosis. We could only expect the brace to hold my curve where it was, and possibly keep it from getting worse. *Possibly.* But "possibly" getting worse was a lot better than *definitely* getting worse, which was what was happening without the brace.

Thanks for nothing, Newton.

Before my diagnosis, I thought I knew everything about who I was and what I looked like. I'm Truth Trendon: daughter of Bob and Sue, younger sister of Charity and older sister of Harold. (My parents, who had two of the most boring names in the world, had clearly tried to get creative with their children.)

My name used to bother me, because people always thought it was strange, but it's grown on me. I like that it's unique.

My sister feels the same way. We used to pretend to be superheroes: Charity and Truth Trendon, fighting for justice and the American way. When my brother was born, I was rooting for a name like Freedom or Virtue, or even Patriot, but they went with Harold. Now he's six and sounds like he's a sixty-year-old.

At least people don't ask him if he can't lie. I get that all the time.

As for looks, I have my father's nose, my mother's mouth, and neither of their eyes. I have curly brown hair, and once in a while I get a recurring zit on my forehead. It used to be I could run the fastest of any girl or boy in the fifth grade, and I could swish a basketball from anywhere inside the three-point line. Then stupid Newton played his cruel joke, and gravity took over my body and bent my spine back on itself.

I first noticed it after a shower at the age of ten, which is way too young to have to realize horrible things about yourself. I stepped out of the tub and turned to grab my towel from the rack, but then I paused, staring at my back in the mirror. It was like a scene in a monster movie—as if my body was changing before my very eyes.

My right shoulder was tilted forward, rolled as if it had always been that way, while my shoulder blade stuck out in back a bit too. No matter how I adjusted my posture, I couldn't make either of them sit normally back in place. I turned to see if my other shoulder stuck out, hoping that maybe I was growing wings or was a half-dragon just acquiring my abilities, but my left side remained as I remembered it. Normal.

I stared at my face in the mirror. Somehow, even my nose, chin, and ears seemed different. My vision started to blur. Then I threw up.

5

Scoliosis—the word hissed just like the snakelike villain it was. It had crept up and caught me without my knowledge. I hadn't felt a twinge of pain or any shift in my bones. Newton's evil changes were silent and so swift that I didn't notice them until it was too late.

The only person I try to hate more than Newton is my doctor. Dr. Clarkson is an orthopedic surgeon who looks like a clown with his frizzy hair and bald spot in the middle of his head, and he talks into a tiny recorder all the time. I've been to see him about ten times, and I think he's said a total of seven words to me.

The first time I visited Dr. Clarkson, he placed the x-ray of my torso up on the screen, and I burst into tears. It looked so terrible—the way my spine rose out of my hips and then, about midway up, began to curve into my right shoulder blade. My mom, dad, and Charity were there with me. My dad, an accountant who covers well when he's upset, stood with his arms crossed over his chest like a superhero listening to a villain's plans to take over the world. My mom, a self-declared "part-time librarian, full-time lover of books" and the person most responsible for my love of reading, put her arms around me as we listened to Dr. Clarkson say, "Truth Trendon, ten-year-old female, scoliotic curve of eighteen degrees. Monitor for a year—"

And then he was out the door.

I made it through fifth and sixth grade okay, going to the doctor regularly to make sure my curve didn't change too drastically. Over two years, it shifted from eighteen to twenty-five degrees, which, according to my doctor, wasn't enough of a change to show concern. I could live with a curve of twenty-five degrees without much worry. So I didn't worry. Much.

Which brings us to this summer, when I found out my curve *had* changed since my previous visit, from twenty-five to thirty-eight degrees. My spine looked like a winding road, and I didn't have the map.

Dr. Clarkson just dictated to his dumb handheld tape recorder, "Truth Trendon, twelve-year-old female, curvature shifted to thirty-eight degrees. We will brace and continue to monitor."

At the word "brace," I felt my whole body go numb. It was as if I'd been smacked in the nose, and I couldn't stop the tears from welling up and crashing over my eyelids, no matter how hard I tried. I badly wanted to believe this was all a terrible dream.

But it wasn't a dream. It was real. And it was my life.

A week later, when Christopher Robertson, orthotic practitioner, walked into the room where I waited with my mom, I was contemplating a possible scientific and sure way to murder gravity. He was holding a huge white whale of plastic, and I almost leaped out of my seat and ran for the door. Instead, I said, "Are you crazy? There's no way that's going to fit."

"I have to cut the brace down to fit you," Christopher said. "Stand up for me."

I did, and he wrapped the brace around me. I was fully clothed, but the plastic dug hard into my skin.

I raised my arms so Christopher could take measurements and push on different levels of the brace. The left side of the brace came up and dug deep into my armpit. It had an opening for my ribs underneath that allowed them to be shoved out the hole while the right side of the brace pushed against my curve—that was how the brace straightened me out. In front, the brace came up too high at the moment, over my "barely-there-breasts" (as Charity called them). Christopher reminded me the brace would be cut down to fit me, so my fear of my chest being mashed to smithereens faded. He also told me he would cut a small gap in the front of the brace to release the pressure on my right ribs.

At least Christopher was quiet and listened to me, even though I refused to speak other than in response to his questions. But I quit listening as he went into more detail, and I didn't make eye contact with Mom, because if I did, I knew I would start crying.

He took the brace off me. "When I come back, I promise this will be much smaller," he said.

When Christopher came back the second time, he chatted with my mom about how he had made a brace for a girl in a wheelchair, and she loved it because it helped her sit up.

"It just shows you should be grateful your situation isn't worse," he said, a bit choked up.

I wanted to kick him. Not only did I have to wear a hulking white monstrosity, but now I had to feel guilty about some poor girl I didn't even know.

"That's true," my mom agreed. She tried to smile at me, but I looked away. She was siding with the enemy.

Christopher wrapped the brace around me and wrote on it with a black marker to diagram a few more places to cut the plastic away. Despite the very thin cushioning material glued to the plastic, the brace was hard and dug aggressively into my bones. In front, the brace still came up just past my bra line, making the elastic of my sports bra burrow into my skin. Meanwhile, the left side of the brace still invaded my armpit and extended down past my hip.

Christopher hadn't lied; the brace was a lot smaller now, but I really didn't know how I would find clothes to fit over it. It was not like a corset—sure, it strapped me in, but it was thick and hard, and it definitely didn't make me more attractive.

The third time Christopher came back, he had put thick Velcro straps on the back of the brace. Now he could tighten it up, and when he did, it actually took my breath away. I felt like all the air had left my lungs and there was no way any was getting back in. He disappeared once more to cut the excess Velcro. This time I cried when he left. It seemed so real now; the thing fit me.

Christopher returned with the finished brace and two stretchy white cotton shirts to wear underneath to keep it from rubbing against my skin. I hated to think of all the other girls at school who would be able to wear tank tops in the hundred-degree August heat, while I'd be trapped in my own insulated plastic sauna. Probably covered in a muumuu. At least I'd be colorful.

Since the clothes I had on weren't going to fit over the brace, Christopher strapped the brace over

my clothes, and I wore it out to the car. It was difficult to walk since the back of the brace dug into my
butt cheeks as if it were trying to mold them into
Silly Putty. I'd never had a tiny rear end, but I didn't
necessarily want a big flat one either.

I couldn't fight back more tears as my mom
helped me into the car. She *had* to help. I couldn't
get in on my own. I bent my knees and she gently
pushed me into the front passenger seat.

I kept crying as she drove out of the parking lot.

"It'll be okay, Tru," she said. "It'll be okay."

I didn't say anything.

After ten minutes, I undid my seatbelt, reached
behind me with my right hand, and pulled the Velcro apart. Immediately the pressure gave way, and
after a bit of fumbling, I pried the brace off and
threw it onto the back seat of the car. Its sides
clacked together like two cymbals, only the sound of
the plastic was short and hollow. It looked huge and
evil, as if it were taking up the entire back seat.

Even if it was going to help me, I hated it.

Mom and I spent the drive home mostly in silence.
She'd wanted to take me shopping for clothes to
wear with my new brace, but I nixed that idea right
off the bat. If I didn't have clothes to wear over it, I
wouldn't be able to wear it in public.

At least, that was the plan until I got home and Mom pulled out a pair of jeans she'd worn when she was pregnant. I tried them on. The elastic band was still a little baggy over the bulky square brace. But I tied a shoelace around the top of the jeans, and that kept them up. Great! Now, rockin' my mom's preggo pants, I could try to live life to the fullest as a freak of nature.

I borrowed Charity's cell phone (a technological luxury granted in my family once we hit high school) and called Megan so she could commiserate with me, but she didn't answer. She was having a wonderful time on vacation while I was trapped in my own personal, portable torture chamber.

At dinner that first night, I tried to make a joke about being trapped in Tupperware, but no one really laughed. Harold just looked at me, sitting in my high-waisted pregnant-mom jeans with my brace showing, and said, "It has to have a name. Herman."

I scowled at him, but Charity grinned. She was two years older than me, a soon-to-be ninth grader, and she knew what cool was. "Herman," she laughed. "That's perfect, Harry."

"You should decorate it," Mom said.

"No way," I replied. "You guys can name it, pet it, and feed it when I'm not wearing it, but there's no way I'm going to attach myself to it. The sooner this piece of crap is out of my life, the better!"

Dad looked at me. He hadn't said much since I'd gotten home and Mom had re-strapped me into the brace—just patted me on the head when I'd tried, somewhat unsuccessfully, to flop onto the living room couch before dinner (I'd crushed my right pinkie under the plastic that jutted out by my hip).

"Think of it as a big, long hug," Harold said. He was getting far too excited about this scoliosis thing. He'd even drawn a picture of the family where everyone else looked normal, but my caricature was a stick-figure with a crooked spine. Mom made him throw it away, but not before I saw it.

"Think if I gave you a big, long punch in the face," I said.

"Truth!" my mom cried.

"I'm not hungry."

I pushed out my chair and stood up. The brace dug into my already sore butt muscles.

"Ow!"

I leaned forward so the plastic didn't dig in behind. Then it dug into my hip bones. "This isn't fair!" I shouted, waddling out of the room. I paused, to see if anyone said anything. Nobody did.

They all felt bad for me.

That night, taking my brace off before bed and letting it clunk against the floor didn't even feel good: in the darkness, the brace's opening for my ribs looked like a wide, smiling mouth that was laughing at me.

Chapter 2
Braced

"How do you breathe in it?" Megan asked. She held up the brace and looked through the middle of it, which wasn't even twelve inches wide. She'd just returned from a family vacation, and I was relieved to finally get to see her again and show her my brace. School was starting in a few days, and after three weeks, I'd kind of grown accustomed to wearing the enormous eyesore. The first few days, I'd worn it for just four hours at a time, building up to wearing it during all waking hours. Figuring out how to do things like use the toilet had been a nightmare—my mom and Charity had found me weeping on the bathroom floor with my pants around my ankles, since I couldn't reach them to pull them up.

"It was rough at first," I admitted, sprawling out on Megan's bright green comforter. I wanted to take advantage of every moment I had out of the brace, so I moved my body in every direction I could.

I saw a book on the bed and picked it up, laughing. It was a dictionary—Megan's goal for the summer had been to read the entire thing. Her bookmark was in the G's, but I don't think she'd even made it that far.

Megan slipped the brace on over her t-shirt and jean shorts, standing there with the three Velcro straps undone. Immediately her expression shriveled to one of disgust. She looked down at it, her long, blond hair covering her hazel eyes.

"Do you want me to strap you into it?" I asked her.

"No way. This totally sucks," she said.

"For me," I retorted.

"Yeah," Megan sighed. "I feel bad for you." She paused as she slipped the brace off. Her hands reached behind her, grabbing each end of the brace's open back, and I watched as she struggled to stretch it around her hips. By now, I'd gotten the hang of it and could rip that thing off in one second flat once I'd undone the Velcro.

As Megan lowered the brace to the ground, her eyes narrowed. I knew she was trying to incorporate one of her new vocabulary words. "I have *fortitude* for you."

That's not what I wanted to hear from Megan.

She was supposed to act like everything was exactly the same as it had always been.

"No. No pity from you. And *fortitude* means strength or bravery." I threw a pillow at her. It hit her in the face, and she dropped the brace on the floor. It thumped against the carpet and shook slightly as it settled there.

"Oh no! Did I break it?" she asked.

"I wish. And I'm serious. Don't pity me."

"I won't." Megan put out her hand and we slapped each other five.

"Remember when Tyler Thompson said the high five would never be cool because we were the ones trying to bring it back?" I said. We'd been trying to make the high five cool again for years.

Megan flopped onto the bed next to me. "Yeah, he's a total jerk-face. And totally wrong! We're bringin' back the high five one hand at a time, girl!"

She put out her hand again. I rolled my eyes at her as I pushed her hand away. "I think he was right."

Megan laughed. "Shut up, Tru." Her face lit up. "Speaking of Tyler Thompson, his sister Hannah told me Brendan knows you have a crush on him."

"No!" I said. I sat up immediately.

"Yes!"

"That's horrific news!" I flopped back on the bed and covered my face.

"Why? You've liked him since fifth grade," Megan said.

No matter how hard I tried to explain it to her, Megan would never understand. She was my best friend, and unless I did something crazy like spread an awful rumor about her or kill her pet cat, Mr. Winston, she would always think of me in the same way: like her.

But now, I wasn't. Isaac Newton didn't have it out for her like he did for me.

I shook my fist in the air, cursing Newton and his love of apple trees. I sat up again and pointed at the bane of my junior high existence.

"That's why," I said. "How can I talk to Brendan when I'm wearing body armor?"

"I'm sure nobody will even care, and it's not that big of a deal anyway," Megan replied.

"Yeah? Well I'm sure Brendan will take one look at me and my square hips and smashed butt and run screaming in the other direction."

"You never know. Maybe that's what he's into."

Megan winked at me, and I couldn't help but laugh. Megan always knew how to make me laugh, no matter what.

"Did you get your class schedule?" she asked me.

"Came in the mail last week." I'd memorized it already, and I blurted out the list.

"Slow down," Megan said. "What's after lunch?"

We compared schedules, and they were the same, except for Gym and study hall. Megan was disappointed because we wouldn't be able to hide in the locker room during weight-lifting class or pass notes in study hall. I was upset because I realized I'd have to find someone else to help me put my brace back on after Gym. My doctor had cleared me to take off the brace for any kind of sports, which was one reason I was especially excited about volleyball starting up soon. Charity had been on the junior high team, and I loved practicing with her and going to her games—this year, it was finally going to be my turn to play on a real team, too. The doctor didn't have any problem with me playing, which was a relief—staying agile and strong was important for keeping good posture when I wasn't wearing the brace and for the future, when I wouldn't have to wear it ever again. That future seemed like a dream. For now, I was just glad for any opportunity to take the thing off. However, I didn't know if there was someone else I could trust to help me with the Velcro straps, and I'd be mortified if I had to ask Mrs. Tomjack, the girls' P.E. teacher.

"I may end up hiding in the locker room every day," I said.

"Knock it off. Gym is one of your favorite classes. Maybe I can sneak out of study hall to help you."

"Maybe," I said.

Megan liked to try to break the rules, but she usually chickened out when it came time to follow through. I was the one who always ended up sneaking out of my house at night to walk the block to Megan's house so she could let me in her open window. She'd only tried it once, and she'd turned around when she'd heard a cricket chirp. I didn't trust her to break the rules in front of her parents, let alone a teacher who might give her a detention.

"I better put it back on." I stood up and lifted the brace under my shirt. I shifted it around my hips and felt the uncomfortably familiar smashing of my rear and the tight cinching of my waist. Megan threaded the three straps through their corresponding metal loops, pulling them as tight as she could.

I liked to wear the brace as tight as possible for two reasons: one, hopefully it would fix my spine and make it straight again (or at least straighten it a bit); and two, if it was flush against my body, maybe no one would notice it.

I'd decided that I would not let wearing this back

brace change me at all. No one would know I was wearing it or treat me differently because of it, and everything would be normal.

"C'mon," Megan said. "Maybe my dad will take us to get ice cream. One last hurrah before school starts."

"School doesn't start for three days. We'll have plenty of time for a last hurrah," I said.

Megan rolled her eyes. "I'm trying to get free ice cream, Tru. Don't ruin it for the both of us."

"Sorry. What was I thinking?"

I followed Megan out of her bedroom and into the hallway. Megan's dad, Mr. Borowitz (Mr. B, as I called him), worked from home as a life coach and inspirational speaker. He came and spoke at our school at least once a year. Last year, he talked about achieving our dreams, and the year before, he talked about the importance of education. He used to joke he was going to step in for the school nurse to tell us about our "changing bodies," and Megan always played along, telling him she'd ask the most embarrassing questions if he did.

"Hey, Pops!" Megan said, as she walked into his office. "Hit us up with some frozen treats!"

Mr. B turned around in his computer chair and smiled. "I just took you yesterday, Megs."

"But Truth is here now, and she really wants to go," Megan whined.

I was always Megan's scapegoat. I didn't mind; apparently I was good at it. She usually got what she wanted.

"Yep," I said.

"I see," Mr. B said. He winked at me. "Well, I just happen to have some time in my schedule. I can work in a quick ice cream break."

On the way to the ice cream shop, I caught Mr. B staring at me in the rearview mirror every so often. I think he was trying to figure out what my brace looked like. Apparently he was fascinated by it and wanted to ask me a bunch of questions, but Megan wouldn't let him. He was probably rolling ideas around in his head for a new inspirational speech.

I didn't want to be inspirational. I just wanted to be "Truth Trendon, normal person."

Not wanting to appear any different than I did before, I sat as still as possible with my hands in my lap. Then I relaxed—I'd never thought about how to sit before, so why start now? I'd probably draw more attention to myself trying to act normal than I would just being myself.

We pulled up to Udder Perfection. It was one of those locally owned shops that had a window you ordered at rather than going inside the building. There were picnic tables next to the building, and Mr. B sat down after giving us money for the ice cream. Megan got a large cone for herself, but I ordered a small because I didn't want to take advantage of Mr. B's money. Plus, ever since I got the brace, I couldn't eat as much as I used to because it squeezed my stomach too tight. I took the change back to Mr. B while Megan waited for our cones.

"Thanks, Mr. B," I said, handing him the dollars and coins. A quarter slipped off my hand onto the ground.

"Oops," he said.

"I got it." I bent over and grabbed the silver coin. Since the bathroom floor incident, I'd become more limber, bending my knees more often and figuring out how to rely more on my waist than my spine. "Here you go."

"Your brace comes down that far on your hips?" Mr. B asked, looking at me.

"What?" I said.

Megan walked up with our cones.

"I could see it when you bent over," Mr. B said. "I didn't know it came down that far."

"You could see it?" I asked him, panicked. No one had said that the past few weeks I'd been wearing it.

"Oh. My. Lord. Dad!" Megan said. She handed me my cone. The pink ice cream was already leaking down the side of the cone, like the sweat droplets that had suddenly formed on my forehead.

"I'm sorry! I didn't mean—I wouldn't even know you had one on if Megan hadn't said you were getting one," Mr. B said.

"It's okay," I said. Though in my mind, I was freaking out. For one thing, my mom and I had specifically shopped for clothes that completely hid my brace. Normally, I wore a size five in shorts, but I had to get a size eleven to find a pair that would come up to the waist of the brace above the hip parts that jutted out. And I had to tie my pants with a shoelace to keep them up, since no belt seemed to work with my plastic torso. Leather, cloth, macramé—they were either too big or rigid, or they stuck out abnormally far from my pants. And there was no way I wanted to risk the possibility of my pants falling to my ankles when I stood up at school, so, shoelace: welcome to my waist.

"Good grief, Father," Megan said. She rolled her eyes. Both Mr. B and I knew she was upset. She only called him "Father" when she was angry with him. He just shook his head. I could tell he felt bad about saying anything.

"Really, Megan," I said, licking ice cream off my fingers, "it's okay."

But I wasn't hungry anymore, and I would have thrown the cone away if Mr. B hadn't paid for it.

The ride home was quiet. After he parked the car, Mr. B apologized again and quickly disappeared into the house. Megan remained in her seat, and after a few seconds turned to look at me. "Truth, I'm sorry. You know my dad can be such a tool. Like, a real wrench."

I knew she was trying to make me laugh. In the next few days, with school starting, I wouldn't be doing much laughing. I couldn't even commit myself to not dropping anything, because I was clumsy with my fingers; pencils always found their way onto the floor, and I'd have to chase them so people walking by didn't trip on them as they passed. Once, our elementary school principal actually tripped over *me*. I, of course, was trying to keep the hallway safe by grabbing a pencil.

Bending over was inevitable. People seeing my brace was inevitable.

We climbed out of the car, and I turned to Megan.

"Here's hoping for oblivious classmates," I said, raising my melted ice cream cone as a toast to the new school year.

"To oblivious classmates!" Megan shouted.

She whacked her ice cream cone against mine, which sent a lump of melted vanilla sailing across the front yard.

We laughed until Megan had tears in her eyes and I had fallen to my knees because I couldn't get enough air. My ice cream had basically melted down the cone and onto my hand, but we shared what was left of it as we walked into the house.

Even though it was difficult to laugh, knowing there was someone to laugh with me rather than at me made me think I could do this. I could survive junior high under the heavy thumb of Newton's law of gravity.

Maybe.

CHAPTER 3
The First Day of the Rest of My Life

My mom told me I didn't have to wear my brace the first day of school if I didn't want to.

I graciously accepted her offer with a loud and excited "Heck no, I don't!"

Therefore, I was actually excited for morning when I went to bed the night before school began.

I'd already laid out my outfit on the bench at the foot of my bed—a habit of mine since kindergarten, when I decided I was old enough to dress myself. I used to try to always wear the wackiest thing I could find. I went through a phase of polka-dot pants with zebra-striped shirts, and jewelry all colors of the rainbow. Some days I wore pajamas. My parents saw it as me becoming an individual, but when I walked into class wearing furry footie pj's, my teacher told Mom it was okay if I was late to class if she needed more time to dress me.

Fortunately, I grew out of that phase. Unfortunately, I now had a complete fear of fashion. It was bad enough before getting a back brace. I was terrible at the whole "layering" look, and most days Megan would stop by on her way to the bus stop to make sure I was presentable. Some people might say that's an insult, but not me. I know my strengths, and dressing cool isn't one of them.

I wasn't worried about tomorrow, though. Megan had helped me pick out a short jean skirt (one my mother might have nixed for school, except she probably felt bad I never got to wear it anymore), a tank top with fabric flowers on the straps, and a pair of teal flip-flops. I was happy I might actually look good for one day out of the whole school year.

That night, for the first time in over a month, I fell asleep with a smile on my face.

The morning of the first day back to school, my head popped off the pillow as lightning shattered the skyline, thunder reverberated off the windows, and dark, dismal clouds bulged across the heavens without an end in sight.

I threw on my summery outfit anyway and ran downstairs. Already dressed for work in his dark gray suit and blue tie, my father looked at my skirt, caught me by the shoulders at the bottom of the stairs, and spun me around to face the way I'd come.

"Coldest day for August on record. Put some clothes on," he said.

"But Da-ad!" I cried. "This is the only chance I get to show people I'm not shaped like SpongeBob SquarePants!"

Harold, who was eating cereal at the kitchen table, looked up at me. "You don't look like Sponge-Bob," he said. "SpongeBob is cuter."

I took off a flip-flop and threw it at his face. It landed in his Cheerios.

"Come on, Tru. Put some jeans on. It's just school." Charity grimaced as she pulled the rubber shoe out of Harold's bowl, dripping milk. It was easy for Charity to act as if she wasn't excited, but I knew she was nervous about starting high school—she'd even had Mom iron her plain white cotton t-shirt.

Junior high (comprising the hormonal craziness of seventh and eighth grades) and high school were based in the same building, but junior high was separated into a completely different section. Moving from one section of the building to the other was a major shift on the social scale. Freshmen were peons to the rest of the grades in high school, while junior high kids were peons to freshmen.

Really, I had three years—seventh grade, eighth grade, and then finally my high school freshman year—left at the bottom of the student ranks, but this year was the dirt-level bottom. The lowest of the low.

"Why don't you have Mom iron your push-up bra too, Charity?" I said, trying to sound as bratty as I meant to be. "Oh wait, it's just school."

"Trendons, unite!" my father shouted in the loud bass voice he saved for church choir solos. We all stared at him. "Knock it off," he said. "Truth, change your clothes. Harold, quit eating that dirty-sandal cereal. Charity, you're going to love high school." He put his hand out as if he were a coach in the middle of a huddle. Nobody joined him. "Break!" he shouted, throwing his hand in the air.

I turned and stomped up the stairs. Dad followed me and grabbed my arm. He spoke quietly. "You're pushing people's buttons, Tru, but we're *on your side.* We're all rooting for you. Remember that, okay?"

He looked up at me from the bottom step and I could tell he meant it. It was hard to stay mad at my dad. He was right. I was pushing buttons. I *wanted* to push them. Because Isaac Newton had already pushed mine.

As I walked to the bus stop, the cold rain stung my skin through my blue long-sleeved t-shirt and jeans. I could have been wearing the stupid brace for all anyone knew. Though at least I had a day off from the skin pinching, bruise rubbing, and constant sweating. One of my personal goals for the day was to come home and still actually smell good.

I met Megan at our bus stop, and she knew instantly why I was upset. Her sympathetic smile didn't erase my disappointment, but it at least helped me hope that the day would be downhill from here.

After the fifteen-minute homeroom period, my first class was Band. And at West River Junior High, Band was not lame and full of dorky kids; everybody who was anybody was in Band. We had almost one hundred members. The high school band had a great reputation, and we all wanted to be a part of the magic when we got there. We were all band geeks and happy about it.

I played the trumpet. When I'd started in fifth grade, I'd wanted something loud because I had always been a quiet person. It was my chance to be the leader, to blast explosive notes like a cannonball shooting out of a cannon. I can play quiet, graceful notes too (I'll admit it—I'm pretty good), but the loud notes are the most fun.

Brendan played the trumpet too. I could barely contain my smile as I saw an open seat next to him.

Megan watched me from the clarinet section, her reed hanging out of her mouth as she softened it with saliva (one reason why I didn't want a reed instrument—gross). She jerked her head, coaxing me to sit down. Then she got a crazed look on her face and jerked her head faster and faster, as if she were having spasms. The girl next to her started to look concerned. I frowned, tilted my head, and mouthed the word *what?*

A blonde blur jetted past me, her swaying hips pushing me back a few steps. Jennifer Henderson took the seat next to Brendan. Megan rolled her eyes at me and shook her head. I knew what she was thinking: y*a snooze, ya lose.*

My shoulders drooped and I sighed, causing the bell of my trumpet to poke Jennifer.

"Can I help you?" she asked, clearly not offering help.

"No. Sorry, Jenny," I squeaked.

I sat a few chairs down. Jennifer Henderson was *that* girl—yep, you guessed it: every guy liked her and every girl wanted to be her. Except me. Not only was Jenny rude, she sucked at playing the trumpet. She'd joined band because everyone else did, and she'd never really learned how to play.

I glared at Jennifer's head, which was turned toward Brendan, for several minutes—hoping that, if

I willed it, I could control her mind and make her give up her seat. It didn't work. Then Mr. Weaver, the band director, called us to attention, gave us a run-down of his plan for the year, and warmed us up.

We played a few new songs, and after I'd built up my self-esteem by proving my sight-reading skills still held up after not practicing as much as I should have over the summer, Mr. Weaver asked me to play the solo part. I immediately turned red, but I played it for the rest of the band. A couple of people clapped and some rolled their eyes, but I didn't care. I liked playing my trumpet.

"Nice tongue work, Trendon," a voice said.

My heart skipped a beat as I turned to look at the marvelous lips that had spoken. It was him.

"Thanks, Matthews," I said. I was hoping to sound cool by also using his last name, but I knew I probably just sounded too excited. Still, Brendan grinned.

"Sounded too spitty to me," Jenny said, staring at me. "Sloppy."

I looked at her, but I didn't say anything. I was floating on air at the thought of Brendan grinning at me. If there hadn't been a herd of musicians in the classroom, I would have danced out of the room when the bell rang. Instead, I waited dreamily for people to stack their chairs and followed the line out of the door. As I wondered what I looked like from behind—if people noticed my shoulder blade jutting out of my back like a shark fin—Megan sidled up next to me.

"Hey, Hot Stuff!" she said.

I let my hips sway a little bit in my form-fitting jeans. I wouldn't be able to do that after today.

Well, I *could*, but my whole upper half would rock back and forth like a fishing bobber.

"Did you hear him compliment me?" I asked Megan, lowering my voice.

"Yeah. Jennifer didn't seem too impressed, though." She winked.

I smiled.

The junior high lockers were nearest the band room, and two people were assigned to one locker, but we were allowed to pick our locker partner. Naturally, Megan and I were together. When we reached our locker, Megan opened it and made kissing noises. She'd brought photos cut out from magazines of several singers and movie stars she had crushes on and stuck them to the inside of the locker with magnets. They gazed out at us with sultry eyes and seriously pouted lips.

I sighed. I missed the pictures of cute dogs and neon cartoon animals.

"When did we get so boy crazy?" I asked.

"When boys started to look so crazy good," Megan said.

I looked once more at the paper faces staring back at us. She had a point. We shut our locker and walked to Algebra together. When we entered the classroom, I saw the desks were made for two people each. Brendan sat in the back, next to one of his friends. His slightly curly blond hair hung just above his green eyes, which seemed to absorb all of the light in the room as he listened to his friend tell a joke. A pale blue shirt covered his broad shoulders. His jaw was square but strong, and when he laughed, it was all I could do to keep myself from dropping my notebook and running to the back row to join in.

Watching him, I wondered just how much I would pale in comparison if I were sitting next to him, or better yet, if my hand were clasped in his, walking next to him in the hallway. When I remembered that after today I would be boxed tightly within my brace, I wanted to cry. Instead, I felt Megan tap my arm.

All the desks surrounding Brendan were taken. Noting this with a sad smile to Megan, I sat next to her in the front row. When the bell rang, our Algebra teacher, Miss Peters, one of the youngest teachers at the school, announced there would be seating assignments. The eighteen of us groaned collectively and slowly crawled out of our chairs.

Miss Peters was wearing a royal blue dress that showed off her small waist and flared out to just above her knees. Her makeup was always just right—not too much. I'd heard from Charity that her favorite days were when students complained—apparently Miss Peters liked the challenge of getting through to crappy students.

She smiled brightly, the ends of her straight brown hair dancing around her chin as she turned her head. "I'm glad I could make you all so happy on our first day back."

Several people laughed, including me.

Miss Peters stood in front of the first desk and pointed to each seat as she called out our names. "Callie Anderson. Megan Borowitz."

I waved forlornly to Megan as Miss Peters called out, "Truth Trendon. Brendan Matthews."

And then I tripped on the chair leg in front of me.

"It's cool. I'm cool," I said, collapsing in my seat, so embarrassed I wanted to self-combust.

"Have a nice trip?" Brendan asked me as he sat down.

I felt a buzzing in my veins; the fine hairs on my arms were standing on end. He was so close.

"Nothing broken, so yes. Yes, I did."

Megan was at the desk in front of us, leaning back in her chair to listen. Miss Peters wasn't playing favorites; she didn't even know us. But this seating arrangement was perfect. I liked having Megan so close to me when I was close to an Adonis like Brendan Matthews. She gave me confidence, or at least made me feel like I couldn't just sit there like a bump on a log.

"Good." Brendan grinned. I smiled and took a deep breath to calm my racing heart.

We didn't talk much for the rest of the class, since Miss Peters explained most of her goals for the year and what we could expect from the assignments and tests for grading.

I found myself sitting very still. My wish had come true. If I moved less than a foot to the right, I would brush against his arm. It was tan from a summer of baseball and basketball camps.

I was tan from going to the swimming pool and my general outdoorsy-ness, but I didn't seem to glisten like Brendan did. I wondered how much of my vision of him was "influenced by my hormones," as my mother would say.

I'd known Brendan since first grade. Back then, he was just another boy in my school. But then, in fifth grade, I ran into him at the grocery store when we both reached for the same box of cereal. I'd just wanted to get my chocolatey, sugar-coated corn puffs, but once my hand brushed his and my blue eyes met his green ones, I was captivated.

"Sorry," he said, and handed me the box. Then he took the next box in the row and walked away.

I clutched his gift in my arms for the rest of the grocery trip.

The very next day, my dad had a bumper-to-bumper accident with Brendan's mother outside a fast-food place where we were picking up burgers, and it felt like fate. Mrs. Matthews wasn't cordial at all (she kicked my dad's tire even though the accident had been her fault), but Brendan was a dream. While our parents exchanged insurance information and we waited for the police to arrive to determine fault (again, hers), Brendan and I talked about our favorite school subjects (his: math, mine: also math), our favorite TV shows (his: some sports show, mine: a blatant lie about the same sports show), and even what we wanted to be when we grew up (him: professional football player, me: zoo veterinarian). I also found out he lived within walking distance of my house, just ten or so blocks away.

Matters were wrapped up between our parents all too soon, but I can still remember the last thing he said to me that day: "See you around, Trendon."

Since then, I was hooked. And now, sitting at the same desk, I had the chance look at, or even speak to him whenever I got the courage, every day in math.

When the bell rang, I pushed away from our desk and stood up, my arms wrapped around my books.

"Glad I'm sitting by someone smart," Brendan said.

"Me too," I said. I wanted him to grin again. He did.

"Is algebra your thing?" he asked.

We started to walk out of the classroom.

"It's up there," I said, disappointed he didn't remember our convo from two years before. "I like English too."

"English isn't for me. But math fits my brain like a glove."

"A numbers man. The world can never have enough."

"Glad to know you feel that way, Trendon. See you around." Brendan smiled and walked down to his locker.

"Okay," I breathed. He'd uttered nearly the same words at our last major discussion.

"Penny for your thoughts?" Megan said from behind me.

"I wouldn't sell them for a million dollars," I replied. I began to skip down the hallway, and Megan ran after me. "That's enough celebration, Tru."

A sophomore walked by us. "Dork," he said to me.

I immediately stopped skipping.

"Ignore him. He's the one going to Algebra for the third year in a row," Megan said.

I didn't even care. My heart was carrying me to my locker on a cloud. And that cloud was fluffed, plumped, and comfortable enough for me to ride it all day. Even though the rest of my classes were incredibly boring and uneventful, I frolicked home from the bus stop that afternoon with light, happy feet.

"Best day of school ever!" I declared as I walked through the door.

"Nuh-uh!" Harold was already at the kitchen table, eating a brownie with my mother.

"It was for me." I dropped my backpack and stuffed a brownie in my mouth. "Kir gra na wha oo espeda?"

"Truth. Some manners, please," Mom said.

I swallowed. "Sorry. These are excellent brownies, Mom. I should have said that right away."

She laughed. "No. Your brother. He had a rough day."

"Let me try again, Sir Harold. Kindergarten not what you expected?"

"No," Harold grumbled. "We're stuck in this huge room, and everyone has their own cubicle they have to keep organized, and there's a guinea pig that everyone in the class gets to take home for a weekend during the year."

"That sounds fantastic!" I said. I wanted him to bring the guinea pig home soon, but I bet I'd never see the furry thing because Harold and Charity both had allergies to pet dander.

"Go on, Harold," Mom said, her voice sympathetic.

Harold paused and then launched into an angry rant. "The stupid pig's name is Hairy, with an *i*, and when the teacher called on me to answer a question, she called me Harry instead of Harold."

"So?"

"Everyone started laughing, and all day they called me Human Hairy, and the guinea pig is just Hairy. I told them to call me Harold, but no one would."

I was trying not to laugh, but I let a giggle slip out when I saw Mom blinking back the tears in her eyes from holding back her laughter this entire time. "Tell the teacher," I said.

"I did. I told her it was all her fault and kindergarten was the most horrible thing in the world. She made me sit in the corner."

"Apparently, Harold got a bit angrier than he's letting on," Mom said. "He'd stuffed Hairy the guinea pig in a pencil box and was going to set him free during recess."

This time I laughed. "You were going to harm a defenseless creature because you have the same name? Come on, Hare. That's not you."

"I wanted to set him free, not hurt him. He didn't like it there either. And he's been there for years. He wanted out more than I did. I could tell."

I patted the top of my brother's head. "It'll get better, bud."

Harold sighed. Ever the grown-up, he shifted his mood and asked politely, "How was your day, Tru?"

Mom chuckled and helped herself to a brownie. Sometimes I wondered if we were her entertainment for the day. Right now, I didn't care.

"I get to sit by Brendan Matthews!" I shouted, with my arms in the air.

Mom smiled. Harold rolled his eyes.

"Look out, Tru. He could have cooties," Mom said, and winked at me.

"Girls are the ones with cooties," Harold said.

"I'm slowly putting all of mine in your bed, so you'll be running rampant with them!" I tickled him and he leaped out of his chair, screaming. At six years old, you'd think Harold would know cooties weren't real, but I liked that he played along.

Thank God cooties weren't real. If Brendan had them, it probably wouldn't stop me from liking him.

"How's your back?" my mom asked, getting serious.

My heart sank to my stomach. "To be honest, I'd forgotten all about it."

Mom curved her mouth sadly. "You'd better—"

"I know, I know. I'll put it on."

I'd discovered the one thing that could bring me down from my cloud, and it definitely wasn't comfortable.

CHAPTER 4
The Visitor

I *wore my* brace to school the next day, rockin' an oversized t-shirt and jean shorts with much-too-wide leg holes. I was terrified someone might notice it. Wearing a back brace sucked; no ifs, ands, or buts—well, there was a butt. Mine. And it hurt.

Sitting at a desk was one of the most uncomfortable things in the world. My plastic brace couldn't press back against my plastic chair without pinching me or making some kind of noise, so I had to find a precarious balance where I could sit without mashing my butt cheeks to oblivion or exposing my hidden brace. Rather than taking notes in class, I kept glancing around the room to see if anyone looked at me oddly or questioned my absurdly straight posture. The time in between classes was a relief, because I could stand up and walk around. But then I just began to dread my next class.

My life sucked indeed.

At least the first week of school was only a two-day week. And at home, at least I could lounge around in loose mesh shorts under my brace with a t-shirt over it. I couldn't wear athletic shorts over my brace, because the slick material and elastic band would slide up my smooth plastic hips to my smooth plastic waist and rest there, giving me a wedgie that was both awful to look at and feel.

I noticed that my mood at home had changed. Before I'd gotten my brace, I'd been the first Trendon child to jump up when either of my parents asked for help. I'd been chipper and happy and friendly. Before-Brace Truth had been someone I liked. But Wearing-Brace Truth was moody and pitiful and rarely, if ever, offered to help out. Though I would begrudgingly do a chore or two, Wearing-Brace me spent more time thinking about things like how my brace had made making my bed more difficult. I wasn't proud of these changes, but I was aware of them. And I wondered what After-Brace Truth might be like.

That weekend, I was sitting in the living room near the door, watching television. In the past, I'd sprawl out on the floor in front of the TV and prop my chin on my hands as I let my mind fizzle out the stress of school and homework into a soft, gleaming haze of soothing voices and pretty faces. I rarely watched one episode of a show all the way through, since I'd get bored with the commercials and click the remote to find another channel. Eventually, I'd be wrapped up in four different plot lines and fifteen different actors before giving up and starting all over again. Now, with my brace keeping me from bending my spine in any way I liked or that felt comfortable, I sat in the recliner and shifted my weight every time a new body part fell asleep. (And I grumbled loudly when anyone else was around—pity-collecting was becoming a new hobby of mine.)

Currently, I was all caught up in two shows: one with a talking cat who was going to try his paw at Broadway, and the other about two teens in love who were trapped by their obvious differences. He was a cool, popular boy, and she was a lovable but nerdy girl, who liked to read and play the guitar—a corny, overdone storyline, but sometimes I watch shows like that. I'm human, and I can't help it.

As I watched, I thought about Brendan. Even I knew I was being pathetic, but I could picture him leaning close to me as I stood by my locker, the magnetic letters Megan and I bought from the Dollar Spot at the grocery store arranged into a telling but understated love poem on my locker door: THE DAISIES ALWAYS WILT / BUT NEVER ON THE PLAIN / OF MY

HEART / WHILE I'M WITH YOU. Brendan would see it and tell me how beautiful the words were . . . how beautiful I was.

The doorbell rang, jerking me from my daydream stupor and alerting me to the string of drool leaking from my mouth.

I sat up quickly, and the hard plastic of my brace jutted into my breastbone.

"Ow!" I shouted.

"Is that necessary?" my mom asked as she passed.

"Yes," I said.

My mom had invited her good friend, Harriet Nelson (Mrs. Nelson, to me), over to work on some Parent-Teacher Association thing. Mrs. Nelson was nice enough. Her son Oliver was in my grade, but I didn't know him very well.

Mom opened the door. "Harriet!" she said, her voice much friendlier than it had been to me. "Come in! Oh, and Oliver, come on in."

I froze. Oliver was here, and my brace was hanging out of my pants. If I stood up, I'd expose the low-hanging plastic digging into my butt. I was annoyed that my mother would play this trick on me. I was also surprised that Oliver would be interested in coming over, because that meant he had to try to maneuver around an unfamiliar home in his wheelchair. Oliver had muscular dystrophy, or MD. This meant the muscles in his body would gradually lose strength and muscle mass. There wasn't any cure. In fifth grade, Oliver's parents had made him present to our class about it, something he'd done without much effort or care, but it had made everyone stop talking about why he was in a wheelchair. At the time, I'd considered him really brave. Now I considered him one of the more intimidating beings to talk to: a boy. Oliver was especially intimidating because he didn't care what people thought of him. He spoke his mind.

He came through the door and looked at me, his expression about as irritated as mine was shocked. His dark brown eyes hovered below a dark mop of hair that curled at the ends.

"Hey," he said, pushing his way toward me.

"H-hello?" I said, posing it as a question to my mother.

"Hello, Truth," Mrs. Nelson said. She smiled kindly, and then turned to Oliver. "We'll only be thirty minutes or so."

"Take your time." He shrugged.

I pressed myself deeper into the recliner and glanced down to make sure my shirt was still covering the front of my brace. While I was leaning back, the brace didn't bite into my pelvis or the tops of my thighs. However, my butt was already falling asleep. I wanted to sit up, but if I moved, I feared the white plastic would show. I remained where I was.

"What are you watching?" Oliver asked.

I'd kept the channel on the show about the nerdy girl and her dream crush. Together, Oliver and I watched the end of the show about the oddly matched couple. They ended up together, despite their friends' and families' doubts about their relationship, and they sang a song together while she played her guitar. I liked it.

"That was stupid," Oliver said.

"Totally stupid," I agreed.

"Liar," he said, grinning at me. "You loved it. I could tell by your goofy grin."

I scowled. I did not like having my face labeled as "goofy."

"You girls are all the same," he said. "Dreaming about some guy that you think is so cool, but really he's just a big jerk. That girl is going to dump that loser as soon as she gets some confidence."

I stared at him. Here he was, a guest in my home, and he was criticizing me for something he knew nothing about. (Okay, so he was exactly right about me dreaming about a cool guy, but he didn't need to know that.) "We can't all be as confident as you are," I said.

"Oh, so you do fight back!" He leaned forward slightly on the right armrest of his chair. "I was just teasing."

"That was teasing? It's difficult to tell. But no, I don't fight. I peacefully protest," I said, recalling something Charity had once said about arguing with teachers.

He snorted. "Okay." He shifted his weight and stared at the television again. "So my mom said you might be going through a tough time right now."

I sat up involuntarily. "What? What are you talking about?"

He sat up slightly straighter, taken aback by my sudden anger. "Never mind. Sheesh. She just mentioned you might bring something up and to be nice about it. Forget it."

"Yeah, I will." We watched television for a few more minutes, Oliver looking bored and me fuming in my plastic case like a hot popcorn kernel about to pop.

"You kids have fun?" Mrs. Nelson asked as she entered the living room.

"A real blast," Oliver said. "I learned I have so much to look forward to as a teenager."

My rear end had fallen asleep, but I said nothing. I stared at my mother with my jaw set firm. One glance and I knew she understood. Talking behind my back—about my back—was betrayal.

As soon as the Nelsons left, she apologized and added, "I just think that talking about it might be more beneficial than trying to hide it from everyone."

"It's not your job to 'think about it,' Mother," I said, my voice as haughty as I could muster. "This is my problem. Let me deal with it as I want to."

She watched me storm out of the living room. I didn't speak to her again until dinner, and even then, I avoided eye contact.

On Monday at school, the intercom in my fourth-period study hall classroom buzzed. "Truth Trendon, please come to the principal's office."

Thankfully, people were always being called to the office because of forgotten homework assignments, lunches, sports bras, and everything else under the sun, so no one called out, "Oooohh, what did she do?" or "*Some*body's in trouble!" I did, however, realize that everyone would be watching me leave the room, so before I stood up, I attempted to physically and mentally prepare myself for the upcoming assault of staring eyes. Then I smiled nicely, slid out of my desk, and moved purposefully down the aisle and out of the classroom without a backward glance.

Feeling proud of myself, I walked past the commons, where study hall was held on long lunch tables, across from the steps leading up to the office. Apparently my pride took over my motor skills, though, because when I lifted my leg for the first step, I didn't lift it high enough. I tripped, nearly nose-diving into the staircase, but regained my composure. A few snickers chased me up the rest of the stairs, and I died a bit inside, but embarrassment unfortunately doesn't kill you completely.

I opened the office door and was surprised to see the school counselor, Mr. Umland, leaning against the desk, waiting for me. The year before during the last week of classes, he'd come around to each homeroom and introduced himself to us. According to Charity, he always wore a sweater vest over any shirt, be it polo, dress, or tee, and for him, "counselor" was a loose term. He was all about helping the juniors and seniors apply to college and find scholarships, but when it came to providing emotional and mental support, he shied away from students like a bleating calf running away from a hot brand. It was rumored he spent most of the day surfing the internet for cheap antiques to sell at flea markets.

"Truth?" he asked excitedly.

"Hi, Mr. Umland," I said.

"I'm glad to see you. Will you please come with me to my office?"

I looked at the secretary to see if there was some other, much more important message I was supposed to take instead, but she just smiled politely. I felt my chin drop and my lip curl involuntarily as I considered what this meant.

"Sure," I said.

I followed Mr. Umland into his stale-smelling office and reviewed my options. Either he was really eager to help me start applying to college, or—

"So your mother tells me you have a back brace."

Son-of-a—

"I can't even tell, to be honest, Truth." I figured that was his way of saying it couldn't be that bad.

"It's pretty hot."

"Now that's a good attitude to have! Keep that up."

"No, I mean temperature-wise. I sweat a lot."

"Oh," he said, clearly embarrassed. I smiled.

"Okay. Well, I think it's sometimes difficult for us when we realize we're different from everyone else."

Really? This was his pep talk?

"I just wanted to check in and see how things are going."

"Well, it's been hard wanting to get up some mornings—"

"And I also thought it might be good for you to visit with another student who is going through a similar problem."

I paused. I was somewhat unnerved that Mr. Umland had just ignored what could have been the start of a very serious admission on my part, but mostly because I was surprised to hear someone else at school had scoliosis. I figured I would know.

"I spoke with Oliver Nelson, and he would love to chat with you."

"Oliver? But he—"

"He just finished physical therapy for the morning and will talk with you before his next class. I thought you could meet with him twice a week for a while, just for fifteen minutes at the end of your study hall, until you become comfortable with your . . . situation."

I was aghast. Not only did I not want to see Oliver after our forced interaction over the weekend, but I also couldn't understand how Mr. Umland thought I could compare myself to him. How could

54

Mr. Umland think wearing a back brace was as bad as being in a wheelchair and losing muscle strength in your whole body? Plus, Mr. Umland had taken it upon himself to tell Oliver my secret, something I'd been trying to keep from him and everyone else.

Oliver was going to think I was a whiner who couldn't deal with a few setbacks. I couldn't talk to him, not about this.

My stomach began to pound against my brace; if I'd already eaten lunch, I'm pretty sure it would have been back to visit us on Mr. Umland's desk.

"Follow me," Mr. Umland said.

We walked to what was known as the Resource Room, where some people went for special education, and others for extra help on a subject in which they struggled. Everyone basically viewed anyone who used the Resource Room as totally "not normal." I'm not saying that's fair; that's just how it was. Fear filled my heart as we neared the doorway. If people found out I was going there, they'd begin to wonder why. I couldn't let them find out it was because I wore a brace, but I also didn't want them thinking I was different for another reason. Labels were difficult to overcome, and that last thing I needed was to be guilty by association. Maybe if anyone asked, I could say I was tutoring someone else.

I could practically hear Isaac Newton laughing at me while I tried to come up with excuses for being there. I also fumed with rage at the fact that my mother had a hand in this deal.

I walked in, and Oliver was the only one there, besides the Special Education teacher, Mrs. Werth. He sat at a long table surrounded by plastic chairs. The wall behind him was lined with physical therapy equipment, including crutches, an exercise ball, and three long, blue mats that were folded up and set against a filing cabinet. The room looked like the storage area of a failed exercise instructor.

Mr. Umland sidled up to Mrs. Werth and spoke quietly. She nodded and then stepped out of the room with him. Neither of them spoke to Oliver or me.

Oliver just stared at me. He wore a t-shirt with the name of a band that I vaguely recognized, though I'd never heard their music.

"Hi," I said, glancing at the table.

"Hey, liar. Long time, no see."

"I'm not a liar," I said, instantly defensive.

"Fine. Poser. Fake. Whatever."

"I didn't ask to talk to you. This is embarrassing enough," I said. "I'm going to go."

"No, wait," he said in a sincere tone. It made me pause. "Sorry. I was teasing. I've heard it's difficult to tell." He grinned. He'd quoted me from the day before.

"Oh. Okay." I wasn't sure if I believed him. I wanted to, but as he said, it was hard to tell.

"So, I'm supposed to encourage you to keep going in life, huh?" Oliver said.

I hesitated. Was he?

"I don't know. I'm sorry. I didn't ask for this."

He grinned again. "The deformity or having to talk to me?"

I liked his grin. It was sincere. "Both?"

He laughed. "Sit down before the stupid matchmakers come back."

I sat down across the table from him, uncertain.

"Here's the deal," Oliver said. "I don't have any suggestions for you. You know as well as I do that I'm not like anyone else in this school and Mr. Umdouche and Mrs. No-werth don't give a crap about you or me fitting in. They just want to get through the eight o'clock to three-thirty bell with no surprises."

I nodded. There was enough evidence to support this hypothesis.

"We're supposed to meet twice a week. That's fine; but don't expect me to tell you what to do to get people to see you as normal. Just be glad you can hide your brace. Once they know something's wrong with you, you're different, and that's that."

I nodded again. He was right.

"You're quiet," he said. It wasn't an accusation or a judgement, but an observation.

I didn't want to admit I was scared to say anything and risk offending him.

Oliver wheeled himself around to my side of the table. We were face to face. I'd never been this close to him. His arms weren't bulky by any means, but to be honest, I was surprised to see he had muscle tone.

"I like that. Most people talk too much."

The bell rang. With a hint of a smile, Oliver pushed himself out of the room, merging into the stream of students already flowing down the hallway. People looked at him and moved out of his way, but it was as if they didn't really see him—he was "different," so he didn't register.

Just be glad you can hide it. That was the secret to normalcy. I already didn't want people to know about my back brace, but now I knew that keeping it a secret was even more important than I had thought.

I could hide what was different about me. Some people, like Oliver, weren't so lucky.

At the end of the day, Brendan walked up to my locker after the final bell and smiled at me.

I nearly dropped the books I'd been picking up. Had he seen my brace when I was bent down?

"Hey, Trendon," he said. He sounded so casual, like he had no idea what those words did to my heart. He had to know how I felt about him.

"Hi, Matthews," I said.

He grinned. "I hear you're going out for volleyball."

"I am," I said. I didn't add that I couldn't wait to have an extra hour or two where I didn't have to wear the brace hidden underneath my extra-large t-shirt and denim shorts.

"Cool."

"Yeah." I could feel the awkward silence creeping up on us, so I continued, "My older sister Charity and I play together all the time. She just made varsity, actually."

"Really? That's cool. I bet you're not far behind."

I blushed and smiled, beaming as if he'd just declared me the prettiest person of all time.

"Well, good luck. I hope you do good."

"Well," I said, automatically copying my mother, the grammar corrector.

"What?"

"Do 'well,' not 'good'—never mind. You do good too. We both do good."

He laughed. I liked that I could make him laugh. "You're funny, Trendon," he said. "I like that."

I felt like my heart was about to burst from my brace and make it explode into thousands of tiny white shards as he turned and walked down the hallway. (Now, that would be something for old Isaac Newton to see.)

I like that, he'd said.

I knew he hadn't said "I like *you*," but I was going to count it as a minor misuse of words—just as "well" and "good" could easily be confused, I figured "that" could sometimes mean "you."

"I like that, too," I said, and no one was there to correct me, which I decided was both well and good.

CHAPTER 5

The Discovery
(Part 1)

"Oh, my gerunds! Did you touch him?" Megan cried. We were standing in front of our locker the next morning.

"Gerunds? Do you even know what a gerund is?"

"I'm gerunding right now!" Megan said.

I sighed, lowering my voice so anyone standing around wouldn't overhear. "No, I didn't touch him. But he talked to me. I corrected his grammar and he said I was funny."

"Ooooh." Megan bit her lip, and I knew she was trying to decide how she should word her next sentence.

"What?"

"Well, no offense, but you have different levels of funny. I mean, his grammar? Did he mean funny 'ha ha' or funny 'weird'?"

"I've been wondering the same thing. I think funny 'ha ha.'"

"Good. That's good."

Then, as if on cue, Brendan walked up. "Ready for Band?" he asked.

"Always!" I said, too excitedly. "Go Team Trumpet!"

Megan's eyes widened, and I immediately regretted my words. However, Brendan laughed. He lifted his hand, outstretched as he waited for a high five. I slapped my hand against his with glee. "Go Team Trumpet," he said, and then he continued on his way, catching up with one of his friends.

"I can't believe it," Megan said, her voice hushed.

"I know. He thinks I'm funny 'ha ha,'" I said.

"No," Megan said, a smile spreading across her face. "We did it. The high five is cool again."

It was my turn to laugh. I knew it was probably just in my head (or my hormones), but my hand still tingled from touching Brendan's. Cool or not, high fives were now one of my favorite things.

It may sound like I was actually climbing the social ladder. Brendan obviously wasn't repulsed by me, even after I started wearing my brace to school, and I seemed to be keeping it hidden from everyone else, too. However, I still wasn't sure what to do about Gym class.

The first day of Gym had just been an introduction, but this week, I'd already figured out a sort of routine. Each day, when the bell rang for class, I would sprint to the locker room to be the first one inside, slip off my brace, and stash it in a locker. It was a rather small, square locker room, with lockers along the walls and a row of them running up the middle and splitting the room in half, with a bench on either side of the row. I also had a stroke of luck. All the other girls chose lockers on one side of the dividing row, so I chose one on the other side. That way, I would have a few extra seconds to hide if I needed them.

If I wasn't the first one there, I would hide in the single bathroom stall inside the locker room until everyone else headed up to the gym. Then I would take off my brace and stash it in a locker several down from mine because it didn't fit with all my other stuff—plus, then if someone saw it, they wouldn't automatically know it was mine. I changed clothes quickly before anyone noticed I was lagging behind. After class, I'd do it all over again, but in reverse. Once the brace was on under my shirt, un-Velcroed with my arm pressed tightly against it to keep it from rattling, I'd sneak out to the hallway bathroom, where Megan would meet me from her study hall to cinch me up. There was the risk of someone else taking the bathroom pass or Mr. Landers, the study hall supervisor for that period, being in a bad mood and telling Megan she could wait five minutes until the bell rang, but so far we'd been lucky.

I got along with pretty much everyone in my Gym class, but I just didn't want to tell them about my brace. If even one of them found out about it, they all would (and I wouldn't blame them—if one of them asked *me* to keep a secret, it'd be all I could do to not tell Megan), and soon the whole school would know. And everyone would officially see me as different. So I continued sneaking out of the locker room.

This day was no different than all the others. I put the brace on under my baggy t-shirt at the end of Gym and headed for the door.

My hand touched the knob, and I could smell sweet victory—fresh air from the hall through the stench of a million body sprays and lotions in the locker room.

"What's that?"

Slowly I turned around. Jenny Henderson was pointing at my rear.

"It doesn't pay to be jealous, Jenny," I said. "Some of us are just born with junk in the trunk."

She rolled her eyes. "No, what's that white thing hanging there?" She lifted her eyebrows together into a judgmental line. Other girls appeared from behind the separating wall. I reached behind my back and felt for what Jenny was talking about. The bottom Velcro piece was hanging out. *Oh my gerunds.*

I thought quickly. Stupidly, but quickly. "Football pads."

"What?"

A few girls laughed.

"Yeah, I'm stretching out some of the new pads for Coach Ericson this week. Extra credit for Gym. It's kind of a secret—the smaller boys are embarrassed a *girl* is doing the dirty work for them. So keep it hush-hush. We could get in big trouble for talking about it." I really emphasized "big trouble."

"Thanks for telling me. I wouldn't want to be caught in the hallway with it showing!" I shoved the Velcro up under my shirt. I heard some girls murmuring.

"Lucky. I need extra credit."

"Football sucks."

"Yeah, I would never do that."

I ran out the door. In the bathroom, Megan was waiting in the third stall.

65

"What took you so long?" she whispered. "I have to get this pass back before the bell rings or I'll get detention."

"I'm in trouble," I said.

"What now?"

"You know Jenny Henderson? Can't play the trumpet, meanly nice, kinda pretty?"

Even though Megan was behind me, I knew she was nodding. "Wants your man—yes, I know her. Who doesn't?"

"Jenny and the other girls saw part of the Velcro. I think they're on to me."

"I doubt it."

I started to laugh. "I told them I was wearing football pads—that I'm 'stretching them out' for the freshman players."

Megan snorted as she pulled the final piece of Velcro through its loop and strapped it down. "You are too special. You couldn't come up with anything else? You could have said it was a tag or something."

"See? That's why I need you in Gym with me. You're a quick thinker."

"Not really. You always come up with something, at least."

Megan pushed the Velcro into place and pulled the back of my shirt down for me.

The bell rang.

"Noooo!" Megan moaned. "Now I'll have to stay after school!"

I knew it was my fault. I grabbed the pass. "I'll tell Landers you're having stomach trouble."

"Eww. No." Megan took the pass back and sighed. "I can take my lumps, Truth."

She left the bathroom with her shoulders slumped and her head down. I felt terrible. It was my fault she was in trouble, but I didn't know what to do. I was afraid if I told any teachers, they would say something about it in front of my classmates, even if by accident. And I had to keep my brace hidden. Megan understood that.

I hoped.

Stupid Isaac Newton! Now he was causing my best friend to get in trouble.

My next meeting with Oliver was during study hall that day. I already felt more comfortable with him—after talking to him last week and earlier this week, I realized it actually was a relief to spend time with someone who understood being different.

Today, he jokingly welcomed me into his office as if he were a psychiatrist. I was still feeling bad about Megan, and afraid she was annoyed at having to help me, so I told him about it. It was easy to talk to him, and he kept up his joke-psychiatrist act, asking, "And how does that make you feel?" in an uninterested voice, which actually made me even more comfortable telling him. It went without saying he wouldn't disclose my secret to anyone. I didn't even have to ask.

"Also, I may have inadvertently joined the football team," I said.

Oliver raised his eyebrows, and I told him about that morning's brace escapade.

"You'd probably be a better lineman than a lot of the guys on the team," he grinned.

I narrowed my eyes. "Aren't the linemen the big ones?"

Oliver laughed. "It's not my fault they're scrawny."

"Well, with this, I could probably take 'em on." I tapped the plastic covering my belly.

"Can I see this plastic clamp that's ruining your life?" Oliver asked.

"I, um . . . I'd have to take off my shirt, and that's a little too PG-13 for me."

He laughed. "Fine. Just when I was hoping the special ed room could become the sex-ed room."

I blushed, but that just made him laugh more.

"You know, a lot of people would say scoliosis is not that big of a deal," he said.

"By 'a lot of people' do you mean you?"

"No, I get it. Now you're different from everyone else."

I nodded, and suddenly I found myself telling him how in fifth grade, the school nurse came to talk to my class about scoliosis tests. She showed us how she would conduct them, by bending forward with her hands pointed at her toes. She was on the plump side and, when she bent over, we could all see her granny-panties through her white pants. A few kids snickered, and I knew they were laughing about the poor woman's underwear, but part of me worried they were laughing about scoliosis. I already knew I had it, but all of the kids in my class laughed and made fun of the nurse after she left.

It was amazing how Oliver just listened. He nudged me along in my stories by just widening his large dark eyes. His mouth stayed neutral, but his eyes seemed poised to be delighted.

When I finished my story, he told me about a time a few years after he discovered he had MD. Trying to acclimate to his new wheelchair, he didn't know how to stop. He was downtown with his mother and they needed to cross the street, but he'd picked up speed more quickly than expected and he shot off across the street before he meant to, narrowly missing a

Ford pickup with a panting Labrador hanging out of its window.

"I didn't care about my mom screaming at me or the driver of the pickup stopping to yell at me. The wind rushing in my face and whipping back my hair felt so good—I knew exactly how that smiling dog felt."

"Dogs don't smile."

"You're not a dog, so you can't know that for sure."

"Were you grounded, or what?"

He laughed at the memory. "No. My mom set the locks on my wheels, sat on my lap, and nearly broke my neck as she hugged me and made me promise I'd never accidently kill myself again."

Suddenly, Oliver fell quiet. "I think about that story a lot, actually."

"Because of the dog?" I asked, knowing he wasn't thinking about the Labrador.

"No." He paused. "You may not understand this, but I don't want to be a burden to anyone, not even my parents."

I felt myself growing warm. I didn't like him calling himself a burden. "You're not a burden," I said. "You can't think that. You might have to work harder than most people to—to be independent. But that doesn't mean your family doesn't love you exactly how you are."

Oliver's eyes narrowed. I suspected he was angry, and I'd overstepped my bounds. He was supposed to be the life coach in this partnership, not the other way around. I was surprised when his face softened.

"I suppose you're right," he said.

I waited for Megan after school. She had to go to Mr. Landers' classroom for a ten-minute seminar. It was the punishment that came before detention: four seminars in one week, and then you had to stay for an hour's detention. I was sitting outside the History classroom, reading *Great Expectations*, when I heard familiar footsteps. If you could give "cool" a sound, it would be Brendan Matthews walking.

"Whoa, Trendon. That book's big enough to make my brain explode," he said.

I tried to flash a nonchalant smile, to show I thought reading was cool. "Well, I guess it's good I'm reading it, and not you, then."

"Yes. Yes it is." Brendan sat next to me. "Just can't get enough knowledge for one day, or what?"

I sighed. "Megan got a seminar. I'm waiting for her."

Brendan nodded. "You're a good friend. I don't think I'd wait for anyone."

I wanted to say "Not even me?" But I didn't. Instead, I played the hero. "It was sort of my fault."

"Oh really? I didn't realize you were a rule-breaker, Trendon."

He grinned at me.

"I'm not. We were just in the bathroom at the end of third period and she didn't get back to class before the bell rang. I was in Gym, so it didn't matter."

"That's a lame excuse for a seminar."

"Yeah."

We were both quiet for a moment. I felt awkward, so I brushed my finger over the gilded title of my book's front cover.

"What are you doing this weekend?" Brendan asked me.

"I have to babysit my younger brother, Harold, tomorrow. My sister, Charity, has a volleyball tournament, and I'd like to go to it, but Harold has a class project I said I'd help with. He and I are going to do that while my parents go watch the games."

"Oh. Hey, you know that sentence structure

worksheet due on Monday for English? You wanna work on it together? I could come over tomorrow."

Yes, yes! A thousand times yes! But I couldn't say that aloud. I wanted my response to sound cool, yet pleased.

"Sure," I said.

"Cool."

Nailed it, I thought. I stared at the cover of my book, and suddenly the words gained much more importance. Brendan was coming over tomorrow—and my expectations for that were pretty great.

The door opened next to me and Megan plodded out of the classroom, a frown plastered across her pretty face. I stood up and peeked through the open door. Mr. Landers sat at his desk, grading papers.

Brendan stood up beside me and walked with us down the hall.

"How was it?" I asked Megan, once we were out of Mr. Landers' earshot.

"All he said was 'Maybe you shouldn't drink so much water before study hall,' and then he had me work on homework for ten minutes."

I wanted to laugh, but I didn't. Megan was obviously upset.

"Megan Borowitz, delinquent student," Brendan said.

"I guess," Megan said. She didn't sound happy, but she blushed, so I knew she was enjoying this new attention.

"I'm so sorry, Megs," I said, for about the fortieth time.

"I guess when you're a troublemaker like me, a seminar is bound to happen." She was smiling now. Brendan smiled too.

I laughed loudly. "Yeah, what risky business, going to the bathroom. Landers was right. Don't drink so much water next time."

Brendan laughed. Megan glared at me. I gave her a sheepish look, and squeezed her hand between my fingers. I was trying to pretend that I just didn't want Brendan to find out about my brace, but Megan could probably see right through me—I was jealous he was paying attention to her.

Since we missed the bus, Brendan offered to see if his mother could drive us home. When she drove up, Brendan opened the car door and asked if we could catch a ride. I smiled and offered a little wave, but she didn't even smile in response.

"We have your equipment to pick up. Hurry up and get in. Be quick about it," his mom said, without looking back at us again.

Megan and I climbed into the back of the car

and listened as Mrs. Matthews rattled off information about some football camp Brendan was attending. She seemed to look more at him than at the road. Megan kept her eyebrows raised and her hand gripping the door handle the entire time, glancing at me every so often. I tried to keep a pleasant look on my face.

Both Megan and I got out at my house.

"Thanks for the ride," I said.

"Uhnnn," Mrs. Matthews said (or something like that).

"Bye, Megan," Brendan said. He looked at me. "See you around, Trendon."

I smiled and said "Bye" as the car pulled away from the curb.

My heart was aflutter as we walked to my house. Brendan had only said "Bye" to Megan, but he'd saved a whole sentence for me. I realized I actually had my hand resting on top of my heart.

"You don't have to worry," Megan said. "I'm not going to swoop in and go 'Boom, I got your boyfriend.'"

"He's not my boyfriend," I said. I felt my face growing hot, even though I usually never blushed in front of Megan. "And I know you wouldn't."

"It just sucks getting in trouble when I didn't do anything wrong," Megan said.

"I know. I'm *so* sorry. How can I make it up to you?" I asked sincerely. I stopped walking, grabbed Megan's hands, and pleaded until she looked me in the eye. I tried sticking my bottom lip out to look pitiful, but I've always been afraid of contracting an underbite, so the expression has no effect on any onlooker. If anything, it looks like I'm attempting to pucker up for a kiss.

"Get your puppy-fish face out of here!" Megan laughed.

"I'm serious! How about I treat you to popcorn and a movie at my house tomorrow evening after my parents get back?"

"Fine. But I want to watch a scary movie."

"Noooo!" I cried. "You know I had nightmares after watching the last one!"

"That's what you can do," Megan said with a stubborn smile. "Mummy nightmares or no."

"Okay." I sighed. "Maybe this time I'll dream that I defeat the mummies instead of the other way around."

"Or maybe you'll dream about Brendan running in to save your life." Megan winked and headed for her house. "Call me!" she yelled over her shoulder. And we were back to normal.

"Okay, now we put in one-third of a cup of cocoa," I said. I reached for the cup over Harold's head and handed it to him.

"Let me," he said. That's all he'd been saying for the past half hour. I was teaching him how to make homemade cupcakes from scratch, and he seemed to think I wouldn't let him do anything unless he blurted out "Let me" in a loud voice.

Harold's project for school was to bring something for show-and-tell that he'd made. He liked to eat, so he decided to make cupcakes. My family is completely opposed to making anything from a box, so when Harold said he wanted to make cupcakes for school, my parents looked at me. They'd taught me years ago, and I wasn't afraid to admit I enjoyed baking.

"Cooking and baking are not signs of domestication," my father said the first time he showed me how to cut shortening into the mixing bowl for pie crust. "Sometimes, cooking is a work of art. But mostly, it is a sign that one can live on his or her own." Both of my parents enjoyed cooking, and it often became a family affair, with everyone pitching in something.

I usually helped—that way, if I wanted to eat something in particular, I could make it. I could have my cake and eat it too. Bada bing, bada boom.

"Okay, you don't want too much," I said. I showed Harold how to scrape off the excess cocoa with the flat side of a bread knife. "I like to guess, but you're a beginner, Prince Harry. Use the exact amounts."

"Okay," he said. He dumped the cocoa into the bowl.

The doorbell rang. I dusted off my floured hands on my colorful frilly apron that my grandma sewed for me last Christmas. I didn't mind the colors, but I wasn't huge on the frills. I'd never tell my Nana that though.

"Don't touch anything else," I yelled back at Harold as I pulled the door open. "Hi!" I said, smiling. Brendan was here, and he was smiling at me with his backpack slung over one shoulder. I had the worksheet he wanted to work on together sitting out on the kitchen table, far away from our cooking mess.

"Nice dress."

"It's an apron that my grandma made, and thank you."

"What are you doing?" he asked, looking past me at Harold, who was trying to find the vanilla extract in the pile of ingredients on the counter.

"Baking cupcakes."

"Cool," Brendan said. "Can I help?"

"Sure," I said, while at the same time Harold shouted from the kitchen, "No!"

Brendan looked taken aback by my brother's assertive negativity, but I laughed. "It's Harold's school project, so he's doing the work. I'm the supervisor. You can help me."

Brendan smiled. "So this is Harold?"

"Yes," Harold said. "I'm in kindergarten and I'm not a guinea pig."

"Perfect," Brendan said. "Me neither."

He leaned on the counter. He looked cute and composed in his plain t-shirt and athletic shorts, and I immediately thought about what I looked like. I knew I might have bits of flour on my face and I hadn't really thought about my hair. The apron was tied loosely around my waist—which was cinched tightly in my brace. Trying to stay focused, I glanced at the cupcake recipe, written in my mother's smooth scrawl:

1 cup flour
1¾ cups sugar
⅓ cup cocoa powder
1 cup butter

4 eggs

1 teaspoon vanilla extract

No call for "hot guy," I thought. Yet here he was, twisting off the cap of the unopened bottle of vanilla for my brother. Harold took the bottle with a pert "Let me" and tried to pour the vanilla into the tiny teaspoon. In his overzealousness, he tipped the bottle and much of the liquid fell to the floor. Dark drops spattered our legs.

"Whoops," Harold said, looking up at me with wide eyes.

"That's how we learn, buddy," I said, ruffling his hair.

He let me pour the vanilla into the spoon and dump it in the bowl. Then we cleaned up the mess. Brendan pretended to pass out from the strong smell. Harold doubled over with laughter as Brendan's face playfully turned red, his limbs convulsed, and he collapsed on the kitchen floor. Harold copied his motions, and ended up jumping onto Brendan's stomach.

"Oomph," Brendan rolled Harold onto the floor and laughed. "You've got strong nostrils, Trendon. Nice evasive action with that smelly stuff."

Harold frowned. "If anyone asks, I put the vanilla in. Capisce?"

"Capisce," I said. "Now come here and let's mix it all up." I demonstrated how to turn on the mixer and then watched as he carefully did it himself. The batter mixed nicely, the chocolaty mixture flowing over and in on itself.

"I've never seen anyone make anything from scratch before," Brendan said.

"It's not much more difficult than using a box recipe," I said.

"You just have to be smart enough to read the recipe," Harold teased.

Brendan didn't smile right away, but then he ran at Harold and said "Oh yeah?" and he tickled my brother until Harold dropped to his knees in giggling screams.

I laughed as I poured the batter into the paper cups Harold had haphazardly placed in the two cupcake pans.

"You think it's funny too, Trendon?"

Brendan came up behind me and put his fingers on my sides. I screamed, not happily, and nearly dropped the bowl.

"No!" I said.

I turned around and looked at the two boys staring at my batter-spattered frilly apron.

"What was that?" Brendan asked. He was rubbing his fingers together; he'd hit his hands on my brace.

"N-nothing," I said. "Excuse me."

I pulled the apron over my head and let it fall to the ground. I ran to the bathroom and shut myself in, leaning against the door as huge, inescapable tears began to fall out of my eyes.

"Truth!" Harold said. He knocked rapidly on the door.

"Just go away," I said, trying not to sob.

He kept knocking. It got annoying and started to make my ears ring, so finally I let him in.

"How come Brendan doesn't know about your brace?"

He sounded so motherly, or counselor-like, and I wanted to kiss him for being so cute.

"I don't want people to know about it," I said.

"Why?"

"Because they might notice that I look different, and it might change the way they think about me."

"That's stupid," Harold said. "You're still Truth Trendon. You look nice. You know, for a girl."

I wiped my eyes, and then I did kiss him.

"Yuck, Tru!" He wiped his cheek and ran out of the bathroom.

I looked in the mirror. If my six-year-old brother could accept my body for how it looked, why couldn't I?

I splashed water on my face, took a deep breath, and walked out of the bathroom, into the hallway. It felt like the walk down the cell block before my death sentence; I felt my heart beat uncontrollably in my chest, and before I turned the corner into the kitchen, I closed my eyes and gave myself a pep talk.

Beauty is in the eye of the beholder. My subconscious rolled its eyes. *Okay, you may look weird to yourself now, but someday, you'll be able to have a rockin' bod without a back brace.* I opened my eyes and faced my executioner. He stood up from his spot at the table where he had his worksheet out next to mine.

"I finished the worksheet. It was easier than I thought."

I nodded. He'd obviously looked at my answers, because he'd moved my paper next to his, but at the moment, I didn't really care.

"I also put the cupcakes in the oven. Harry went upstairs to his room to get a timer. I told him the oven has one, but he said his is better," Brendan said. He watched me carefully, as if anything he did might cause me to erupt into a crazy, tweenage monster that would rip him apart, limb from extraordinary limb.

"I should apologize," I said.

"For what," Brendan replied. It wasn't stated as a question. He knew full well what I was talking about.

"I freaked out because you touched me, and I don't want people to touch me."

"Ooookay. I won't do it again." He frowned.

"No, that's not what I meant. I—I have this . . ."

I considered Oliver's warning and then took a deep breath. "I have scoliosis and I have to wear a back brace for it, and it's gross and I hate it, and I didn't want you to know because I like you."

I covered my face.

He didn't say anything. I peeked between my fingers.

"What?" he asked.

I reached underneath my shirt and pulled my brace's three Velcro straps apart. Thank goodness for elastic pants, I thought, as I lifted the brace away from my body and pulled it out from under my shirt.

I watched Brendan's face. He was clearly intrigued. I felt like Iron Man revealing my true identity. So much for trying to be like everyone else.

"I have to wear this. For my back," I said.

"All the time?"

"During the day. For two years or until I stop growing."

He took a step forward, then stopped. "Can I . . . touch it?"

"Yes," I laughed. "I'm sorry I freaked out on you. I just didn't know you were behind me and then I didn't know what to do."

Brendan lifted my brace. "How do you fit in here? The middle is tiny!"

"It's nothing short of a miracle," I said, rubbing my skin where the brace pushed against my ribs.

"Why were you afraid to tell me?" He tried to put it on himself, but he couldn't stretch it enough.

"Because everyone laughed at the chubby nurse."

Brendan's dark blond eyebrows drew together in confusion.

I started to blush, but then I just told the truth, the same story I'd told Oliver.

"It was devastating," I said.

"I remember that." He eyed me carefully. "I don't think I laughed."

I smiled gratefully.

"But you shouldn't be so nervous. Everyone has their problems," Brendan said. He handed the brace back to me.

"Please don't tell anyone," I pleaded.

My face must have contributed to my petition of sworn secrecy, for Brendan immediately looked serious and sad.

"I won't."

"So you don't think I'm disgusting?"

"Are you serious? What kind of a person do you think I am?"

A very handsome person, I thought. Instead, I said, "I was just self-conscious. That's all."

"Well, I'm glad you told me. I won't try to tickle you again."

He held up his fingers as if they were broken.

I laughed and pushed Brendan's shoulder. "Now you know not to just tickle random girls. We have deterrents to keep pests like you away." I shook my brace at him.

Brendan smiled. "I've learned my lesson, believe me. The next time I want to tickle you, I'll ask first."

Next time. That time I couldn't stop myself. I blushed.

Chapter 6

BFF Duty

The week after Brendan learned my secret, Megan and I started volleyball. In junior high, anyone could join volleyball. The junior high teams only played for a few weeks out of the year, and we really only scrimmaged each other, but it was fun nonetheless. I'd played with a lot of the other girls on city league teams in fifth and sixth grade, so we were already familiar with the positions and rules. We were stationed in the "old" gym, which hadn't been updated since the seventies and carried an aroma of body odor and bleach, while the high school team got to use the new and larger gym.

With Megan's help, I was able to get out of and into my brace after practice without any of the other girls finding out. We were late to practice a few times—once when Jennifer was smoothing lotion all over her legs and going on and on about how her older sister said moisturizing was the most important aspect of lasting skin care, and another time when

Michelle Arlington was discussing a school project with Megan. She just kept talking, and I couldn't change into my practice clothes without her seeing everything. Eventually I mumbled something about having to use the bathroom and changed in the stall. Megan headed upstairs and Michelle followed, giving me privacy to stash the brace into my locker.

I loved volleyball practice. I could move without the anchor of my brace tying me down. It was different from Gym class because in Gym, I spent so much time worrying about how I would hide my brace and then get it back on. With Megan there, I had almost no fear. As soon as the brace came off, I imagined my body as a light bulb, my torso shining brightly and illuminating every inch of the ways I could move. I was basically giddy. My classmates even commented on the noticeable change.

"Did you eat too much sugar today?" Ruth asked.

"Yeah, calm down, Truth," Jennifer said, after diving out of the way of the ball she was supposed to pass with her arms. "You nearly hit me with that last serve."

I smiled. "Yeah. You're supposed to pass the ball, not be afraid of it."

She glowered, and I continued to smile, happy that even if it was crooked, my body could still do something I loved. And if I do say so myself, I was pretty good at volleyball.

Having that outlet changed my outlook for the days I had practice. If I could make it to the end of the day, I could have fun. I could sit through seven hours of class, deal with the excruciating pinching of my skin against various bones, and if I got a bit sweaty, it didn't matter because we all sweated at practice anyway.

As the weeks went by, I also found myself hanging around Brendan more and more. I couldn't believe how easy it was to talk to him now that he knew my secret. Between classes, he'd come talk to me at my locker, and once, he squeezed my arm after I loaned him a pen.

Now that we were growing closer, he and Megan were growing chummier as well. They joked and talked through Algebra as if they were old friends. She practically ignored me during class and focused entirely on him. Her chair was always turned around, facing our table. Miss Peters had to ask them to quiet down at least once a class period, and she'd threatened to move them twice. She'd look at me, and I'd shrug and turn back to my homework, trying to appear studious while also keeping tabs on Brendan and Megan's conversation.

Besides class, Brendan was in football practice while I was at volleyball, and sometimes we'd pass each other in the hallway afterward as we headed back to our locker rooms. Twice he winked at me, and I waved back. Twice my teammates cooed at my blushing reaction, and twice Jennifer made jealous eyes at me before grabbing her two closest friends and pulling them into the locker room first.

I mentioned Brendan so many times to my mother that she finally demanded I invite him over for dinner. My parents knew of him from his various athletic events—which were sometimes written about in the local newspaper—and after the cupcake escapade, Harold declared him "an enjoyable person." Charity was impressed with me because she thought he was cute.

"I didn't know you could snag a buck like that, lil' sis," she said, spying Brendan sending me a smile after practice the day he was coming to dinner. She was waiting for me outside the locker room. Mom picked up Charity, Megan, and me now that we couldn't ride the bus after practice, and we'd take turns waiting for each other to finish up.

"I didn't either," I said. I rapped my knuckles against my stomach armor. The tap, tap, tap said it all. "He did say he likes *The Terminator*. Maybe he just sees me as a way to live out his dream of killing an unstoppable cyborg."

"Knock it off. You're a good catch yourself."

"You're biased. We look alike."

"Liking someone shouldn't be based off looks, Truth," Charity said, her older-sisterliness shining through. Her attention shifted as the varsity football team appeared at the end of the hallway. A slight grin played across her lips and she nudged me. "Though it doesn't hurt."

Megan finally emerged from the locker room, her face ashen.

"Cool," Charity said, oblivious to Megan's demeanor. "Let's go."

"Wait, Char," I said. "What's wrong, Megan?"

"I overheard a few girls. They're—they're planning something."

"Something what?" I asked.

Megan stared at the floor. "Jennifer's mad at you. She . . . she put sand in your locker."

"What?" I asked, alarmed.

"She says you keep attacking her during practice, and she's copying something her mother did when she was in school, dumping sand in the lockers of girls they wanted to quit the team. But Nora saw me sneaking out; she knows I saw."

"She did what?" Charity asked. "Let me in there. I'll take care of this."

"No," I said, stopping Charity with my arm. "This is my battle, Charity. I need to settle this. If you do it, I'll just get made fun of." I looked up at her, hoping she knew who I meant as I continued, "Maybe by everyone."

She hesitated, but then she relented for good. "Fine. But you have to do something. You can't let bullies get their way."

"We need a 'timely' accident," I said, pacing the hallway. "Nothing too damaging, but something that will show her what it feels like to have sand in her shoes."

"And in her bra and underwear," Megan added.

"Really?" I said, disappointed. "That's gross on more than one level."

"Be glad I warned you," Megan said, nodding in agreement.

"Well, at least I only have my gym clothes in there. And now I can bring new ones with me tomorrow."

Charity nodded. "Yeah, imagine if your brace was in there. You'd probably be trailing sand behind you for days."

I immediately shushed her for using the b-word in public.

"Sheesh, Charity," Megan said, rolling her eyes. "You should know better."

I could tell Charity wanted to roll her eyes right back, but she didn't.

After a moment, I smiled. "If Jennifer wants a trip to the beach, we'll bring her the ocean."

"Okay, Miss Metaphors," Megan said, rolling her eyes. "But remember, she'll know exactly who it was."

As we waited for my mother, a plan was hatched against my nemesis (okay, one of them. I haven't forgotten about you, Mr. Newton)—a plan that involved warm, day-old tuna fish and a locker door.

"So, Brendan," my mom said, spooning peas onto his plate at dinner that night, "how's football going?"

"Yeah, how's football going?" repeated Harold, energetically. Charity kicked me under the table and smiled. Harold hated all things sports, and he'd refused to even pick up a football when my dad tried to teach him how to throw a spiral last year. I'd learned instead.

"It's going good," Brendan said. "I like my coach, and he thinks if I keep practicing I could be the team's quarterback when I'm in high school."

"That's impressive," my mom said, though I could tell she wasn't all that impressed. We Trendons enjoyed sports, but my parents thought too much pressure was put on kids to play and play well.

Mom and Dad had agreed that if we wanted to play school sports, we could dedicate as much time to them as we wanted as long as we got our homework done. I thought that was a good philosophy. It was nice to have a foot in more than one pond, as long as that foot wasn't buried in sand.

"I hear Charity's volleyball team is doing well," Brendan said.

"Yes, they won their last two tournaments these last two weekends," my dad said.

I glanced at Charity. I didn't know if she'd be able to talk about volleyball without disclosing my plan. My sister was known to crack under pressure. I had truly taken a risk trusting her with knowledge of my planned revenge. However, life in the trenches of the girls' locker room seemed to have hardened her resolve.

She smiled at Brendan and spoke with her usual poise and candor.

I smiled. Mission "Something Smells Fishy" was still on.

After dinner, I walked Brendan to the door. "Thanks for coming," I said.

"Thanks for the invite."

"I was worried you might say no after the last time you were here," I said, surprising myself with my blatant honesty. I liked to conceal my feelings until I first knew how other people felt, a habit that had gotten worse after getting my brace. I wanted to fit in, no matter what.

"I told you, it wasn't a big deal. Besides, I haven't told anybody about your brace. I promised I never will."

I don't know why, but I blushed. His willingness to keep my secret was the same as him telling me I was the prettiest person in the world.

"Thank you," I said. "You have no idea what that means to me."

He turned his head as if glancing for strangers who might overhear, and then he shrugged. "I have an idea," he said.

The strains of a popular love song echoed out of my bedroom's open window. Charity was probably doing her homework while she listened to music. "I like to stimulate both sides of my brain at the same time," she always said. I was better just focusing on one thing and getting it done, so we had to find separate times to study.

"That's really loud," Brendan said.

"Yeah—I like it," I said. Megan and I listened to it almost every day.

"You like this song?"

"Yeah. Why shouldn't I?" I asked. I realized I had no idea what Brendan's taste in music was.

"It's sappy and lame," he said. "I hate this song, but every girl I know loves it. Even my sister does, and she's sixteen years old."

I decided I didn't need to agree with him on this, since every girl he knew didn't either. So I sighed, deciding I'd have to let Brendan in on a secret of the female heart.

"Only a handful of girls get love songs written about them," I told him. "So the rest of us have to settle for the idea that a guy might at least think about us that way."

"Oh," he said.

I smiled, happy I'd gotten through to at least one stubborn boy.

"I still think it's a lame song."

I shoved his shoulder playfully. "Get outta here!" I said.

Brendan chuckled. "Yeah, I'll go before your terrible taste in music rubs off on me."

"Is Truth Trendon going to have to beat up a star quarterback?" I threw up my dukes and chased him down the steps to the sidewalk, swinging my fists at the air.

"You can't punch this face," he said, throwing his hands over his glorious visage. "Your will power isn't that strong."

"You're right," I said, without thinking. "I can't ruin such a perfect thing."

Brendan didn't say anything for a moment, but before I could try to explain my crush-induced word-vomiting, he leaned in. His lips brushed against my cheek, and then he was off, jogging in the direction of his house.

"See you tomorrow!" he called over his shoulder.

I attempted to wave, but I don't think my hand moved. I couldn't move anything. I was stuck in the ground as if Cupid himself had planted me there; a tree of love, unabashed hope, and stomach-swirling embarrassment.

"Okay, missy, get in the house! It's past your bedtime."

Harold stood at the door with his hands on his hips. My mother's laughter waterfalled behind him as she grabbed his shoulders. I saw her eyes sparkle in the dimming light.

"Better listen to him, Tru," she said. "He means business."

I walked in the door with an incredible bounce in my step. Isaac Newton: one. Truth Trendon: one million.

Even in my brace, I was winning.

CHAPTER 7
Something Fishy

The next morning before classes started, Megan met me in the locker room. Sure enough, when I opened my locker, about a gallon of sand puddled onto the floor. Another gallon remained inside. Yeesh. At least it wasn't a surprise!

Megan took a few pictures with her phone for proof, just in case, and then we started to clean up the mess. That was irksome enough for me to start begging for Megan to hurry up and complete step one of our plan.

Megan could pick any lock with a bobby pin; a pure master of the art of doorknob keyholes. She'd often helped me break into the bathroom when Charity was taking forever. She'd scrunch her brow, pull out a bobby pin from somewhere behind her ear, and bend it to slide into the tiny hole in the doorknob. In a matter of seconds, the door would be open, and she'd kiss her fingertips.

"Delicious," she'd say.

I tried to do it myself once, but it took me over half an hour, and Charity opened the door before I managed to pop the lock. She popped me on the head instead.

Now, at Jennifer's locker, Megan was visibly shaking and kept glancing over her shoulder.

"I'm only picking the lock," she whispered. I could barely hear her. "Then, I'm out of here. I refuse to get caught in this horrendously ripe revenge."

"Don't worry. I'm the one holding the fish, Megs," I said.

"Don't say my name! Someone might be listening!"

I rolled my eyes. "Just hurry up. I don't want to get caught either."

Megan had a stick pin with her, just in case the bobby pin was too thick. It wasn't. She pulled out the bobby pin, and in less than a minute, Jennifer's locker was open.

We stopped for a second, just to see what she kept in there. "Hey!" Megan set down her phone and grabbed a perfume bottle. "I've wanted this scent for weeks!"

She was about to spritz herself when I stopped her. "You don't want people to know you're involved, and yet you don't think Jennifer will find it fishy if you smell like her perfume?"

Megan sighed. "She'll find *something* fishy."

I laughed and held up the bag of tuna I'd commandeered that morning from a can at home.

Megan worriedly put the bottle back in the locker.

"We're lucky tuna sandwich is an option for lunch today," I said. "She won't suspect a thing."

"We're lucky I always know what's for lunch," Megan replied. But she still looked nervous. To be honest, I was nervous too. Megan and I were not rule-breakers, let alone personal space violators. If we got caught, I didn't know if either of us would be able to handle the guilt.

Taking a deep breath, I opened the plastic baggie. "Where should I put it?" I asked, suddenly feeling less confident in my revengefulness.

"I don't know. Her shirt, or something."

I grimaced and dumped some tuna onto the collar of her shirt and left it there. The guilt was overwhelming, but then I thought of how I'd be slipping and sliding on the gym floor in my sand-covered shoes. I added another clump of fish for good measure.

"Okay, that's enough," Megan said, plugging her nose. "Let's go."

I smiled to myself. *Stay away from the Truth and Megan: Bully Beaters.*

"Fighting for justice and the American wa—" I

101

said, just as the locker room door opened with its telltale hinge squeak. I slammed the locker shut and slid the padlock back into place. We headed for the door, just as Nora turned the corner.

"Hi," she said.

"Hey, Nora," Megan said.

"Ugh, it kinda smells in here, doesn't it?"

"Yeah," we both agreed. Megan nudged me, because I was smiling.

Nora went to her locker, and after fiddling with the lock for a few minutes, reached in and grabbed a hair tie. She pulled her hair into a high ponytail before sniffing once more. "Gross. Well, see you in English."

She left and we followed a few seconds later, relaxing immediately now that we were out in the open.

"We shouldn't have done that," Megan said.

"Are you kidding? It was a rush!"

I threw up my hands; I felt invincible. Together, Megan and I could do anything—defeat any foe, defend any friend, eliminate crime and torture.

We walked over to Band. Just as we were parting ways to get our instruments out, I stopped. "Oh no," I said.

Megan turned toward me. "What?"

"Your phone. Did you leave it in the locker?"

"No." She fumbled in her pockets and then in her backpack. "No, no, no! I did!" Megan grabbed both of my shoulders, and hissed, "What am I going to do?! She's going to find it!"

I winced. "Maybe she won't know whose phone it is?"

"Are you kidding me? We're dead! I need my phone back!"

The bell rang, and we gave each other a final panicked look before heading to our seats.

All through Band, I felt a huge ball of guilt and dread building in my gut. I forced myself to smile at Brendan when he waved at me. I refused to make eye contact with Jennifer, though I knew she followed Brendan's every move, even just a shift in one of his facial features. The worst guilt was that I'd led happy, conscientious Megan astray down a bad, can't-go-back-to-the-innocent-life kind of road.

Jennifer would discover the phone in third period, after Algebra. We'd be excommunicated. Poor Megan would be banished as a social pariah from all school functions, and I would be the evil monster that ruined her future. No sleepovers, no dates, maybe only dances where we could lurk in dark corners as we solemnly watched the girl who had forced our hand: Jennifer Henderson. She'd probably be crowned homecoming queen and everyone would worship her and she'd date Brendan Matthews . . . I wanted to puke.

Then a miracle occurred. Jennifer left Band early. According to whispers down the trumpet line, she was going home sick.

"Megs!" I said, running to her after Band. "We've—been granted—a revenge—miracle!" My breath finally caught up with me.

"I've had enough of this, Truth. We should have just cleaned up the sand and acted like it never happened."

"No! She's going home sick! We can get your phone out without her ever knowing!"

Megan's eyes flashed with surprise. "Fine. Meet me there during my study hall. But after all this, you owe me *two* horror movies."

Wasn't the horror of the junior high girls' locker room enough for her? I also wanted to remind her I hadn't left *my* phone in someone else's locker, but I didn't want to upset her more.

"Deal!" I agreed.

We went to Algebra, where I sat with bated breath waiting for the bell to ring. I even found myself ignoring Brendan altogether. Luckily, he didn't seem to notice. Megan held his attention for most of the class period anyway. I could tell she was annoyed with me over this whole tuna fiasco, and she was trying to punish me by ignoring me.

Worse than her ignoring me, however, was her extra buddy-buddy-ness with Brendan.

Recently, Megan had been acting like she didn't understand new assignments in math. It bothered me. It drove me nuts, in fact. She was better with quadratic equations than I was, but she'd rarely get through more than three problems in class because she'd talk the whole time (mostly to Brendan) about how it didn't make sense. Then, in study hall, she'd fly through the assignment and just sit there, bored.

My mood was beginning to be as rotten as day-old tuna fish, and I was glad to get away from Megan's overly chipper voice. A guilty conscience does not a good Truth make—I was itching to get Megan's phone out of the locker and be free of this situation.

In third period, I faked a cramp during Gym. Mrs. Tomjack was in her sixties and was one of the kindest women in the whole school. Unfortunately, we took advantage of that whenever there was a game of kickball we didn't want to play or when we wanted to get out of jumping rope. This was another one of those times.

"Are you hurt?" she asked.

"Yes. A cramp," I winced, holding my stomach.

"Do you need to be excused?"

"I think so," I said, weakly.

She nodded, and I limped away. Once I was out of sight, I ran like I was on fire (which I would never do—I would stop, drop, and roll until the fire was out. But maybe the body's instinct is to run; luckily, I don't know for sure). Better yet, I ran like I was trying to keep the friend I loved from being caught in a terrible act of reverse bullying.

I ran into the locker room, turning the corner to slide several feet across the slick tiles on my sandy shoe bottoms.

Megan was already there, in tears. "What's wrong, Megs?" I asked her. "Break a nail?"

She looked at me with hatred in her overfilled eyes, more sparkling tears spilling over her bottom lids every time she blinked.

"The janitor caught me trying to break into Jennifer's locker," she said, anger spewing at me in specks of spit from her lips. "She went to get the principal. She said if I left, she'd make sure I was expelled."

"Oh no!" I said, sincerely worried for her. "Did you get your phone?"

"No, I didn't get my phone, Truth!"

I sighed. "Now Jennifer's going to make both of us look stupid—"

"That's all you care about, isn't it? How you're going to look in front of everyone. In front of stupid Brendan Matthews!"

"You seem pretty intent on impressing him with your own stupidity," I muttered.

"What?" Megan almost screamed.

I was being a horrible friend. I felt ugly and mean and downright pathetic. Before-Brace Truth Trendon would never have stooped so low as to involve a friend in an act of breaking and entering, let alone commit revenge in the first place. Before-Brace Truth was a peaceful person.

"Nothing. I'm just trying to fix this."

"You don't even care that I could get detention or—or—suspended. People are going to think I'm a thief!" She threw up her hands.

"That's not true." I grabbed her arm and, with a burst of heroic pride (and my attempt at saving our dangling friendship), I said, "Get out of here. It was me the whole time."

"No. They'll know."

"How? The janitor doesn't know your name. I'll take care of this. It's my problem."

Megan wiped her eyes and considered my offer.

"Thanks, Tru," she said. Then she ran out the back door of the locker room, avoiding the main entryway.

Immediately, I regretted my decision. Alone in that big gray cement room, my world was going to end. I knew Brendan Matthews would hear about this. Everyone would. *I* would be the thief, and I didn't even know how to pick a lock.

I took a deep breath and then wrinkled my nose. The smell was pretty bad.

I waited a full minute before I considered leaving the crime scene, and the moment I gathered enough courage, the principal entered the locker room with the janitor right behind her.

"What do you know. She did stay here," said the principal, Ms. Eastin.

"I knew I'd scared her," the janitor said. She grinned wickedly, and chuckled a deep, throaty laugh. She was a short, stout woman, and she had long dark hairs sprouting above the edges of her lips. Her eyes were beady and narrowed as she glowered at me. I understood how she'd made Megan cry.

When her gaze met mine, I saw a flash of confusion play across her face.

I smiled, trying to act like this was all a misunderstanding. "Hi," I said.

"Hey, did you change clothes?" the janitor asked me.

"Nope," I said.

Her forehead furrowed and her chin jutted forward—she clearly didn't believe me. But Ms. Eastin quickly took charge of the situation.

"Hello," she greeted me. "What is your name?"

She asked the question like she might know the answer, but didn't want to be wrong and suffer the embarrassment.

It was a small school, so I was a little miffed she didn't remember me. I was memorable, wasn't I? I liked to think that what Ms. Eastin did all day was sit and stare at pictures of students, memorizing their names so she could go out in the hall and yell at the misbehaving and miscreant during class breaks. That's what I would do if I were principal. I'd yell at everyone; no one would be safe from my reign of authority and rule. No child left behind. Imagining being able to terrorize my fellow students: that's the kind of mood I was in.

"Truth Trendon," I said.

"Trendon. That's it. Your sister is Charity, right?"

"Yes." *Of course she'd remember Charity's name.*

My brain zapped with an idea. They didn't know who I was. They didn't know this wasn't my locker.

"I'm sorry. I forgot my key at home, and I really need . . ." glanced at the janitor and then at Ms. Eastin. "You know, a girl thing. I was just too embarrassed to say it before."

Ms. Eastin smiled. "Oh good grief. Let her into her locker so she can get back to class, Patty."

"Thank you," I said, relieved. I hoped Jennifer had a tampon or something I could grab so I didn't look like the liar I was.

The janitor (or "Patty," as I would forever know her from then on) pulled a small key from the ring on her belt and unlocked Jennifer's locker. She glanced at me once more, shook her head, and looked away as Ms. Eastin asked her about her plans for the weekend.

While they were busy talking, I was able to grab Megan's phone and put it into my right pocket. I also saw I'd left the bag of tuna. My conscience took over, and, hiding behind the locker door, I tried to scrape out the large hunks of fish from Jennifer's shirt (though I didn't try *that* hard) and put them back into the bag. Then I slipped the bag into the left pocket of my mesh gym shorts.

"Thanks again," I said.

I smiled politely and headed for the hallway. Since I'd already broken so many rules that day, I left the locker room to walk past the open study hall, which was also the cafeteria. The hallway was quiet, and my sand-covered shoes were even more slippery on the hard tile floor than the gym floor. I spied Megan sitting forlornly at the end of a table, her books closed and her head propped up by her hand.

Look up, I thought urgently. *Look at me, you sad angel.*

As if reading my mind, she glanced up and we made eye contact. I pulled her phone out of my pocket and waved it around, smiling. Her eyes widened and she smiled, relief washing over her troubled face and tense shoulders.

"Can I see a hall pass, Truth?" Mr. Landers asked, looking up from the front table.

I'd forgotten there were other people there.

"I—um, forgot it. I'll go get it," I lied. As I turned around, the bell rang, and I walked back to the locker room to change clothes. But when I got there, I saw two eighth-grade girls on the side where I usually changed by myself. The locker I had shoved my brace into was now open, and they were standing in front of it. I quickly sat down on a bench on the other side.

"What is that?" one of them, a girl named Katrina, asked.

"It looks like a cast or something," Brandy, the other girl, said.

"Should we tell Mrs. Tomjack?"

"Naw, she probably stored it there herself. Probably something we'll talk about in health class," Brandy said.

She kicked the brace's plastic hip with her shoe, and they laughed as it shook against the metal of the locker.

They finally left. "Hey, Truth," Brandy said as they passed.

"Hello, goodbye," I said, and they laughed.

The warning bell rang. I had a minute to get to class. I looked at myself. Girls wore athletic shorts and t-shirts all the time, and my clothes were fresh from home that day. And I liked the idea of not wearing my brace for the rest of the day. If nothing else, I could blame Jennifer and my immature volleyball teammates (myself included) for not being able to wear it.

I slammed the open locker door and put my school clothes in my designated locker a few rows down, now sans sand. Happy, I practically skipped to lunch. My torso was free for the afternoon.

112

I was especially happy when I went to see Oliver during my fourth period study hall. He smiled when I rapped my knuckles on my stomach, and nothing but the soft *plump* of skin on skin sounded forth.

"You're something else," he said.

"What do you mean?" I leaned casually against the wall.

"Well, you know you're going to have to put the brace back on once you get home, right?"

I nodded, sad but aware.

"So why are you so happy right now?"

"It's relief, a break. My body is free for the afternoon."

Oliver looked down. Not at his legs, but like he was considering something. "Oh."

I felt my freeness melt away. Oliver couldn't leave his wheelchair like I could take my brace off. We were supposed to meet to commiserate, but maybe our meetings were a bad thing for him; I'd only been thinking of myself, but I never meant to make him feel worse.

"Will you help me with something?" he asked, after several moments.

I didn't even hesitate. "Of course."

"Not today. Maybe next time."

"What is it?"

"Nothing difficult." He didn't say more, and I didn't push it.

After a while, I brought up homework and how much easier elementary school was, when parents would help with the dioramas and papier-mâché projects. The tension was palpable in the room, and I wondered if Mrs. Werth could feel it when she came back.

I left early, feeling uneasy, but Oliver smiled and said he'd see me next week. I pushed away from the wall and waved, getting a whiff of my armpit. Not great. The stress of the day had already gotten to me, and it was far from over.

Even though I'd gotten Megan her phone back, she avoided me all afternoon in sixth period Science and seventh period English. This was annoying because in Science we were building miniature bridges out of toothpicks and, though Megan wasn't in my group, she was directly behind me, and this would have been an opportune time to joke around and discuss how gluing toothpicks together would turn us into engineers.

Instead, she kept her back to me the entire time.

I was chastised three times by our teacher for trying to tell Megan she had nothing to worry about, so I gave up. Once, while stepping around a fellow bridge builder to help hold a piece of suspended pick, I swear Megan even tried to kick me.

In English, her gaze remained focused on the chalkboard as sentence structure became the topic of the day, for about the fifth day in a row. I finally grabbed her before eighth period History and forced her to stand there while I talked. She relaxed as soon as I said it had all added up to nothing and we weren't going to get in trouble.

"But you did look pretty when you were crying," I said.

"Yeah, right," she said. "Pretty pathetic. Why couldn't I have thought of something like that?"

"Because you're the brawn of this operation, Megs. You've got the right tools to get the job done. I've got the brains," I said in a sinister voice.

She laughed, but not as much as I expected. "Next time, Brains, remind Brawn not to get involved in your reckless shenanigans."

"What are you two talking about?" Brendan appeared next to us in the hall.

"Nothing," I said. "Girl stuff."

I winked at Megan. She smiled.

"Okay, I'll stay out of it then."

Brendan walked us to the History classroom and dropped us off. I hung back to talk to him.

"Did you change clothes?" he asked me.

"Yeah, I didn't have time to change back after Gym. Do I smell that bad?" I asked, joking.

"Not that bad. You look a little wrinkled."

"Oh," I said, looking down. I guess I did carry my gym clothes to school crumpled in a ball at the bottom of my backpack.

"I think I can still smell the tuna from lunch, though," Brendan said, looking in the direction of the cafeteria.

The warning bell rang, and he headed off to his class.

I set my books down on the desk next to Megan's and talked with the girls around us until the final bell rang.

"Take your seats. Let's get started," said Mr. Landers. "We've been a bit slow this semester and have some catching up to do."

I plunked into my seat, bumping against the metal bar that connected the seat to the desk.

As I sat, a loud popping noise sounded from within my shorts. Everyone looked around; luckily they didn't seem to know where the noise came from. I looked around too, hoping I had a confused expression on my face, rather than the terrified one I feared was plastered there forever.

The bag of tuna. It was still in my pocket. I had completely forgotten about it. Only now, it burst forth like a ray of sun through the clouds and shone itself all over the inside of my athletic shorts. No wonder Brendan still smelled tuna from lunch; a ripe bag of it had been in my pocket the whole time.

"That was strange," said Mr. Landers.

Unlike a lot of the faculty, especially Mr. Umland, Mr. Landers was very thoughtful in his speech and spoke slowly so we could catch every word. And though he was serious about history, Mr. Landers often strayed off topic, something we took advantage of whenever possible.

"Speaking of slow, you know what truly tests my patience?" he said. "Well, besides grading your essays. Traffic on I-80 during rush hour. The speed limit is seventy-five, but there are just too many cars to be able to drive that fast. I was on it this weekend and there was road construction. I went from seventy-five to a complete stop in less than a mile."

"How long were you stopped?" Erwin Bowden asked.

"Fifteen minutes."

"Geez."

"You're telling me. Years ago, the first time I got stuck there, I was driving an '83 Thunderbird. Now, this car was pristine!"

I glanced at Megan while Landers talked about the "souped-up" interior of his first car. She was staring at my pocket. Liquid tuna juice (yuck!) was leaking out from my mesh shorts (double-yuck!).

Megan flung her hand over her mouth to keep from gagging. I wanted to blow chunks myself, but I also wanted to avoid drawing attention to myself at all costs. I didn't remember there being so much water left in the can when I dumped the fatal fish meat into the plastic baggie that morning, but apparently my left thigh was a good pressure-strainer.

Gingerly, I shifted my bodily girth to my other leg. I considered sliding the plastic baggie out from my pocket onto the floor and trying to get the class to accept it had been there the whole time, but I knew that wouldn't work because one of the Klafken twins sat behind me, and Tina was too observant to be unaware of a toxic-smelling fish carrier just appearing on the floor. She was probably watching me as I squirmed in my chair, cognizant of the permeable, synthetic mess ruminating near my underwear.

"And I'm telling you, the cop that pulled me over did not care that I had dropped my favorite Rush CD; he gave me a ticket anyways. Do you smell that?" Landers put his nose in the air and rolled his head right, then left. "Unpleasant."

Several people nodded in agreement. I plugged my nose and bobbed my head along with them.

"Yuck," I mouthed to Megan. She snorted and covered her eyes.

"It reminds me of the time I went to a fishery on a field trip in fifth grade," Landers said.

He ran his fingers down his tie as he spoke. Then he paused and stared at the back wall of the classroom, the fluorescent lights reflecting off his just-barely-balding forehead.

Something was happening. Something big. I looked around the room; my classmates had noticed it too. We'd reached a new level of Landers' stratospheric storytelling and opened a new door to endless possibilities of childhood recollections. We'd heard about his memories from high school before, but now we were diving into the elementary school era of Landers' life.

I gave myself a mental pat on the back. Even though I would never admit it to anyone but Megan, this new unleashing of brain matter was my doing;

my "fishtastrophe." With Landers' epic reminiscent meandering, we'd probably never have to read another chapter about the Mesopotamians again. So, even though I was more uncomfortable than ever, I sat quietly through the rest of eighth period, listening to the story of Landers' most beloved field trip.

As a class, we successfully coaxed him into reenacting his classmate's fall into the human-constructed river: he perched on top of his desk, all six feet three inches of him, leaned back, and then jumped to the ground behind it. Fluidly he transitioned to telling us about the bus ride to the river and then the bus ride back as he maneuvered between the rows of desks just like Ol' Jimmy did with the long yellow bus.

His memories flowed nonstop. Next we heard about his favorite backpack; a bird pooped on it when he stepped off the bus and his mom threw it out. He panned out to the layout of his hometown, stretching his arms wide in his yellow shirt and showing off the even-more-yellow sweat stains in its armpits. I swear, at one point I even saw tears in Landers' eyes. We applauded. We cheered. Wc encored until the bell rang.

Mr. Landers smiled at all of us, proud, as we left the room. I walked out the door clutching my messy pocket in my hand.

I made it back to the locker room without anyone realizing a can of tuna fish had manifested itself in my shorts. Changing into the clothes I'd brought for volleyball practice, I couldn't stop grinning. When I emerged into the hallway to wait for Megan, Mr. Landers passed by and high-fived me, along with every other student he passed. I smiled as I watched him go. It was a good day for both of us.

Chapter 8

The Discovery (Part 2)

L ife was rockin' and rollin' for me as a seventh grader at the end of September. Brendan was hanging around me even more, my team had won the most scrimmages in volleyball, Megan was no longer angry about her seminar for being late back to study hall because of me or our fishy revenge, and I had a listening ear and confidant in Oliver.

Jennifer Henderson had grown outwardly nicer to me for some reason, even if she didn't seem sincere. After she pulled out her t-shirt with the chunks of tuna I'd left behind on it, she briefly analyzed it, shook it out, and then pulled it on over her head. I leaned around my side of the lockers to watch. She glanced at me, and I held her gaze. But I didn't mention the sand, and she didn't mention the tuna.

Every day she walked by my locker when Brendan was leaning on the one next to mine, and she smiled and waved, but I saw the glare in her eyes. In Gym she'd inquire (nicely, too nicely) in front of all the girls if I was still testing out football pads. They would laugh while I shook my head, with an enormous fake smile plastered across my face.

"Not anymore," I answered every time. "But I can let Coach know you're interested, Jen."

She hated to be called Jen, and I smiled politely every time I said it. She would smile politely back, and we'd part ways, each wishing the other would just disappear from the school grounds.

My biggest fear was that Jennifer would discover my real reason for sneaking out of the locker room and expose me to the rest of the school. Changing for Gym and volleyball was difficult, but at least I had Megan with me standing guard for volleyball. Gym was frightening. Every time I ran to the locker room, trying to beat everyone there so I could separate the noisy straps of my brace and shove it into an unmarked locker, my heart would race as if I were guilty of breaking and entering.

Nevertheless, I was either becoming more careless, or Isaac Newton had discovered I was triumphing over his gravitational hold and had upped the ante. In the middle of English one day, I sneezed, and my brace's top Velcro strap ripped apart with a sound reminiscent of a fighter jet taking off, making my blood freeze in my veins.

I immediately sat up and looked around the room with my peripheral vision as Mrs. Pike lectured about complex sentences, but no one seemed to have noticed the sound. For the rest of the class, I kept my arms straight from my armpits to my hips, to keep the two sides of my brace from pushing the fabric of my shirt out in the back. As a result, my notes weren't legible, and I got a ninety-two percent instead of my normal ninety-eight average on the quiz the next day.

At my next appointment with Christopher, he replaced the Velcro for me, but he wasn't very sympathetic.

"I'm terrified that if I sneeze or cough, the brace will explode off me in a glistening white fury, taking my clothes with it," I said.

Christopher scrunched up his face, a look that reminded me of Harold when he suffered constipation. "That won't happen. At least not the clothes part. The Velcro does wear down though. That's why I replace it for you every visit."

He didn't seem to appreciate my humor, though I did get a laugh from my mother, who sat in the room and said polite, appropriate things.

Christopher was, however, impressed by how tightly I liked to wear my brace, and he hacked off more from the middle, making it even smaller and tighter.

"Usually I have to fight children to wear the brace tighter, but you're a piece of cake!" he said.

I didn't like being called a child, but I smiled. Then he told another sad story about a heavy-set girl who hated her brace. I understood the girl in his story; I hated my brace too. I just didn't like floating around in the middle of a plastic prop. And most important, there was a significantly smaller chance of people seeing my brace if it was fitted tighter to my body.

I was happy when the appointment was over. Christopher's a great guy—he always made me feel like I was absolutely normal for having a spine deformity. But it was still nice when I was able to leave his office and know I wouldn't be back for about three months. And I was really looking forward to the day when I could walk out of those sliding glass doors for the last time, knowing I'd never have to go back in.

Actually, against my will, I was growing more comfortable in the brace. The constant pinches and digs into my skin had become normal, and my early morning and afternoon sweats were expected. But I still couldn't wait until the end of the day when I could take it off. Every day, my damp skin burned as I pulled the thing off, tossed it on the ground, and threw my arms up in the air, spinning in circles and letting the cool, refreshing air envelop me.

Volleyball practice and scrimmages remained my favorite part of the day. Those were the only times when I felt in complete control of my body. While other girls groaned at having to run sprints, I was the first one at the line, ready to take off. When the coaches told me to jump, I launched as far off the ground as my legs would allow. If the ball was about to smack the floor, I rolled, sacrificing life and limb to punch it back into the air. It felt amazing.

I played outside hitter, and though none of us seventh graders could hit especially hard, we were at least hitting the ball over the net most of the time. I whacked the ball every time with relish, and whenever possible, I aimed for Jennifer. She'd stopped squealing and getting mad and instead would pass it back and then try to hit me. It was a battle, but I enjoyed it immensely.

We scrimmaged every Wednesday and Friday. Megan and I had ended up on the same team. She played the position of setter, partially because she didn't like having to receive serves and partially because she was actually pretty good at it. She liked to set it to me, shout, "Truth pound!" and then cheer wildly if my hit connected with the floor, which was called a kill.

One afternoon I had three kills in a row, and all of my teammates began shouting "Truth pound!" whenever I jumped up to hit it. I felt adrenaline kick in, and the next time Megan set it to me, I thought of the stupid brace sitting and waiting for me in the locker room. I could feel it wrapping around me and stealing my breath away with each Velcro strap. I imagined knocking Isaac Newton senseless as I launched into the air and slapped the ball. *Take this Truth pounding, Newton.*

Unfortunately, this time the ball slammed into the net instead of over it—then bounced back and hit me right in the stomach. Oof.

"Darn," Megan said. "You looked so angry I was sure you were going to kill it again."

I bit my lip and rolled the ball to the other team to serve. I hadn't realized my rage for my brace had been showing on my face.

Megan high-fived me anyway. "Let's try it again!"

Though I hated having to put my brace back on, it seemed less daunting after doing something I really enjoyed. No matter how hard Newton might try, he couldn't take away my spirit, at least where volleyball was concerned.

However, Newton crossed the line when he started messing with something very important in junior high: hygiene.

One day while walking to Band, I passed two eighth-grade girls. One of them pointed at me and waved her hand back and forth in front of her face as her nose wrinkled. Then she mouthed the words "she smells."

I fought the urge to cry and then the urge to run away from school and never come back. Instead, after Band I went straight to Megan.

"Do I indeed carry the stench of a trillion sweaty socks?"

Megan laughed.

"Be honest. Does it need to be burned to eliminate the stink?"

After a long, dramatically overdrawn sniff, she shrugged and said, "It wouldn't hurt to wash it, I suppose."

That made me realize I couldn't just ignore the brace after I took it off at night. The last thing I needed was to smell like a boys' locker room. So I began wiping the inside of my brace with rubbing alcohol, which Christopher said would get rid of daily body sweat and odor.

On weekends, I washed it in the tub ("like a

puppy," according to Harold) and let it dry overnight. It seemed to help, but it was a hassle, and I awarded ol' Newton one more point for another contribution to ruining my life.

One Saturday afternoon (post brace bath), my mother took me with her to Oliver's house, where she was meeting his mom to do some PTA work.

"'PTA work'—pssh, you're really just going to be talking about how wonderful I am," I said. "What could be better than talking about me?"

"Believe me, there are options," my mother said, eying me from the driver's seat. She smiled. "But not too many."

"You know, you're really pushing this friendship with Oliver, Mom. Are you trying to arrange a marriage or something?"

"Don't be silly. You're too young to even think about that." My mother rolled her eyes.

"So you're saying it's our age you don't like, and not the fact he can't keep his hands off my turtley body?"

"Truth Trendon!" My mom parked the car in front of Oliver's house and turned to face me.

"I'm kidding!" I said.

"I hope you don't talk like that in front of your friends."

I widened my eyes and shrugged, dramatically feigning innocence.

My mother narrowed her eyes but got out of the car. "I give up," she said, wrapping her arms around my shoulders as she guided me out of the car and up to the door. "I'll tell your father we're done with you. You're as good as you're going to get."

"You really are the lucky ones," I said.

She kissed the top of my head and rang the doorbell.

Oliver answered. Again, just as it had been at my house, it was strange to see him outside of school. I didn't expect him to be out of his chair or anything, but I felt almost as if I'd been zapped to another dimension.

"Hey," he said.

"Hi," I said, imitating his nonchalance.

"Oliver!" My mom stepped into the house like she owned the place and hugged him. "Truth has just been saying the nicest things about you!"

I thought about what I'd said in the car and I burst out laughing.

"What?" Oliver asked, his gaze flitting between my mother and me.

"I'll tell you in a minute," I said.

My mother squeezed my arm and muttered under her breath, "You better not."

I stifled my laughter and followed Oliver down the hallway. He turned left into a room that would have been brightly lit, had it not been for the navy curtains covering the windows. My eyes took a moment to adjust to the dim lighting compared to the sunlit entryway we'd just left.

"So," I said, feeling suddenly aware I was alone with a boy in his bedroom. Besides Harold's bedroom, I'd never been in a boy's room before. I felt as if I'd leveled up or crossed some threshold nearer to teenagedom than ever before. "Am I the first girl to see the man cave?" I winced as soon as the words left my mouth. I wasn't off to a stellar afternoon of self-confidence and poise.

"No," Oliver said, raising his eyebrows at me as if he were talking to a child who'd just said the grass was blue. "I do have friends outside of the ones forced to come visit me."

"Of course you do," I said, suddenly blushing. "I—I n-never meant—"

"Truth, calm down. Have a seat before you hyperventilate."

I took a deep breath and sat on the edge of his

bed, which was really the only place to sit. Oliver had moved to his desk, where he started typing on his keyboard while a group of computer-generated characters fought on the screen of his laptop.

"I'll be done in a second."

"It's fine," I said, taking the opportunity to look around the room. I was surprised to see several toys, mostly building-block sets portraying various spaceships and scenes from different fantasy and science-fiction movies, sitting on the bookshelves on either side of his bed. There were a few framed posters, one of a band I recognized from his t-shirt, and another of a warrior hero from some movie I wasn't deemed mature enough to see yet. There was a stuffed animal sitting near his pillow.

I grinned and grabbed it. It was a stuffed moose with a plaid scarf around its neck. "This guy got a name?"

Oliver looked up, and to my surprise, he blushed. With surprising swiftness, he closed his laptop, wheeled over, grabbed the stuffed animal, and shoved it in his closet.

"Moose," he said.

"Don't you think it's a bit rude to shove Moose away like that? Maybe he's afraid of the dark."

"Shut up," Oliver said, but he grinned at me. "So,

what have you been telling your mom about me? I'm just too much of a man that you can't keep your hands off me?"

I laughed so hard I nearly fell over onto the bed. I told him what I'd said and he laughed too.

We calmed down, and I wiped my eyes. "Sorry if you're bummed I'm here," I said after a beat. "I know we're being forced to spend a lot of time together lately."

"You know, you're not actually that bad. Some people might call you downright tolerable."

"Yeah? What a compliment. You know just how to warm a girl's heart."

"Naw. I just know you."

I'd been teasing, but Oliver's voice sounded serious. I tried to lighten the mood. "What's the deal with all these toys? You afraid to grow up or something?"

"Yeah, Peter Pan visits me at night and I fly away. These floppy legs are actually great wings."

I stared at the floor. I never knew what to say about his physical disabilities.

"You don't have to be afraid of offending me, you know," Oliver said, after a few moments of silence.

"I don't like to upset people," I said.

"Well, I'm not 'people.' Your popularity isn't going to be affected on account of me."

"I . . ." I hesitated. When I was with Oliver, I honestly didn't think about my social status. Whenever I told him a story of nearly being caught with my brace or tripping up the stairs, I just cared about his reaction.

"Fine, but I don't want to upset people I care about," I said, my voice sounding less chipper and more serious than I'd intended.

To my surprise, Oliver didn't tease me. Instead, he nodded. "That's an admirable quality." He narrowed his eyes. "I guess."

I laughed and shoved his shoulder.

He grabbed it and winced.

"Oh my gosh!" I said, standing up and covering my mouth. "Are you okay? I didn't mean to hurt you—"

His loud laughter sent my fear reeling into annoyance.

"That's not funny!" I said, hitting him again.

He finished laughing and then sighed with satisfaction. "I was just seeing if I was someone you care about," he said, teasing me.

"Not anymore," I said.

"Yeah, right," he said. He left the room and I followed him to the living room. He climbed from his wheelchair and lifted himself onto the couch, where he reclined and extended his legs out onto the foot-rest. His feet moved once in a while, and I realized he was moving them on his own. Interesting. He turned to look at me once he'd gotten comfortable.

"Thanks," he said.

"For what?" I asked, baffled.

"For not looking at me with pity, like nearly every-one else I know does. Even my parents do once in a while. But you just observe. It's refreshing."

I sat down on the other end of the couch, leaving a seat between us.

"You're welcome?" I said. "I wasn't aware of my refreshingness."

He laughed. "Good. If you have to think about it, it's not as refreshing."

We sat together on the couch watching a rerun of an old sitcom, sometimes in silence, sometimes dis-agreeing about the quality of it (he thought it was predictable and bland; I found it hopeful and encour-aging). I realized how comfortable I felt—not once did I worry about what Oliver thought about something before I gave my opinion. I felt more like Before-Brace Truth. Confident and happy and content to be me. To be honest, it was a very "refreshing" feeling.

The next morning, though, Newton's plans for my demise were already back in full swing. Brendan stopped by my house—he'd won a local scholarship for football camp that summer. His mom and older sister had gone shopping, but he wanted to share the news with someone, so he'd come over to tell me. I was flattered and honored.

"That's awesome!" I said, excited that he was excited. I invited him in to join me at the kitchen table, where I was drawing a picture for Megan of her cat, Mr. Winston.

"I brought the letter," Brendan said.

"Cool," I said as I started working on my sketch again. "Read it aloud to me."

"No, I'll feel weird. Like I'm being cocky or something. And you'll read it faster than I can, anyway." He tried to hand it to me.

"Come on, Brendan," I said, "I'm almost done with this. Just read it. I won't think you're bragging or anything."

I looked back at my sketch of the cat. He needed more fat rolls.

"I don't want to read it," Brendan said.

"Fine, then don't."

He was silent, and out of the corner of my eye, I realized he was staring at the floor.

I looked up from my sketch, curious. Brendan had never acted like this before.

"I can't," he said quietly. He had turned bright red. He looked at me with such embarrassment in his eyes, I thought maybe my belt shoelace had come untied and my pants had fallen down. But I was sitting down. That wasn't possible.

"What do you mean, you can't?" I asked him.

"Can I tell you something? You have to promise not to tell anyone."

I immediately thought of my reveal nearly a month before, when Brendan was so easy-going and accepting of my brace. I thought about how nervous I'd felt before I opened the bathroom door and faced him.

I sat up straighter and looked him in the eye. "I promise," I said.

"I can't read," Brendan said.

If he had said he was a zombie or that he had a tiny fairy that lived in his ear who gave him his athletic ability, I would have been less shocked. I realized my open jaw might appear cruel, so I quickly shut it.

He started talking so fast I could barely understand him "I know it sounds impossible," he said, "but when I was little, none of the letters made sense, so I just pretended to understand. And my parents were too busy fighting to notice."

"What?" I asked, a bit too loudly. But I was actually thinking: *That's your superpower? Illiteracy?*

"And don't pull the 'dumb jock' stereotype on me. I'm a rock star with numbers."

"I don't get it," I said, shaking my head. "You've gotten through seventh grade, and you can't read? Nothing? Not even *Goodnight Moon* or *Calvin and Hobbes?*"

"Don't mock me, Truth. I'm not proud of it. I've just found ways around it."

"But there are tests and book reports! I mean, restaurant menus! Texting! The internet! Technology!" I covered my mouth to keep myself from shouting more random words.

Brendan hesitated. As cute as he was, this little— or, rather, *big* fact—could ruin him. "Look, I know some things, and with the rest, I make do. My sister has old copies of her book reports. I just type them up and hand them in. If I need a specific book, I match the title to free essays online and hope it fits the assignment well enough."

"But—"

"As for tests, there are neighbors who forget to cover their answers. And when you're nice enough to people, they sometimes just give you the answers you need to pass."

"But you'll get caught!" I said.

Brendan shrugged. "Haven't yet."

"Oh my." I sighed.

I didn't know how a living, breathing—don't forget stunning—intelligent person could actually function in a world where he couldn't read. I knew Brendan was smart, because he was good at math. It made me feel like I'd been going through my life assuming many things about people that weren't even true. Maybe Hairy was actually a female guinea pig, or my father was from Russia and was now an agent for the CIA. My world was upside down. Pretty much everything important I'd ever learned was from a book. That wealth of knowledge was missing from Brendan's life. He may have been more popular than me, but no way would I want to trade places with him.

Finally, he sat next to me at the kitchen table. He stared at the letter on the table—what must have been almost gibberish to him. "Tru, you have to promise me you won't tell anyone."

If only I hadn't made him promise about my back brace. My instinct was to run to my parents so they could tell Brendan's mother, but I knew that would catapult me off the popular ladder like a rock from a slingshot. I'd shot a slingshot before; the rock popped out the back of it and hit me in the eye. Being the "girl who destroyed Brendan Matthews" would only backfire on me, even if I had good intentions.

"If I could do something to change my back, I would do *anything*," I told Brendan. "You can change this; you can make it better."

He continued to just stare at the letter.

"I promise I won't tell anyone," I said. "But you *have* to learn to read. I can help you."

And then we can run away together, because you'll realize even more how awesome I am because I know things, like books.

Brendan's silence was starting to make me feel stupid, even though he was the one who couldn't use the alphabet.

Finally, he looked at me and smiled. "You're bearable enough, Trendon. You've got a deal."

"Right-o," I said. To distract my swirling brain, I looked away and drew another fat roll onto Mr. Winston. His plumpness was just about perfect.

"Uh, Tru?"

"Yeah?" I looked up again.

"Can you read me the letter?"

I slid my chair closer to Brendan's, abandoning my drawing, and I put the letter flat on the table.

I made him repeat each sentence after me. He did know more words than I thought, and (disappointingly) his breath was worse than I thought. I wondered what my breath was like as I leaned away. Then my mom walked through the back door.

"Hey, Tru! Hello, Brendan!" She had been doing yard work, which always put her in a cheerful mood. I leaned further away from the attractive boy in our kitchen.

"Hi, Mom," I said. "Did you conquer the leaves in the backyard?"

"They shall live to see another day. My rake will not. Never bet on a plastic rake head when you drop it against cement," she said sadly. She shook her head and drank a glass of water. I smiled sympathetically and looked back down at the letter.

"Whatcha working on?" she asked. "It looks like you're decoding a cryptogram."

I felt Brendan's entire body stiffen.

"Oh, it's about football," I said, wrinkling my face to show my detestation. "Brendan's explaining it to me."

"Ah, I understand," my mom said, winking at him. "You must have a lot of patience, Brendan."

"I try," said Brendan. "And that's probably enough for today," he continued. "I don't want Truth's brain to be overwhelmed."

Even though I knew he was joking, something about the way he said it made me want to crumple up his letter and force him to eat it. But then he looked at me, smiled gratefully, and brushed his hand against mine as he folded up the letter. He smiled at me once more at the door and then left after he said goodbye to my mom.

"That smile," I sighed, when the door shut behind him.

"What?" my mom asked.

"I, uh—umm," my mind was awash with words from his dazzling incisors and canines. "I got nothing. That boy is hot," I said.

My mom burst out laughing.

"I thought you'd be mad," I said.

"Mad? Of course not! It's normal for you to have feelings like that," my mom said.

"Whoa! Back up 'The Talk' train, Mom. I don't need that today."

"Chug-a-chug-a-chug-a." My mom moved her arms in rolling motions as she walked toward me.

I leapt out of my chair, laughing and running away from her.

"I swear I'll scream," I said.

"Oh, quit it. But it's normal for you to be interested in someone you find attractive."

"Who would have thought he'd be interested in me?"

My mom immediately lowered her wheel-arms and furrowed her brows at me. "What? How dare you say that! We Trendons are the most interesting people in the world!"

She forced me back into my chair and sat next to me.

"You aren't even technically a Trendon," I said. "You're genetically a Smith."

"And no one lets me forget it. Boring ol' Sue Smith."

I frowned. "You're calling yourself boring? You just did a train impression for a full two minutes despite a negative response! How can I believe you when you say I'm *not* boring?"

"My name! My name was so boring!" Mom dropped her head in her hands, then popped back up. "But that's beside the point." She grabbed my hands. "You are one of the most caring, intelligent, and lovely young ladies in the world. How could someone not be interested in you?"

I patted my rib-hump. "Uh, the fact that upon seeing me, most people probably think I'm related to Frankenstein?"

"Scoliosis does not make Truth Trendon," my

mom said. "The Truth I know would make scoliosis whatever she wanted it to be. If that meant she joked about it and let everyone know it didn't control her life, or accepted it was a tiny pimple in the wonderful life she's going to have, that's what she'd do."

I sighed. It was hard to convince the woman who carried you for nine months and then pushed you out after ten hours of labor that you weren't worth a dime. "Thanks, Mom," I said.

I lugged myself out of my chair and walked up to my room, where I lay on my back and pulled out *Great Expectations*. After a few moments, I'd forgotten about my brace as I became lost in the world of Pip as he met the very past-obsessed Miss Havisham.

When my dad yelled at me to come down to dinner, I put the book aside, returning to the real world in a bit of a haze, briefly disappointed to have to come back from the faraway world of the book. A sad thought struck me—Brendan didn't know that feeling. He had never experienced reading a good book.

Maybe everyone had something that held them back, whether they were willing to admit it or not.

CHAPTER 9
A Brief Lesson

*B*rendan and I decided to meet inconspicuously at the public library after school three days a week after junior high football and volleyball ended in mid-October. After volleyball was no longer an option, it was nice to have time with Brendan to look forward to. Even if it meant wearing my brace.

The library was within walking distance of the school, and I knew the library building well, since my mother worked there. I planned on avoiding the afternoons when she worked, and if someone caught us, we could always lie about having a school project to work on.

Brendan appreciated my assistance with bettering his reading ability; I, however, still appreciated just being in his presence.

For our first meeting, I sat at the back table in the corner that was hidden behind three rows of nonfiction bookshelves. No offense to West River residents, but I wasn't worried about someone deciding to take up learning Latin and coming back to this corner to get the library's single tome on Latin language. Not a hot commodity, that Latin book. As I scattered my books across the table, I considered checking out the Latin book just because I felt bad for it, but then Brendan walked up and the thought vanished.

"You're sure no one will find us?" he whispered.

"You don't have to whisper," I said, in an equally quiet voice. I was positive we were safe in our secluded little corner, but I also didn't want to be wrong and disgrace him. I'd dubbed him my "valiant reader" and part of me felt like I was his hero; I was the only girl—the only person—he'd ever told.

He sighed and set his backpack down on the table. "I only have about half an hour today. My dad's picking me up from my mom's to go watch a football game."

"That's okay," I said, masking my disappointment like a champ. "We just need to see where you're at." I'd found an *Introduction to Reading* book at the library and thought it would be a good place to start. The moment Brendan sat in that chair, I leapt into "Truth Trendon, teacher" mode.

"Do you know the alphabet?" I asked.

"Truth," he said. I could tell he was insulted.

"I need an answer."

"I'm not an idiot."

I stared him down.

"Yes," he said.

"Great. Let's hear it."

"You're kidding."

"Not at all. I captain a tough ship, but we aim for nothing but results." I pointed my finger at him and winked. He wasn't impressed.

Brendan rattled off the letters faster than I could say them in my head. I thought about asking if he realized each letter was different and not part of one long word, but I didn't want to make him regret telling me his secret.

"Good!" I said, a bit too excitedly.

"I'm not an idiot, Truth," he said again.

"I know!" So I jumped in, talking about parts of sentences. Brendan immediately grew interested because he knew what nouns and verbs were—he pictured them in his head; he just couldn't write out a full sentence that was seventh grade material. So it wasn't about connecting words to images or meanings; it was just about the words themselves.

After about fifteen minutes, I discovered we were basically nowhere. He'd just brushed up on one-word nouns he knew. "Okay," I said slowly, looking at the table so I wouldn't see if Brendan's eyes grew angry from another demeaning question, "so what about the different sounds the vowels in the alphabet make?"

"What about them?" *So far, so good.*

"Do you know what they are? Like what sounds an "A" can make?"

Brendan stared at me, and then blushed bright red. I'd struck a chord in his brain, or in his blood's ability to get to his face—which I suppose comes from a demand in his brain.

"No. Well, I don't know for sure."

"Good!" I said, once again too eagerly. Now we had a starting place. I grabbed my introductory reader and we got through the vowels in the remaining fifteen minutes. I'd forgotten how many different sounds the letters could make; it was amazing to me that humans could comprehend all these letters and create words that made sense not only to themselves but to each other.

Whose hand had created these lines of communication? Who did I have to thank for advances in human understanding? Immediately "Isaac Newton" came to mind, but I swatted my hand at his science. Gravity was evil, so therefore he was evil. My joy lay in the written word. I suppose Shakespeare fit in there somewhere, but he certainly didn't create the entire language. As Brendan repeated all the sounds for the letter "E," I leaned back in my chair to contemplate human intelligence.

A moment later, I said aloud, "Robots will never take over the world. We're way too smart."

Brendan's lips were pursed as an "ooo" left his mouth. "For real, Tru. You're weird," he said. I just smiled, and he continued going through the sounds for "U." He could already spell simple words such as "dog" and "cat," so we wrote out a sentence together: "The dog quickly chased a cat onto the veranda."

Smiling after he wrote it, he handed it to me. "The 'a' makes two different sounds in that word," he said. "Veranda."

"'A' for effort today, Mr. Matthews!" I said, beaming.

"Don't patronize me, Truth," he said. But he still had that spectacular grin on his untarnished, perfect face.

He stood and slung one backpack strap over his shoulder. I continued on like I hadn't heard him. "I think you should make goals for each week. That way we'll know what we're reaching for."

"I want to fly to the moon by next Friday."

"Reading-related goals."

"Okay, I want to be able to read by next Friday."

"Read what?"

"Everything."

"I think it will take longer than that," I said slowly.

"I know." He sighed. "You know, it's not that I don't know a lot more words; it's just that I get so nervous, and I forget for a few seconds and then my mind goes blank, especially in class where there are a lot of people. It's hard enough in front of just you. The more people, the blanker my mind gets. It sounds really stupid, I know."

"No, it doesn't," I said sincerely.

Brendan paused. "A picture book. I want to read a picture book by the end of next week."

"Done."

I expected him to walk away and leave me there; after all, he had a football game to watch. But he stood there, among books with words he couldn't form in letters, and waited for me to organize my mess of books and papers.

We walked out of the library together in silence. I was always silent when I passed through a library. I don't have an explanation for why, and it wasn't out of respect for the people reading. It was out of respect for the books, I suppose. Libraries reminded me of churches or cemeteries—full of old souls and characters, leading us to find answers.

Who knew more about death than cemeteries? Who knew more about history than books? Whenever I picked up a book, I felt a connection to both the author—who had formed those words on those pages just so that someone like me would read them—and to the thousands or even millions of people who had already been witness to the story.

I wanted Brendan to feel that way too.

"Ugh," he said, as we walked out of the large, wooden doors into the sunlight, "libraries are so boring. They make me feel depressed."

"Oh," I said, disappointed. "I like them."

"I know," he said.

"They remind me of dead people."

He raised his eyebrows at me.

"I mean, they feel like they deserve respect. People shelve their brains there." I wrinkled my smile at him. "Do you get what I mean?"

"No. But that's okay. Maybe when I can write more than a sentence and understand it, I will."

He laughed, so I did too. But part of me felt like he was laughing at me, rather than at himself.

The next time we met, Brendan picked out the book he wanted to read. It was a picture book with a dog on the cover. Along with the sentence he'd written, we seemed to have a dog theme going, and I suggested to Brendan that perhaps the dog was our reading spirit animal.

With the book opened on the table, Brendan sat for a moment in silence.

"You know that first word," I said, encouraging him.

He rolled his eyes. "I know it's 'the,' Truth." He sighed and then cleared his throat. "It's just, you know, intimidating to sit next to someone and read out loud. You could read this book in a minute."

I felt bad as he stared at the open book. "Well, it might take me longer. I usually stop to look at the pictures."

He let his face drop against the book. "I'm never going to learn. Let's give up."

I gingerly lifted his head up, pressing my fingers against his forehead. His blue eyes met mine, and I immediately retracted my hand, suddenly nervous.

"You wouldn't give up on learning a football play, would you?" I asked.

"No," he said. "But that's easy."

I nodded. "For you," I said. "For me, it would be like learning a new language. You can do this. It's just learning a new play."

He sat up, his mouth lifting to a resolute pout. "Fine. But don't help me. Let me figure it out."

He began reading quietly, his reading voice much more stilted and low than his regular speaking voice. I thought of my mother, whose reading-aloud voice usually resounded higher and happier than her general speaking voice. I wondered if Brendan's voice was happier and higher when he was doing something he enjoyed.

Pausing on only two words, Brendan finished the book in seven minutes and twenty-five seconds. I didn't want to time him, but he requested that I do it so he could work on shaving off time in the future.

"Speed isn't our goal. Slow and steady wins the race, you know."

"Not in my experience," Brendan said.

I let it go and he read the book again, this time remembering "interesting" and "honestly" as he turned page after page.

He read another picture book at our next meeting. Then Brendan had his sights set on a chapter book by the end of the month.

I was proud of the leaps and bounds Brendan made. After two weeks, he even tried to write a poem (after I prompted him to, of course). It read:

"Roses are red

Vilets are blue.

I wrote this poem

Just for you Tru."

Needless to say, despite the spelling error and lack of punctuation, I melted. Brendan said he even kind of understood my respect of libraries. I took him at his word.

During one study session, I stopped to look at several busts of authors and philosophers placed within the shelving units as decoration. They'd been in the library for ages, but I'd never stopped to see who they depicted. Inscribed below each person's name was a quote. I walked past Mark Twain, Willa Cather, Shakespeare . . . the next statue caught my eye. I knew that strong nose and puckered forehead, and I hated it. Isaac Newton. The worst. If no one else had been in the library, I would have thrown Newton to the ground, ironically shattering him with the force of his own science. I stopped to read his quote.

"If I have seen further it is by standing on the shoulders of giants."

I scoffed. A woman in the nonfiction section glanced my way. Crossing my arms, I contained my rage. Newton was trying to come off as being humble. But I saw right through him. He's standing on those poor giants' shoulders, adding more weight to their spines than they can hold, giving them scoliosis!

I stood up straighter, if that was even possible in

my erecter-set bodysuit, and thought defiantly: *New-ton's not bringing me down!*

I walked away when I heard Brendan whispering my name. As I passed the bust of Shakespeare, I wondered if Brendan resented the Great Bard like I did Newton. Would Brendan learn to love Shakespeare, or avoid his work for the rest of his life? Maybe we all just needed to learn to love the historical figure we hated.

At home that evening, I felt crabby. My sympathy toward Newton had dissipated. As I climbed the stairs to my room and felt plastic digging in to my hip bone, I knew it was too late; I'd already been Newton'd. And I wasn't a giant by any means; what could Newton gain by my having scoliosis? It was so frustrating. The time of Before Brace seemed so long ago. I'd tried to be a good person my whole life; why had I been singled out to have this deformity?

"It's not fair!" I shouted. I dramatically punched the bedroom wall, and then whimpered as I cradled my hurt knuckles in my other hand and curled up on my bed.

"Feel better?" my mom asked, passing by the bedroom with her laundry.

"Much," I said. "Thank you."

She paused and looked at me for a moment and then continued on. I sighed. At least Brendan was making progress, so his problem was getting better. I just wished my spine would, too.

CHAPTER 10
Rollin' in the Blues

"*How come you're* so good at math?" Megan moaned. I rolled my eyes. We were working in groups on FOILing binomials, and I knew Megan knew how to multiply as much as *she* knew she could. She was just trying to get Brendan's attention.

"How come you get it so quickly?" Megan whined again.

"I don't know. Once the directions are clear, the numbers just come easy," Brendan said.

Now I knew why Brendan always asked to do the first problem with me at our table. He wasn't sure what to do until I read the directions. Then he could fly off on his own like an eager beaver, devouring the problems until he came to a new section, and then I'd explain that one too. I felt guilty about it, as if I were helping him cheat—or helping him cheat himself—by not letting him figure it out on his own. He'd been getting by on other people's work for years. I found myself growing resentful of his questions in

Algebra, wishing he had a different table partner who didn't know his secret.

"What about this problem?" Megan pointed to number twenty-five as Miss Peters walked up to our group.

It was a new section. Brendan paused and stared at his book. He ran his finger along the printed words. I could tell he wasn't reading it; he was just putting on a show in front of Miss Peters, waiting for her to move on. I would have been mad if I couldn't relate to his panic: Jenny had almost caught me taking off my brace in the locker room the other day, but I'd managed to throw my jacket over it before she turned the corner. No one wants to be outed for being different. I wasn't about to let that happen to Brendan right in front of me.

"It says we need to use the FOIL method to multiply the binomial equations together," I said.

"That's easy," Brendan said. He wrote the numbers on his piece of paper:

$$(3x-2)(x+1)$$

"You just multiply the first numbers: three x times x is three x squared. Then the outer numbers: three x times one is just three x. The inner numbers equal negative two x, and the last numbers, negative two times one equals negative two. So your final answer is three x squared plus x minus two." He wrote:

$$3x^2+x-2$$

"What are you missing, Brendan?" Miss Peters asked.

"What do you mean?" he said, checking his answer again.

"Read the directions," she said.

I took a breath as I prepared to answer for him, but Miss Peters spoke before I could.

"Read the directions, *Brendan*," she said. She looked at me when she said it. I shut my mouth just as I released my breath, and it turned into what accidentally sounded like an exasperated sigh.

Brendan turned bright red. His finger was under the word "FOIL," the only word he was positive about because it was related to math and we'd seen it a dozen times already.

He continued to sit there in silence until Megan, who had been staring at the book and was oblivious to the building dynamic of fear in our group, said absently, "Show each step of the FOIL process."

Miss Peters looked at her and nodded. "That's right. Show your work."

She stood there a few more seconds and then walked away to the next group.

"Okay, so how do we do that, Brendan?" Megan asked.

Brendan scribbled the steps onto his paper and then moved on to the next problem. He wouldn't look in my direction for the rest of the class, but he continued to answer Megan's questions. When the bell rang and we left the classroom, he grabbed my arm and pulled me down the hallway to a secluded corner. At first, I thought: *a romantic gesture!* But then I remembered he was mad at me.

"How could you do that?" he asked.

"Do what?" I still didn't quite understand why he was so angry.

"Try to answer for me and then sigh like that—like 'Good luck, Miss Peters, but this idiot can't read!'"

I almost laughed. "Are you kidding? That was an accident. I was trying to answer for you but she stopped me. Did you see how she looked at me? I probably have a hole in the back of my head from that glare." I turned so he could look.

He didn't say anything, and he didn't look amused.

"My ponytail probably covers it," I said.

Definitely not amused.

"Thank God for Megan," he said.

I scowled. "What's that mean?"

"Well, at least she covered up for me."

"She doesn't even know you can't—"

I stopped short because I realized I was practically shouting and anyone could overhear us. "How could she have covered for you when she had no idea? She was just answering Miss Peters' question."

Brendan shrugged. I didn't know what else to say. I just shook my open hands in his face and walked away. I wasn't big on confrontation, especially when something wasn't my fault.

Jenny sauntered past me in the hall. "Lovers' quarrel?" she asked, with a smirk.

"Idiot's quarrel," I mumbled under my breath.

Later that day, during study hall and my visit with Oliver, I tried to vent without giving away Brendan's secret.

"Megan's just vying for his attention by acting dumb," I said. "It's so annoying."

Oliver tilted his head and playfully tugged his mouth to the side in mock thought.

"Seems to me you're the one who wants Brendan's attention."

I immediately shut my mouth and tried to keep from blushing. "No, I—I just know she's smarter than that, that's all."

"Uh huh." Oliver pushed himself away from the table and leaned back in his wheelchair while gripping the wheels, doing what he called "stationary wheelies."

"You girls seem to keep all kinds of secrets, and talk bad about each other behind backs. Why don't you just tell Megan how you were feeling? Stop being so immature."

"*You're* immature," I retorted.

I scowled at Oliver's confident grin, and this made him smile even more.

He lowered his chair so it was on the ground again and then rolled closer to me, leaning so his face was inches from mine. "Tell me I'm wrong."

His brown-eyed gaze stayed steady on mine, but I could feel my own gaze jumping back and forth between each of his dark pupils. I felt my face flush and my heart race, and I stood up, certain my heart was going to leap out of my chest from his close proximity.

Oliver snorted. "Point proven."

The worst part of it all was that I knew he was right, but I still didn't want to admit I had been wrong.

The rest of the day went by slowly and horribly. My brace seemed to be digging into the meatiest parts of my skin with utmost abandon. I left English just to go to the bathroom and undo the bottom strap. I tried to stretch in the stall to relieve stress, but it didn't help. Then Jenny and her horde of girly goons followed me down the hall between classes, giggling about Brendan and Jenny soon being a couple.

Worst of all, when I went to my locker at the end of the day, Megan was there, tossing her hair and laughing loudly—with Brendan. He gave me a quick glance and then turned to walk down the hall with Megan. If this was a scene in an average high school television drama, sad music would be filtering in as tears rolled down my cheeks and I ran wildly to the bathroom. Instead, I stormed down the hall and practically knocked Brendan over when I grabbed his arm.

"Can I borrow him for just a moment, Megs?" I asked with a huge smile, while really thinking, *Stay away from my Kool-Aid, traitor!*

"Of course, Truthy," Megan said, in her most chipper manner, but I could tell she was disappointed I was pulling him away.

I dragged Brendan back to my locker so I could put my books away. He was dragging his feet as if they were glued to the floor. I shoved the books I needed into my backpack and then I looked Brendan squarely in the face.

"I didn't tell anyone your secret."

"I know."

"So why are you mad at me?"

"I was just—" He paused and looked away. "I was scared. If people find out about this, I'll be laughed at. I'll be put in the remedial classes. You think a kid who can't read at thirteen is going to get into college?"

"Yes," I said, picking up my bag and swinging it over my shoulder with a thump. "You are." We started walking.

"It's harder than you think."

"No, you're making it hard."

He sighed.

I stopped walking. "Look at me."

He did. I looked around to see if anyone was watching. Then I rapped my knuckles against my plastic ab.

"I trusted you with my secret. You can trust me with yours."

Brendan grinned. Good grief, I liked that grin.

"Okay, Trendon. You're right." He put his arm around my shoulders as he walked me out the door to the bus.

"So, I heard you're going to be dating Jennifer Henderson soon," I said.

"Jenny?" He looked as if he'd thought about it before, and then he laughed. "No. Why?"

"Her brigade was taunting me with information about how you two were going to fall in love and run away together to, I don't know, the moon? Or Jenny's dreams, apparently."

Brendan laughed. I loved making him laugh.

"You're ridiculous sometimes, Tru," he said.

"It's true," I said.

"That's what I said. Tru."

"No, I meant—" Even when he was confused, I didn't want to look away. "Never mind," I said. "See you tomorrow."

He jerked his chin in a forward motion, one of the lamest forms of acknowledgement guys have invented. I rolled my eyes as I turned and walked onto the bus.

Megan had saved me a seat, as usual. "Everything okay, then?" she asked.

Good ol' Megan. "Yep," I said.

"Good," she said. Even though I knew Megan wanted me to be happy, I could tell she wasn't exactly enthusiastic about this particular outcome.

Apparently Newton wasn't happy about it either.

In late October, I went in for my three-month check-up after having my brace, and it wasn't exactly the best news.

"Well, the curvature is holding. That's good." It was the least clinical thing I'd ever heard Dr. Clarkson say.

"What does that mean, exactly?" my mom asked him.

"It means that while braced, her spinal curve is pushed to a lower degree. When it's not braced, it goes back to its original starting point."

He was entirely focused on my mother, ignoring the fact I was sitting right there.

"Okay," my mom said. "So by wearing the brace until she's done growing, Truth's spine will stay at thirty-five degrees?"

"We can only hope so," Dr. Clarkson answered, without an ounce of sympathy or consideration.

"You mean my back can still get worse?!" I burst out, loudly and angrily.

"Well, yes," Dr. Clarkson said. "Your spine may continue to curve. We brace it to slow its progress during the growing period, hopefully keeping it from progressing past the bracing point."

"Are you kidding me? Why am I even wearing this thing?" I asked.

"I just said—to keep your back from getting worse."

"I thought this was guaranteed to make me better."

"Even with surgery, there's no guarantee your back will hold. The body is an amazing thing."

I almost leapt out of my skin. "*Surgery?*"

"I don't think you'll ever have to worry about surgery, but it is an option," Dr. Clarkson said.

"Really?" my mom said. She had tears in her eyes for the first time in any of the doctor visits I'd had. "You don't think she'll need surgery?"

"If her spine continues to hold like this, I don't think she will."

I didn't point out that Dr. Clarkson continuing to say "I think" meant he could easily be wrong.

My mother and I left the longest and second-worst appointment I'd ever had. Right behind the one where I'd found out I actually needed a brace.

"Maybe you should get a rolling backpack," my mom said, as we drove away. The way she abruptly broached the topic, I knew she'd been considering this for a while.

"Hold up that thought-plane," I said. "Alter your course, Mama Dearest. I am *not* using luggage as a backpack."

"I think it would be best for your back."

"No."

"Well, I'm going to get you one."

"No!" I didn't usually get mad at my parents. I didn't buy the whole "teenagers need to be obstinate" thing; my parents were good, nice people. I could be that to them, too. However, with this abominable idea lingering between my mother and me, I felt anger growing inside my belted body.

I crossed my arms and waited in the car when Mom stopped at a department store. I leaned my chair back and watched the people who filed in and out of the sliding glass doors, carrying their nice new purchases. None of which were rolling backpacks.

It was bad enough I had to miss school to go to these appointments (okay, so missing school was pretty awesome), but now when I went back to school, I would have a new, piece-of-junk suitcase to put my books into.

"I swear she picked out the biggest, ugliest one she could find," I said to Megan and Brendan, whom my mom had let me invite over for pizza and a movie after I arrived home from my appointment. It was a Friday, and I couldn't wait to bash my new school accessory.

"It's not that bad," Megan said.

"Are you kidding? It's big enough to fit you inside it, Megs, and the only pattern it came in was old lady floral."

"The flowers are pretty lame, but it's really not that big of a deal, Truth," Brendan said.

I sighed. Even though Megan and Brendan were being nice about it, I knew people would make comments about me behind my back—and behind my backpack.

I pressed play on the movie, and *Newsies*, one of my favorites, blasted on the screen. I was hoping the soothing voices of singing and dancing newspaper boys would calm me down for the weekend, so I could get my mind off the dreadful sound of wheels rolling across cement and tile, which reverberated in my brain like a bad song.

It was all I could do to keep myself from breaking the backpack when my mom wasn't looking. Instead, my spirit was broken.

With his invisible clutches, Newton had dragged me down to a new level of uncoolness.

CHAPTER 11

A Biting Accident

Chunk. Doonk. Rowl. The rubberized plastic wheels of my new backpack clamored against the cement steps of the hallway. As each wheel clonked or bashed against a stair, I vented my irritation with choice words my mother wouldn't have appreciated.

I rolled my backpack quickly through the high school side of the building, comprising overconfident sophomores and even more zealously confident freshmen, to the junior high hallway. To my relief, no one said anything about the girl with the backpack on wheels roaring behind her.

Paired with my brace, my jeans were too tight. I hadn't done my laundry that weekend, so when it came time to dive into my wardrobe that morning, I'd been up a creek. Meanwhile, my pants were up my crack. Even though the summer months had come and gone, my personal temperature was always hot. But as sweaty as my plastic pal made me, I suffered through each day wearing long, loose shirts that hung past the indentation from my brace and would hopefully offer some sort of air movement for my extra-warm torso.

I approached my locker where Megan already stood, talking to Brendan. Shockingly (I almost dropped my rolling inanimate buddy), Jenny Henderson was there as well. She smiled, nicely for once, and said something that made them all laugh. Remembering my conversation with Oliver about backstabbing, and knowing Jenny had just looked at me, I felt certain she was talking about me. Maybe she'd pulled Megan and Brendan over to the dark side and I'd have to wheel away, dejected and alone. Or worse, maybe they'd told her about my brace.

I picked up my pace. My right foot caught my "study-luggage," as Harold had called it, and I tripped mid-step but kept going. I rolled right up to the trio I didn't fully trust, ending up almost in the middle of their small circle.

"What's up, trendy Trendon?" Megan said.

"Hey, Tru. Nice backpack," Brendan said. He winked. I should have smiled, but I didn't.

"Hi," I said, in a voice that was too loud and full of suspicion.

"Hello, Truth," Jenny said. "How are you?"

I wanted to mimic her chipper voice back with: *I don't know, Jen. How are you when your best friend and maybe-boyfriend are talking happily with your nemesis?*

Instead, I murmured, "Fine," and unloaded books from my school suitcase. Meanwhile, Megan, Brendan, and Jenny fell quiet. An awkward, they're-probably-staring-at-my-backpack-and-back-to-my-brace kind of quiet. I felt like I'd interrupted the Three Musketeers in the middle of becoming BFFs.

"So Megan tells me your mom forced you to get a backpack with wheels."

Immediately my limbs, mid–book shelving, stiffened. Jenny was not supposed to know about the backpack. Obviously she could see it, but I didn't want her to know I'd gotten it because of my curved spine.

I slowly turned around, making eye contact with my so-called best friend for a split second. She looked away quickly. Too quickly.

"Yep. Here it is." I kicked it. It hurt my big toe. "Ouch," I said.

"That sucks," Jenny said, shaking her head. "My mom tried to make me get one too. I refused though. She bought one, but for the first week I had it, I carried my books in my arms in protest. She eventually took it back, because it cost seventy bucks and she didn't want to spend the money if I wasn't going to use it."

My ears perked up. A fellow repressed daughter? "That was smart," I said. "I should have done that. I think I've committed myself to it now though. I don't even know where I'll put the thing during the day. It won't fit in a locker."

"You could put it in the locker room. I'll go with you," Jenny said.

"That's a good idea," Brendan said.

I couldn't tell if he was referring to storing my backpack or having Jenny accompany me.

"Okay," I said slowly.

Jenny grabbed the backpack's handle and began rolling it down the hallway. I gave Megan a quick glance again. She just shrugged her shoulders. Jogging to catch up to Jenny, I watched as she walked. She was so confident. Her stride was long and her hips swung back and forth like a perfect pendulum. Her long, blonde hair swayed in straight, shiny strands just below her shoulder blades.

Part of me wanted hair like hers instead of the frizzy curls I always pulled up into a messy bun-combination-ponytail on top of my head. The other part of me wanted to yank on Jenny's golden mane, hard.

We passed the freshmen and sophomores again. We passed by Charity, who was so engaged in conversation with her group of girlfriends, she didn't notice her sister rolling by. To her possible doom. Jenny could kill me in the locker room. While my body would be found eventually, she would probably corroborate her story with Megan and Brendan, and the tracks of my new suitcase rolled into my skin would show I'd been killed in a horrible accident of death by backpack. Not by a pretty, popular girl.

I sighed as I opened the door for Jenny and she rolled my backpack into the lair of fruit body mists and vanilla lotions.

"There you go." Jenny stood the suitcase up so I could take the handle.

"What?" I asked.

"Megan told me how embarrassed you were about dragging this thing through school," she said. "I wanted to help."

"Oh," I said. "Thank you?" I still wasn't sure how to feel about this.

"You know, it's not a big deal you have that. No one's going to care as much as you think. If you drop it off here first and carry your books the rest of the way, you won't have to backtrack in the morning."

"That makes sense. Thanks," I said, sincerely this time.

"Okay, see you in Band!"

Jenny turned and walked out the door.

The first bell rang.

I stood there, confused. Jenny Henderson was supposed to be my nemesis, the evil I went throughout my day to avoid. She had put sand in my gym locker. Now she was trying to be my friend? I couldn't fight the urge to believe there was something underhanded or sneaky behind Jenny's actions, but I had to admit, it was kind of nice. Rather sisterly. My own flesh and blood, Charity, hadn't even wanted to walk in the door with me that morning, because of the eyesore she thought I'd be. She sympathized, but she also had a reputation of her own to protect. I understood that. Now, the girl I had considered the most selfish, cold-hearted person in the world had risked her reputation for me.

"What a confusing world we live in," I said aloud, to no one in particular. No one answered.

I rolled my boxy backpack into a corner. To my friends, it probably seemed like I was making too much of a commotion over just a bag, but there was more to it than just my dislike of its physical appearance. Having to use a rolling backpack was like admitting defeat and committing myself to the fact there was indeed something wrong with me; something different about me. But I wouldn't give in to Isaac Newton. Not yet.

In Band, I watched Jenny as she sat next to Brendan. Her flirting was natural: she ran her hand through her long blonde hair and pulled it away from her face; when Brendan said something, she laughed, slapping his shoulder playfully. I watched as he smiled at her, her pretty face crinkling into a toothy grin. Her laughter was high and flute-like, while I knew I guffawed like a trombone.

Band always put me in the mood to compare things to instruments. Jenny was a smooth saxophone, while I was a buzzy plastic kazoo. She had the slim body of a violin, while I was curved like a tuba. The only thing we had in common physically was that we were both female. And she was better at being female than I was.

I blew hot air into my mouthpiece and pushed on the spit valve. Four quick droplets leaked onto the cement floor. *Wasted DNA*, I thought. *Ending up on the bottom of someone's shoes.*

At the end of fourth period, I visited Oliver in the resource room. I collapsed in the chair across from him.

"Hey," he said. He began to motion toward the back of the room. "I was thinking you could help me today."

"I can't. I'm an abomination," I moaned.

"Finally she admits it!" he said, smiling. "All these weeks just waiting for you to say it so I didn't have to!"

"Shut up," I said.

"What's up, Drama Queen?"

I spoke without thinking. "My mom made me get a backpack with wheels on it. It's the worst."

"Are you kidding me?"

I immediately looked up from where I'd buried my head on the table.

"I basically *am* a rolling backpack," Oliver said. "Am I an abomination?"

"No. That's not what I meant—"

"You know, I let you complain a lot without saying anything back, but I think you need to put some things in perspective, Truth."

I felt myself grow incredibly hot. For several seconds, I thought my skin would melt right off my body. I didn't know if I should look away or look at Oliver to see what he would do, so I ended up swiveling my head in various directions until my gaze came to rest on his face.

Oliver was watching me, waiting to see what I would do next.

"I'm sorry," I finally said. "I overreacted."

"Now we're getting somewhere!" he shouted, throwing his arms in the air. He offered a smile, but I could tell he wasn't enjoying our visit anymore.

"I'm really sorry, Oliver," I said.

I reached out for his arm, several feet away, but my hand shook uncontrollably so I pulled it back. I didn't know what else to say. So many thoughts ricocheted in my head that they all seemed to hit each other and implode, so I had nothing left.

"Here's the deal, Truth. I'll wear your back brace for a day and you can roll around in my wheelchair. Do that, and I'll believe you're sorry."

I looked at him and didn't say anything. I couldn't tell if he was serious or not.

"That's what I thought."

I lowered my head and looked at the floor. We were both quiet for a long time. I lifted my head after I couldn't take the silence any longer. "Didn't you want my help with something?" I asked weakly.

"Not anymore." Oliver sped by me and left the room, and I sat until the bell rang, wondering how I could be so stupid, but certain I'd just deeply hurt a friendship that meant more to me than I'd realized.

At that moment, my day seemed to fall apart. I stood, and my brace seemed to have found new places to dig in to. I tugged on the part right below my chest while I walked to lunch, though I tried to be discreet. I couldn't stop thinking about Oliver, and the more I thought about him, the worse my brace seemed to dig into my hip bones and ribs.

I was about ready to fake being sick and see if my mom would pick me up to take me home after lunch. Megan could tell I was down.

"What's wrong, Truth?"

"Everything. Nothing. Just me," I said, my head buried in my hands on the cafeteria table.

"Oh yeah? I bet I know what will cheer you up."

"Prince Charming asked you to marry him and you're taking me to Paris to plan your wedding and live with you, so I don't ever have to work a day in my life?" I asked.

That was our dream for Megan: to become a princess. For years, she'd covered her notebooks with doodles of herself as a stick figure doing princess-y things, such as riding unicorns and speaking to squirrels.

"Sonthday," she said.

I looked up. I knew she had said "someday," because that's what she always said when discussing royal betrothing. But it came out weird because

Megan had two straws on two of her bottom teeth, "lower laterals" as my dad called them, and they stuck straight up in the air in front of her face.

She made a wild face as she looked at me.

"You do realize people can see you, right? This isn't the table of invisibility," I said.

"You reawize yer bein' a craffy person." She gnawed her teeth a couple of times, slowly, with her eyes open wide, and I buried my head again.

"I know you didn't just call me a crappy person," I said, "because that wouldn't cheer me up at all."

Megan just kept making the face. No one was really paying notice to us, so I let her keep going. She leaned across the table, crossing her eyes, spilling drool over her bottom lip. Enough was enough. I wasn't in the mood for gross Megan. She was obviously craving attention from me; maybe I had been neglecting her more than I thought.

"Eat your food, Strawface," I said. I grabbed the straws, one in each hand, and yanked them out of her mouth. Blood trickled over Megan's lower lip with her drool, and she stared in horror at the end of the straw in my right hand.

I mirrored her gaze and almost dropped the plastic tube into my applesauce. Her tooth was stuck in the end of it.

"Truth!" Megan yelled.

My name bounced across the cafeteria walls and then from people's mouths as they turned to see what had just gone down. I'd performed a tooth extraction in the middle of hamburger day. Huge tears were forming in Megan's eyes, and she held a napkin where the small bottom tooth used to be in her happily complete mouth.

"I'm sorry!" I said. "I didn't know I pulled that hard!"

Megan grabbed the straw from my hand, angrily and accusatorily.

I started to turn bright white. Blood didn't make me pass out, but it made me think of all the other things that make up a body: guts, veins, arteries, a pumping heart, encased only by layers of thin skin. . . . That always made me feel nauseous.

"You'd better go to the nurse—" An image of all of Megan's teeth exploding out of her mouth appeared in my head. Dizzy, I stopped breathing as Megan pulled another napkin to her mouth. The lights above me seemed even brighter, Megan's face blurred in front of me, and just when I thought the white spots that had filled my vision were fading away, my head met the tiles of the cafeteria floor.

I opened my eyes just as someone poured room-temperature chocolate milk onto my face. Megan was already gone.

"Wait! Where's Megs?" I asked, wiping the liquid from my eyes.

"She went up to the nurse's office to call her parents." There was Jenny Henderson for the second time that day. She was leaning over me, blocking out the light. I focused on a freckle above her right eye. It was perfectly round and a light brown color. Chocolaty liquid dripped onto Jenny's designer shoes from the sides of my face.

I sat up, realizing a horde of people surrounded me.

"What's going on here?" Miss Peters, out of the math classroom and on lunch duty that day, ran over.

"I thought about veins," I said.

"What's that on your face?"

"Unrequested rogue dairy," I said. She handed me a napkin and I wiped my face.

"Can you stand?"

I did. I told her about Megan and she told me to go with her to the nurse's office. I liked Miss Peters.

She liked me; I was a good student. I did my work, and I didn't cause trouble—until today, that is.

Megan sat by the office door with a washcloth over her mouth. She wouldn't make eye contact with me when I got there.

"I'm sorry," I said quietly.

"This way, Truth." Miss Peters directed me toward the nurse.

"I'm sorry, Megs," I practically shouted, wanting to know she'd heard me even if she hated me.

She pulled the washcloth away from her face. "You've been a shoddy friend this year, but this tops it all. Crappy friend award goes to Truth Trendon." She pulled out her cell phone and took a picture of me. "Great. I can frame that one."

I didn't know what to say. My heart hurt.

"I'm giving you a break on that one, Megan," Miss Peters said. "Phone away until you leave the school grounds." She pulled me by the arm into the office. The nurse, a large woman with graying curly hair, patted her hand on the leather table. I sat down.

"You passed out?" she asked me.

"Yes."

"Did you hit your head?"

"No."

"How—"

"Well, I think maybe I did after the passing out part, but I passed out because I saw Megan bleeding and then I thought about blood and how it runs through the body and how insignificant human beings truly are to have existed for so long with such weak exteriors, and then I quit breathing and passed out."

The nurse looked at me and then wrote two words in her notebook. She looked back up. "I see. How long were you out?"

"A couple of seconds. Not long. I got milked."

"Excuse me?"

"Someone poured milk on me. Chocolate. But I was cognizant before it hit my face."

I thought she'd be more impressed than she was with my use of the word "cognizant," but she just wrote down a few more things and then shut her notebook.

"You'll be fine. Go to class when the bell rings."

"What about Megan?"

"That's confidential."

"She's my best friend," I pleaded.

The nurse sighed. Then she smiled slightly. "Her parents are coming to get her to take her to the dentist. They'll see if they can save the tooth or if she'll have to get a bridge. Very expensive, and sad, really, for such a young girl."

Looking at the nurse, I wondered if she ever really cared about vanity. Her chest rested comfortably on her stomach, and instead of wearing scrubs, she wore elastic white pants and a tight white jacket over a black shirt. She had several large moles around her neck, creating the illusion of a brown, bumpy necklace.

I wanted to vomit. Not because of the nurse, but because of what I'd done. Not only was I going to cost the Borowitzes a ton of money, but now Megan was going to be miserable. She had only been trying to cheer me up, and I'd basically ripped a bone from her face. Megan was right; I was the shoddiest.

The rest of the day passed by in a fog of drudgery. Newton struck again—I seemed to be weighed down by gravity itself. My shoulders, head, and even my knees drooped toward the floor as I walked through the halls. But when the final bell rang at the end of History, a light shone through my dark cloud.

Brendan stood in the doorway, smiling at me as I rose out of my seat.

I felt as if I were floating on top of the cloud instead of buried within it, my arms lifted out like an angel. When Brendan grimaced, I realized I had actually put my arms out and was slowly moving them from side to side. I dropped them fast, and stopped outside the doorway to talk to him.

"Can't talk now," he said quickly.

Mr. Landers was looking right at us, and he didn't look happy. I stepped back to get out of his death-glare, and Brendan stepped inside the classroom. I was surprised when Landers shut the door behind him.

I stood by the door as everyone around me threw books into their lockers and laughed and gallivanted off to their afternoon activities, hoping to overhear what Landers was saying to Brendan. Teachers never closed the room doors except when lunch was going on, and it was too hard for us to focus with the sounds of gossip floating down from cafeteria.

In less than three minutes, the hallway was clear. Except for me.

I wanted to know why Landers was keeping Brendan after school. I felt deceitful, but I also felt like Harriet the Spy, one of my childhood heroes, listening for clues to solve the mystery.

Looking over my shoulder one more time, I pressed my ear against the door. I couldn't hear anything. There weren't any cracks or vents either. I cursed the door for being solid wood. However, the bottom of the door was about an inch off the floor. With my back brace and taller stature, it seemed a long way down.

Harriet would have her ear at the hole and be taking notes already, I thought.

Squatting downward, I put my hands on the floor and lowered myself flat against it.

No one walk by, please, I prayed.

I could hear them, almost as if I were sitting at the desk right next to Brendan.

"You copied her," Mr. Landers said.

"No, I didn't."

I turned my head to look under the crack with one eyeball. All I could see were shoes. Brendan's white sneakers moved every so often, jittery, while Mr. Landers' brown dress shoes were planted decisively on the floor.

"Then why are your answers exactly the same?" I could tell by the way he shifted his weight that Landers had crossed his arms.

"I don't know. Did you talk to Jessica?" Brendan said.

I frowned. How dare he try to blame someone else! It was obviously him. My moral upbringing had me wanting to leap up to my feet again to open the door and tell Mr. Landers Brendan was a liar and a cheat, but my heart held me down on the floor, keeping me from revealing the secret I wished I didn't know.

"Yes. I did. And it's clear she wasn't copying you because she actually finished each question."

Brendan leaned back and put his feet out, a self-assured stance. "What if we chalk it up to coincidence, teach?" he said, in his playful, you-must-like-me-because-I'm-funny-cute-and-confident voice. But Landers wouldn't have any of it.

"This isn't acceptable, Brendan. You do good work. Why would you cheat on a test?"

"I didn't!" he said, pleading.

Liar!

"I think we need to talk to Ms. Eastin," Mr. Landers said.

Brendan didn't try to argue anymore. He stood up and they walked toward the door. I was about to push myself up off the floor when I heard footsteps behind me.

"What are you doing?" Ms. Eastin, the junior high principal and the woman who had unknowingly helped me remove fish from the locker room, loomed above me.

"I—" I tried to think. *What would Harriet say?*

The door opened on my other side.

"What in the h—?" Mr. Landers cut himself off when he saw the principal.

"I fell," I said quickly.

To stand up, I would have to knock over one of the parties standing over me, so I just lay there.

"Are you hurt?" said Ms. Eastin. She shook her head in disbelief at Mr. Landers. "So many students have been injured today."

I grimaced as I thought of Megan. "No," I said.

"Well then, what are you doing?"

I looked at Brendan. He hardly made eye contact with me. He was looking at the test in Mr. Landers' hand.

"I just wanted to—I mean, I fell and then I couldn't get up, because I have a back brace. It takes a little bit of time to get up." I rolled from side to side on my stomach, somewhat like a turtle on its back, trying to get clearance. The faculty members backed away. I rolled onto my side, and from there pushed myself up to my knees. The sad part was that's exactly how I did have to stand up. There was no exaggeration on my part.

"Huh," said Mr. Landers. "I couldn't even tell you were wearing a brace."

I beamed at him for saying what I considered the best compliment ever. Then I knocked my knuckles against my brace. "It's not comfortable, that's for sure."

"Well, I'm glad you're not injured," said the principal.

"Me too," I said. "Oh, and promise me you won't tell anyone about my brace."

"Of course not," said the principal.

I looked at Landers. I thrust my finger at him menacingly. "Anyone! It's embarrassing enough I have to wear it."

He smiled at me kindly. "I had to wear head gear with my braces until I was a sophomore. I get it."

"Thank you," I said, smiling back.

Landers looked at Ms. Eastin and then back at Brendan. Glancing at the test, he sighed. "We'll discuss this another time, Mr. Matthews," he said.

Ms. Eastin walked away, her heels clicking on the floor. I was mad at myself for not hearing them when she walked up; I'd been so engrossed in the classroom situation, I hadn't even noticed them.

Landers lowered his voice. "But if I find you *are* cheating, you will get an F for the semester. Got that?"

"You won't," Brendan said, relief spreading across his cute countenance.

"I hope not." Mr. Landers smiled at me once more and went back into the classroom.

"At least the head gear paid off," I said.

"That's enough brown-nosing, Truth," Landers yelled from his desk. But he was still smiling.

I walked with Brendan to his locker. He didn't talk and he didn't have his usual confident bounce in his step. I really wanted him to thank me. I'd gotten him out of another pickle. Finally, I couldn't take the lack of appreciation anymore. "I guess my brace is a lifesaver now too, huh?" I said.

"Yeah," he said. "Thanks."

"You could be a bit more grateful," I said quietly. I wanted to add, *I just told them my secret in order to keep yours, you jerk*, but I kept my mouth shut.

Brendan slammed his locker. He opened his mouth but then grabbed my arm and led me down the stairs and out the door. As we walked, he watched to see if anyone else was around.

"Do you think I like copying other people's papers?" he asked, angrily.

I didn't know what to say.

"Do you think I like pretending to flirt with girls, leading them on and telling them, 'I didn't study so can I maybe check some of my answers with yours?'" he said, mimicking himself as he spoke.

"Yes?" I said, joking.

He didn't laugh. He sighed and took my hand. "I hate it, Tru."

I didn't like that he admittedly flirted and led girls on, but at least he was honest about it.

"But thank you, you did save my butt," he smiled. "You do realize you looked like a fish out of water back there, don't you?"

He nudged me with his shoulder. I jabbed him back, a little harder than usual. I was mad he'd tried to blame Jessica for cheating, but I considered that enough revenge, especially if Brendan had been flirting with her.

Once again, I'd missed the bus, so Brendan's mother gave me a ride home.

"I'm going to have to start giving you gas money," I said, when I climbed in the car.

"It's my kids who owe me," Mrs. Matthews said. "I have to come pick up Brendan, take him to football, and then go get Melissa when she's done with volleyball and go back to pick up Brendan."

The short season of junior high football had ended over a month ago, so Brendan was playing with a club league in a town twenty minutes away a few days a week. He called it "camp" since they didn't play a lot of games, but focused on the fundamentals. Not many people could afford to send their children to play club ball.

"Sorry, Mom," Brendan said. Clearly, he wasn't sorry.

"Well, maybe that arm of yours will pay us off

someday, huh?" she smiled, but I couldn't be sure if she was joking or not.

I sank into the car seat as she eyed me in the rearview mirror.

"Is this the one you were talking to your father about on the phone?"

"Shut up, Mom."

My body warmed from my feet to the tips of my ponytail. Brendan talked about me at home!

"What did you say?" I asked innocently.

"Nothing good, Trendon," Brendan said, turning to wink at me.

"What do you do?" his mother asked me.

"What?" I asked.

"You play any sports or anything?"

"Volleyball. And I play trumpet in Band."

"Hmm," Mrs. Matthews said.

She ignored me for the rest of the ride, but I didn't mind. I didn't say anything. I was trying not to shout with joy in the back seat of the Matthews' car. Brendan talked about me at home! To his father! I held my hands in my lap and happily looked out of the window. I had a chance with this gorgeous guy!

As we passed shedding trees and piles of fallen leaves, I pictured my dream date with Brendan. But just before we could climb onto the horses on the beach in my daydream, Mrs. Matthews pulled into our driveway and the rear tire of the car caught the curb, jarring me back to real life.

"See you tomorrow, Tru," Brendan said.

"Okay. Thanks for the ride, Mrs. Matthews!"

I climbed out of the car. Brendan rolled down his window.

"Thanks again," he said.

A pang of guilt flashed through my gut. Because he hadn't gotten in trouble, I still felt as if Brendan was cheating himself.

But staring at his smiling, appreciative face, I couldn't stop myself.

"Anytime," I said.

CHAPTER 12
Losers and Winners

"Are you going to be a dentist, then?" Mr. Borowitz stood on our front stoop, his arm around Megan. He'd obviously forced her to walk the block to my house to show me the gaping hole in her mouth. Mr. B was grinning from ear to ear. Apparently, Megan still had a few baby teeth left, and the one I'd extracted had an adult tooth behind it, itching to come out. "You were able to get it out of there with no pain and hardly any blood. Mrs. B and I have been trying to take her to have all those tiny teeth pulled, but this one is hard to persuade." He patted Megan's shoulder. "I'd say you're destined for a career working with teeth, my dear!"

I smiled. Megan didn't.

"I don't think so," I said. "Mouths are gross." To Megan, I said, "I didn't mean to do it."

"I know," she said, stepping into the house while Mr. B talked to my mom. "But he keeps going on and on about what a miracle it was and how you've saved him money. Right now, I'm just hoping this tooth grows in straight. The last thing I need is braces."

"I'm sorry," I said.

Megan smiled. I couldn't even see the hole I'd left, because her bottom lip covered it.

"I know. I forgive you," Megan said. She took a deep breath. "So guess what my dad's talking your mom into right now?"

"A motivational talk at the library about speed-reading?"

"No, but I'll suggest it to him. The three people who go there every week will be excited."

I rolled my eyes. "Yes, my two friends and I will be very excited. So, what is it?" I asked.

"Sa-leepover!"

I smiled, and in my mind I performed death-defying mental backflips; Megan was still my friend— despite my having drawn blood.

But just as I thought she was completely over it, she said, "Just don't go anywhere near my face. I don't want to end up wearing a neck brace or something hideously embarrassing like that."

I frowned. That cut deep. Too deep. I crossed my arms and leaned against the wall.

"I didn't mean it like that," Megan said. "No one

even knows you have a brace, Tru. Everyone can see I have a tooth missing."

I didn't say anything. She had a nice, brand new tooth coming in to replace the tiny baby one; I didn't have a nice, sparkling new spine to replace my crooked one. And Oliver wouldn't have strong muscles to replace his weak ones. Even though she said she understood what I was going through, I didn't trust Megan's empathy anymore.

Just like Oliver was apparently alone with muscular dystrophy, something in my gut told me I was on my own with scoliosis. I grimaced at the thought of the word. *Scoliosis.* Absently, I pulled the front of my brace away from my ribs, enjoying the brief rush of air that touched the sweaty cotton shirt under my oversized t-shirt.

We waited in silence until our parents finished talking.

"We've got clearance, Meg-pie!" Mr. B said. "Let's go get your things!"

"See you in a bit," Megan said, but I could tell neither of us was overly excited about our prospective evening.

"What a great night I'm going to have," I said to my mom.

"I thought you'd be ecstatic," Mom said. "Megan

hasn't spent the night since summer."

"She's mad at me."

"Her tooth will grow back. It was an accident, and she knows that. Don't worry about it."

"Easier said than done."

My mom smiled at me. "I know, but if anyone can handle a challenge, it's you, my dear daughter."

"Why do I have to have so many?"

"Challenges? I don't think you do. You're pretty lucky, Truth Trendon. You're smart, talented, kind-hearted, and you're pretty."

I rolled my eyes. My mother throwing vague, unoriginal adjectives at me didn't do me any good. "You've just said what billions of other mothers tell their boring, less-than-average children."

"I know," my mom said, her eyes twinkling. "But unlike those poor children's mothers, I have the Truth."

My mother loved a good play on words with my name. I didn't consider this a good play.

"Nice try, Mom," I said, walking upstairs. "Still depressed. Better try a little harder if you're going to win Mother of the Year."

"I won last year!" she yelled after me. "I can take a year off. Even the best need a break once in a while."

And the worst don't get a break from the challenges, I thought.

With each thump of each foot on the stairs, I cursed Isaac Newton. As if it wasn't hard enough trudging along through the muck of junior high. And I hadn't even been in the thick of it yet.

We ate supper early because Charity had a volleyball game. It was important because it was a sub-district game, so if the team won, they'd go on to districts, and if they won that, state. If they lost, the season was done. The West River Lady Bucks weren't favored to win over the Panthers, but we Lady Buck fans were prepared for a win anyway. ("Lady Bucks" doesn't make sense at all, I know. I petitioned to have the name changed in third grade, but to no avail. No one wanted to be the Deer. I liked the fact we wouldn't need to pluralize the name on t-shirts, but the Bucks stayed, and I declared as a nine-year-old that feminism was dead.)

As usual, I was excited to go and watch Charity play. I wasn't quite as excited about sitting next to Megan. She was wearing a cute, tight blue t-shirt and straight-leg jeans that showed off her few curves, while I was stuck in my extra-large t-shirt, the front of it tucked into my elastic cargo pants and the rest of it draped around me like a curtain.

I picked at my salad and baked chicken. I wasn't very hungry. Charity had already left to support the girls on the junior varsity team. As the season had progressed, Charity had become a major contributor to the Lady Bucks' winning season. She had about seven kills a game and she passed like a maniac. I wished I could bump a ball directly to the setter like she did.

I tossed a cherry tomato in the air and pretended to serve it at Harold. He leapt out of his chair to avoid the failed missile, which I'd caught in my hand.

"That's enough, Truth," Harold said.

Megan and I laughed. Harold was going through a stage where he tried to imitate my dad. He lowered his voice, dipped his head forward, and frowned at me, his finger pointed straight into the air as he tried to correct my misbehavior.

"I agree with your miniature father figure," my mother said. "Let's not throw food."

"We're not cleaning up, anyway," my dad said. "We'll leave it to Captain Tooth Puller and her partner in victimless crime, the Walrus."

My father thought the whole tooth incident was hilarious. Something about the way he played down my villainy and showed how Megan had participated in her own tooth's demise made me feel better. Megan didn't mind either. She had already demonstrated how she'd stuck the straws over her teeth, and laughed along with the rest of us at her own immaturity (one point to a Mr. Oliver Nelson).

Harold thought it was hilarious too, but when he snorted after drinking his milk and it purged out his nose like a sinus rinse, he cried. It wasn't the cleanest of Trendon dinners, the milky snot mixing in with Harold's peas and carrots, but then again, Harold ate his boogers—a habit unique to him within the Trendon clan, which my parents weren't sure how to break—so he didn't seem to mind.

Our arrival at the volleyball game coincided with the fifth and final set of the junior varsity match. It had clearly been a good match, and with the score tied at 13–13, the excitement was building. Usually, the gym was pretty empty for JV matches, but since it was going on so long, the crowd had already arrived to watch the varsity game and was in their seats, cheering on the younger girls.

I saw Brendan sitting with some other seventh graders on the student side of the bleachers. His sister Melissa was a sophomore and played mainly for the JV team. He waved, so after conferring with my parents and shoving Harold in their direction, Megan and I headed over to him. He scooted over and made room for us.

"Good game, huh?" I asked.

"Yeah," he said. "Melissa and that giraffe on the other team have been going head to head the whole time. I think they've blocked each other about fifty times."

I looked at the "giraffe" Brendan was referring to. The tall, pretty girl with a long braid hanging down her back spiked the ball past Melissa. The ball hit the floor as two Bucks splayed across the gym in their attempt to dig it up. The score was now tied 14–14.

"I think she's pretty," I said.

"She's a monster," Brendan said.

I knew he didn't mean to sound so rude—he was clearly referring to the girl's height, since she had to be around six feet tall—but it bothered me he'd be so quick to criticize a stranger. I had become particularly sensitive when people judged others for their looks.

The Panthers ended up winning, and the crowd clapped appreciatively for each team, but it was clear no one really cared. The atmosphere changed as the varsity teams walked onto the floor, though.

People were chanting and on their feet throughout warm-ups; as a sub-district game, there definitely more significance to its result. It was fun to watch Charity. She was my older, more graceful (much more graceful!) sister, and from my seat on the bleachers a few rows up, I could see a fire in her eyes I usually saw there only when she was angry with me for using her perfume or nail polish or hair straightener without asking.

"Charity looks good," Brendan said.

"You lookin' at those tight shorts, Matthews?" Megan said, leaning across me to be heard in the loud gym. I raised my eyebrows at her, and then at him.

Brendan laughed. "I meant she looks like she's warmed up."

"She's got fire in her feet," I agreed.

Megan nodded as we watched Charity jump and spike a ball over the net, snapping her wrist around as she spanked the ball against the hardwood on the other side.

"Wow," said Megan.

We watched without talking as the girls finished warming up. Then the high school pep bands for both teams played "The Star-Spangled Banner" together from opposite sides of the gym. It was the first time such a feat had been attempted in our school—rival bands playing together in unity and patriotism before each team's fans jeered and swore at the opposing side. The final note echoed back and forth as the directors looked at each other for the cutoff.

The crowd cheered, and the referees blew their whistles.

"Game on," I said.

Brendan put his arms up, trying to get a double high five. I started to lift my arms when Megan leaned around me and thrust herself toward him, slamming her palms against his. I fell against his chest, which was actually rather nice, though I didn't want to violate his personal space.

"Go Bucks!" Megan shouted.

"Easy, Megs," Brendan said, laughing.

Megs? I thought. *When did he start calling her Megs?*

"Sorry! I'm just pumped up," Megan said, jumping eagerly with the rest of the crowd as the first Lady Buck prepared to serve the ball.

The up referee who stood on the ladder signaled for the serve. To the Bucks supporters' horror, the girl tossed the ball and barely hit it with her fingertips. It didn't sail through the air; it sank. It didn't even reach the net. To *my* horror, in the silence of the ball toss, Brendan leaned across me and said, "You look nice tonight, Megan."

From that second on, it was bad luck for the Bucks. And for me.

"Thanks," Megan said, a chipper smile on her face. "It's a new shirt."

"Newton doesn't understand fashion," I mumbled.

"What?" Brendan asked me.

"I hate that I can't wear cute clothes," I said, tugging on my t-shirt.

"You don't need cute clothes," Brendan said quietly. "You're already cute enough."

I blushed and felt myself start to sweat. I looked at Megan. From the scowl on her face, I knew she had heard him.

Beads of perspiration dripped down my back. There was no way I was leaving the gym tonight without sweat marks all over my shirt. And the more I sweat, the more the Bucks let the Panthers pound them. I would have felt really depressed about the Bucks' loss, for Charity's sake, but Charity was playing out of her gourd. She dug every ball that came remotely close to her; she hit around and over the Panthers' blocks; and she hit the ball so hard, the back row Panthers had red marks on their arms from digging her hits, which they usually shanked off into the crowd.

In fact, Charity was the only reason the Bucks even had a fighting chance. They lost the first set

14–25, the second 18–25, and finally won the third set 25–21. The crowd was raring and ready to go, cheering the Lady Bucks on; ready to follow them into a forest, leap over streams, and avoid getting hit by cars on the highway; but the volleyball players refused to lead us into a metaphorical or actual win. They sat back on their heels, looked tired, and moved ungracefully—very unlike the deer they were supposed to be. (Then again, a panther would obliterate a deer in the wild and never the other way around, so maybe this was nature's way of showing us that our mascot was jinxing us).

Either way, halfway through the fourth set, with the Panthers ahead 12–4, most of the crowd was seated and not paying much attention to the game. Brendan had lost interest two sets ago, giving up hope after we'd lost the first set. He kept talking to the guys on his left, and Megan and I were left alone to talk to each other.

"I think they just need to take a time-out. Right, Brendan?" Megan asked.

Brendan had turned around and was talking to eighth grader Mave Johnson, whose shirt was even tighter than Megan's. The problem with Mave was she always talked especially quietly, so you had to lean in to hear her. While maybe this technique worked to get guys closer to her, I, for one, did not like having another person so close to my face that I could see the individual pores on their nose.

"I don't think he's listening," I said.

"What?" Brendan asked, finally responding.

"Do you think a time-out will help?" Megan nodded her head toward the court.

"I think a miracle would help," Brendan said.

I sighed. I was tired of sitting in my sweat and losing feeling where my brace pinched pieces of my flesh. "I just want to get out of here," I said.

"Sorry we're such bad company," Megan said, rolling her eyes.

"I'm not talking about you," I said, restrained anger leaking through in my voice.

"Problems in BFF paradise?" Brendan asked.

I widened my eyes at him, hoping he got the message: *shut up.*

"Don't get me started," Megan said.

The Panther fans stood up and clapped as their team served the final point. The ball went over the net directly to Charity. She passed it to the setter, who set it right back to her. She ran up for a quick set, where the ball isn't set as high, and hit it over the net. A Panther barely splayed herself out in time to pick it up, but they hit it back over, past the block, and it landed with an assertive bounce. That was it. We'd lost. All the Bucks looked sweaty, beaten, and depressed, but Charity was clearly devastated. It wasn't so much the losing that bothered her, but I knew she was sad the season had ended. Volleyball had been her life for nearly four months. Now it was over.

"Finally," Brendan said.

I stood up and waited for people to filter out of the gym. I needed air; I wasn't claustrophobic, but during that game, I'd found myself growing more and more agitated, needing space. Maybe it was from my brace; maybe it was from Megan's coldness. It was an irrepressible feeling that made me want to run for days. Or punch a wall. I couldn't decide. Instead, I walked across the gym and gave Charity a hug.

"Yeesh," I said, wiping my hands on my shirt as she peeled her sweaty self away from me.

"You're pretty clammy yourself," she said.

"Well, you know us Trendons: the sweet, sweaty sisters!"

"Shut up, Tru," my sister said, tucking a few loose strands of hair behind her ear. "We're in public."

"So?" I turned and saw a cute older boy walking toward us. "Who's that?"

Charity looked giddy. She jumped up slightly on her toes as she said, "Hi, Jacob."

"Hey, volleyball star," this Jacob character said.

I squinted my eyes at him, scrutinizing his initial demeanor. I'd never known Charity to be boy crazy, so I was hesitant to accept this new but attractive guy. I was worried Charity hadn't done her research and conducted a thorough background check on him. Then again, I was interested in a guy who couldn't read, cheated on tests and homework, and had basically ignored me for the last hour and a half. Besides, asking Jacob for a urine sample now would probably scare him off.

"Hello, *Jacob?*" I said, emphasizing his name as a question. I wanted him to be aware he was not to be trusted.

"Hi?" he asked back.

"This is Truth, my little sister," Charity said. She gestured toward me and sort of shifted her hips. I shifted my hips right back, not caring about my brace shoving my butt-fat out further than it already was.

"I would hardly say 'little,'" I retorted.

"I can tell. You're both the same kind of pretty," Jacob said.

I melted. "Abubloga," I muttered—gibberish. I

couldn't form words; an older, hot guy had just said I was pretty.

Charity laughed, obviously embarrassed. She turned her back on me a little bit. "Thanks for coming," she said to Jacob. "Sorry it was such a sucky game."

"No way! You were awesome!" Jacob said. He put his arm on her shoulder. "We were shouting for Killer Charity. Didn't you hear us, Killer?"

"Charity doesn't even like to kill bugs," I said, putting my arm on her other shoulder. "I'd rethink that nickname."

"Tru, I think your friends are waving to you over there," Charity said, pointing to where Megan stood next to Brendan while he talked to a group of guys. Megan looked really ill at ease, and I could tell she felt out of her element.

"I don't care," I said. "I'd rather stay here and harass you. I'm your annoying 'little' sister, remember?"

Charity sighed. "You're my mature little sister, okay?"

"You know it. See ya, Jake!" I slapped him a high five and walked away, deciding I'd done my younger sisterly duty of making them both uncomfortable.

As I crossed the gym, a familiar set of wheels rolled across my tracks.

"That was quite a game," Oliver said.

"A blow-out. Those Bucks didn't stand a chance," I said.

Oliver grinned. "Walkin' roadkill."

Megan was glaring at me. I hadn't really talked to anyone about Oliver, and I sort of liked it that way—I wasn't sure Megan would understand our friendship.

"Look, about our last visit—"

Oliver waved his hand. "Forget it," he said. He wrinkled his face. "And don't call it a 'visit.' It makes it sound like a retirement home or a hospital."

"Gotcha, Gramps," I said, relieved he was still willing to smile at me.

"Hey, you know that thing I wanted your help with? Could you—"

I had to cut him off. "I'm sorry, I think Megan's using her psycho best friend telepathy to tell me she needs me."

Oliver glanced over his shoulder. "Ah, yes. I think I'm feeling some of her powers myself. Those eyes are spectacular."

"Spectacularly scary."

"Go about your business, then. I'll see you around."

He left before I could respond. I hollered farewell after him, but if he heard me, he chose not to reply.

I couldn't erase the guilt I felt staring at the back of Oliver's brown curls. I wanted to chase after him, but my best friend duty called me onward in the opposite direction.

"Thanks for blowing me off," Megan said, as I approached.

I kept myself from rolling my eyes. "I was telling my sister she did a good job. Why didn't you mingle? You're the best mingler I know."

I gestured to the gaggle of guys beside us.

"With a missing tooth? They'll either think I'm weird or in kindergarten."

"Hey now, I lost a tooth in fifth grade. Let's not mock the old loose-toothers."

Megan smiled slightly, but she put her hands in her pockets and shrugged her shoulders, a very un-Megan-like move.

"Come on," I said, pulling her toward the group. "Matthews!" I said. Brendan turned and smiled at us.

"Your sister is awesome!" one of the eighth-grade boys said.

"Yeah, she is," I replied.

"And she's hot," said another.

I didn't know how to answer that. Should I defend my sister's honor and claim my feminist roots? Part of me knew Charity would like to hear this, but she would probably be embarrassed too.

It got quiet. I knew it was my fault. But I couldn't think of anything to say.

"Truth pulled a tooth out of my mouth today," Megan said suddenly. A round of voices leapt excitedly from the circle.

"I heard!"

"Lemme see it!"

"Is the tooth fairy still a thing at your house? That tooth's gotta be worth at least five dollars."

Brendan pulled me aside since his friends were distracted with Megan's now elaborate story. Already her fingers were up by her mouth, representing the straws she'd jammed on her teeth. She'd clearly come out of her funk.

"I need your help with History," Brendan said, as he led me to a secluded corner of the gym. I could see candy wrappers and pieces of chewed gum under the bleachers. The metal bars of the bleachers looked old and rusted. Kids used to play on them, but now they didn't even look fun; just dangerous and full of tetanus.

Ever since running into Oliver, I couldn't concentrate. My mind kept struggling to keep up with the people in front of me. I kept staring at the bleachers, my eyes glazing in and out of focus.

"Landers' History class," Brendan said, drawing me back to the light of the gym.

"His story or *his* story?" I said, pointing at two different people.

"Very funny, Trendon," Brendan said, smiling.

"I'm just here to bring some razzmatazz to your life with my wordplay," I said. "What do you need help with?" I'd been having him read through the chapters at our study sessions, and he was improving at a surprising speed.

"Well, we have that big paper due, and I can't risk copying someone else's because of my last test."

"Yeah. How long is that again?"

"Three pages."

"Three? That's nothing!"

"Good. So you can knock it out this weekend and get it to me?"

I felt as if I'd taken a cannonball to the stomach— without my plastic shield to protect me. "What?"

"It's due Monday, right? Is the weekend enough time?"

"Brendan, I'm not comfortable with writing your homework."

"It's no biggie, Trendon. You can do it." He

smiled at me, and that toothy grin still had its dazzling effect, even though I wanted to run away and never have to talk to him again. While I was wrestling with my moral and ethical values inside my head and heart, he seemed to think I was worried about the subject matter being too difficult. I had my own paper to write about art and the artisans of Mesopotamian culture.

"You're smart. I know you can write it in no time."

"What's yours about?" I asked, trying to think of another way to shift the guilt to him.

"The Assyrian Army. I told Landers it would be about weapons."

I considered myself a pacifist, and I hated weapons. Weapons meant blood and blood meant a woozy Truth.

"Not my forte," I said. "Better find someone else."

"Come on, Truth," Brendan pleaded. I'd never seen him so terrified. I instinctually looked around, to see if anyone saw how sad he looked. I didn't want them to think I was the cause. He spoke barely above a whisper. "You know you're the only one who can help me."

I knew he was trying to persuade me, but I actually thought about it. Was I the only one? Supposedly I was the only one who knew he couldn't read, but everyone liked him. He could ask anyone to jump through hoops for him and he or she would do it. And didn't he have his sister's papers?

I frowned at myself. I was trying to come up with ways for him to cheat, acting completely against everything I stood for, even my own name.

"I'm sorry, Brendan," I said, sincerely. "I really like you, but I can't help you cheat. You're only hurting yourself. I don't want to be a part of that hurt."

"Whatever," Brendan said. He sighed. "I get it. You're too good to help people like me."

"People like you? What's that supposed to mean?" But I was thinking: handsome princes. Illiterate, handsome princes.

"People who need help."

"That's not true! I've been helping you ever since you told me you couldn't—couldn't *you know,* and you've made progress! You're underestimating yourself, Matthews!" I slapped him on the shoulder as if I were one of his football buddies. He raised an eyebrow.

"You're impressed by my strength, I see," I said.

He looked away. "Impressed isn't the right word."

We walked back to the group of guys who were now captivated by Megan. She was talking about her visit with the male dentist, who had a long ponytail that had continuously threatened to land in Megan's mouth. I was a bit miffed. She hadn't shared this story with me.

The boys all laughed as Megan pretended to vomit hair. Even though we weren't on the best of terms, I was happy Megan had some interested onlookers. Maybe by the time we got home, she'd like me again.

Just as I was about to join in the conversation and point out Megan hadn't described my heroic part in her tooth story, Charity ran up to me and yanked me from the group.

"Jacob just asked me out!" She grabbed my hand and jumped up and down. I stared at her. Who was this girl? Surely not my sister, who was practical about everything, right down to the white tennis shoes she wore every single day to school.

"Good luck," I said. "You're not sixteen. Mom and Dad are going to say no." Even though it was sad, I sang out "no" in a happy tune, hoping not to pop her metaphorical balloon of bliss.

"I didn't think about that." Charity's face was crestfallen. Balloon popped. "I already told him yes."

I saw my parents and brother waiting to talk to Charity. Wanting to congratulate her again, and also keep her ego in check from the praise I knew Mom and Dad would give her, I followed in a slow saunter. More sweat leaked down my back, causing me to involuntarily shiver. *Gross*, I thought.

"We really are proud of you, Charity," I heard my dad say. "You played so hard. I'm marking this as a win in the Charity Trendon column."

"But an utter annihilation on the Lady Bucks' yearbook page!" I said.

Charity barely looked at me. "Jacob asked me out," she told Mom and Dad.

"Jacob?" said my mother. She nodded and looked around. To my surprise, she wasn't as surprised as I was. She had heard of this Jacob before.

"I know you've thrown the number sixteen around before," Charity said, "but I'm really close. I'll be sixteen next summer?" She pulled her shoulders up to her ears, trying to pull off a cute, pleading stature. She did; she looked convincingly cute. I, however, wasn't sold. I looked at Mom and Dad.

My parents turned toward each other and huddled together; as in an actual huddle. They put their heads together, their hands on each other's shoulders. Harold stood between them, looking up with furrowed eyebrows.

"Really? What are you doing?" Charity said.

She looked around to see if anyone else was

watching. Some people were. I thought about joining the huddle to make Charity even more embarrassed, but I had my reputation to consider too.

My parents whispered back and forth, glancing periodically at Charity and then at me. Harold shook his head, adding a few noes. My father winked at us a few times, and my mother nodded a lot. They were putting on a show. Clearly they'd had this conversation before. Finally, they shouted "Break!" and turned back to us.

My mother faked tears. "We never thought this would happen. We know you're a good catch, but for someone else to notice, it's just heartwarming."

"My heart is very warm," Harold said, nodding and patting his chest.

My father crossed his arms, stern and stoic. "And what are this boy's intentions, dear daughter?"

"He can probably hear you. He's right over there," Charity said, through clenched teeth.

Mom and Dad grew serious, content they'd performed their parental duty. "You may go on a date," my mother said.

Charity's face lit up.

"One date," Mom added.

"As long as Truth goes with you," my father added.

The color drained from Charity's face. "No!"

"Hey! I'm fun! I can make a jolly good time for those around me!" I said, insulted.

"That's why she can't come!" Charity said, gesturing angrily at me. "She says weird things, and she's just going to try to embarrass me the whole time."

"Those are the conditions, Chary-bear," my dad said.

I put my hands on my hips and looked at Charity, a huge smile on my face.

"Fine," she said.

She ran over to Jacob for a "good-news, bad-news" session. For some reason, it didn't bother me that I was the bad news.

"It's nice to see her so happy," Harold said, resting his hands on Mom and Dad. "We did this."

My dad squeezed his shoulders, and Harold smiled up at him.

"So, who are you going to bring along on your double date?" my mom asked me.

"Whaaaaat?" I asked. "I thought it was just me."

"You can bring a *friend*," my dad said. "The gender doesn't matter, but it is just a *friend*."

"Oh," I said, pleased. "I'll think about it."

Mid-sentence, on the word "think," I began walking toward Brendan. He was talking to the few boys still meandering around the gym. Mostly everyone but the team and family members had already left. I waited until he had finished talking to them, and then I pounced.

"Wanna go on a date?" I asked, embarrassed I couldn't contain my giddiness.

"What?" he asked, surprised.

"Okay, so it's not a date. We'd be going as friends—chaperones, really—with Charity and this Jacob guy, if that is his real name."

"When?"

"I don't know. Maybe tomorrow. She's talking to him right now."

"Hmmm."

I couldn't believe how long he was taking to say yes, he'd love to go. I wanted to shake his cute features until they fell off his face.

"If you write that paper, I'll go with you."

A ton of bricks fell on me. I was sure of it. Maybe a hurricanic wave had just swept me away and knocked me out cold in the middle of the ocean. I was certain I hadn't heard correctly. I'd imagined it. He didn't like me enough to get some crappy fast food and go to a movie without getting something in return?

"S-seriously?"

Brendan's face drooped. "I just thought if you liked me enough to ask me out, you'd like me enough to write a paper for me." He took my hand. "But if you really want me to go, I'll go."

I should have thrust his hand away, pushed him down and stormed away, but I felt sorry for him. If he really thought I was the only one who could help him, maybe he felt as helpless as I did when I changed clothes for Gym. I didn't want anyone else to experience the same anxiety I did every day. As I stared at him, I felt as if the weight of the world was on my shoulders. I knew Newton was there, standing on them and laughing hysterically. The only way to find relief seemed to be to give in.

"Okay. I'll write the paper," I muttered softly.

He dropped my hand. "You're the best, Trendon! I can't wait for our date. Call me with the deets!"

"The what?"

"Details," Megan said, as Brendan ran after his friends. She had walked up behind me. "So you and Brendan are an item now?"

"No," I said.

"Well, he said you're going on a date."

"It's not a date. We're chaperones."

"Don't be weird. Parents are chaperones. You're dating." She crossed her arms. For some reason, I'd expected her to be happy for me. Instead, she was cold and harsh. I knew she didn't know about the paper, because Brendan wouldn't want people to know, but I could tell she was angry with me.

I also didn't like that she'd called me weird. It was one thing for my sister to say it when she was annoyed, but the way Megan was saying it felt as if Isaac Newton was now tap dancing on my shoulders.

"Whatever," I said.

We met up with my parents and Charity, who was beaming as if she could light up the night, and left the gym. As I thought about the possibility of Brendan just using me for homework and not actually liking me for who I was, I felt another dribble of sweat snake down my shoulder blade.

For the rest of the evening, my chest hurt, and it wasn't from Megan's refusal to say more than two words to me all night. I couldn't believe Brendan had wrapped me around his perfect little finger, convincing me to go against my moral upbringing, my ethos, for him. As I lay in bed in the shadowed darkness, I caught myself thinking of ways to write a good introduction to a paper about weapons.

The Assyrian Army was made of dedicated rulers and citizens whose goals were to build an empire and maintain lasting loyalty.

Loyalty. I scoffed as I thought about the word, mouthing it to no one in the dim bedroom. I wasn't even loyal to myself.

My head wanted to dial Brendan's number and tell his mom to have him read to her out loud—to point out the nouns and verbs in sentences, so he'd expose himself for the cheater and liar he was.

But my heart wanted to be loved.

It wanted all of us—my brain, personality, and crooked body—to be loved.

CHAPTER 13

Double Date

"Just one decision you make that seems really minor at the time can change the rest of your life," my dad said. The way he said it, I knew this was a monumental Papa Bear Trendon quote I would hang on to for the rest of my life. I knew he was talking to Charity, since she was the one going on an actual date, but I couldn't help applying it to myself and my inability to tell Brendan I wouldn't write his paper for him.

"Yeah, yeah, Dad," Charity said, rolling her eyes. "Don't worry. You've got good kids."

She tugged on my hair, pretending to mess up the hairdo Megan had spent hours helping me create. We had pulled my long, frizzy hair into a side braid, tucking the frizziest pieces behind my ear. The final result had only taken a total of three minutes, but deciding that was the one to go with had taken forever.

While Megan was jerking on ponytails and running curling irons through my hair, I'd wondered if the accidental tugs on my scalp where she exclaimed "Oops! Sorry!" were really accidents. I knew she was mad about my date with Brendan, but I didn't want to talk about why. I'd even let her put some mascara on my top eyelashes, with several swipes that nearly cut through my corneas. If she was that upset about my "date that was not a date," why would she help me get ready for it, let alone still be talking to me?

Since we were going to a movie and the theater was sometimes cold, I took a zip-up hoodie to wear over my fitted white long-sleeve shirt and dark jeans. I wore a long necklace with a gold heart at the end of it, and hoop earrings. It was a simple outfit, but it was awesome because I didn't have to wear my brace.

Brace-free for the night. Isaac Newton could do whatever he wanted. If I had wings, I would have lifted off the ground and flown—his gravity would have no effect on me.

As I checked my foreign-feeling mascara one more time in the bathroom mirror, the doorbell rang. I heard two young male voices greeting my father, who sounded more serious than I'd expected him to be.

Charity ran out of our room and grabbed my arm. "Come on. They're here." She sounded a little nervous, but I knew she didn't want to leave the guys in the clutches of our protective father for long.

"We're coming," she called down the steps, as we began our descent.

I suddenly felt silly, as if this were some kind of practice for prom (my mom had already taken pictures of Charity and me, and she'd promised she wouldn't ambush us again). But then Brendan looked up at me, and I was pleased to see his eyebrows lift in surprise when he saw me. He had on a plain blue t-shirt and fitted khaki pants, and he'd styled his hair with some kind of gel, so it lifted at the front above his forehead. I stared at his smile, gripping the banister railing so I didn't lose my footing on my way down the steps, and smiled back. My initial embarrassment faded as I met him at the bottom of the steps.

"You look great," he said.

"You too," I said.

"Yeah, but you look so different."

I looked away and tucked a renegade curl behind my ear. I knew I looked better without my brace on—I felt way better about myself too—but I hadn't expected Brendan to comment on it. Was my brace as physically repulsive to him as it was to me?

"Come back right after the movie, okay girls?" Dad said, his arms crossed. My mother was putting together a puzzle with Harold in the living room, but she stopped to watch us go.

"Yes, Dad," Charity and I said.

Jacob smiled politely and thanked my parents. "We should be home by nine-thirty. Have a good night," he said. He seemed nice enough.

"Bye, Brendan," my mom said.

"See you later, Trendons!" he said.

We walked out to the car. Jacob and Charity walked ahead of us.

"You look great," Jacob said to her.

"Thanks," Charity said. "So do you."

Charity didn't blush or giggle nervously like I expected her to. She seemed really comfortable around Jacob. He opened the door for her and she slid gracefully into her seat, while Brendan and I climbed into the back.

Brendan was talking about a football game he'd been watching before Jacob picked him up. "I didn't get to see the end. It was tied 14–14 and the Broncos had the ball at the thirty with a minute left on the clock."

"You're annoyed you had to come?" I asked him.

He frowned. "Not at all. I'm excited.."

"I'm excited to see this movie," Charity said.

"What is it again?" I asked.

"A chick flick," Brendan moaned.

"It won't be that bad, man," Jacob said, looking at Brendan in his rearview mirror.

I liked Jacob's attitude. "Yeah, man," I said, playfully punching Brendan in the shoulder.

"Oh yeah?" Brendan grabbed me by the waist and tickled me. I screamed with laughter as Charity turned around in her seat.

"Truth!" Out of the corner of her eye, she looked at Jacob. He held his composure, his face forward. "I am not here to babysit you," she said.

My neck flushed with anger, annoyed that I, the youngest person in the car, had been singled out. "I *am* here because Mom and Dad don't trust you with boys."

Charity's eyes widened and I knew if Jacob hadn't been there she would have cuffed me like a lioness swatting one of her cubs. Luckily, Jacob laughed and the tension eased.

"Your sister's funny," he said.

"That's one word for her," Charity said.

"That's three words," I said. Jacob laughed again. I realized I was too focused on being an annoying sister, rather than a mature seventh grader on a (chaperoning) date with another mature seventh grader. I leaned back and looked at Brendan, jutting my

229

chin in what I thought was an easygoing gesture. "Ya know, if you're counting," I said.

"I wasn't," Brendan said. He yawned.

We finally pulled up to the movie theater. Jacob tried to drop us off, but Charity insisted we could all go together. I could tell she didn't want to be left alone with me and Brendan like a babysitter. As if I needed a babysitter.

"You can drop Brendan and me off," I said. "We'll wait for you inside."

Brendan leapt out of the parked car as Charity said "Ooookay." She was hesitant, but she didn't dislike the idea.

"Let's go, Truth," Brendan said, standing on the curb. I thought he might open the door for me, but instead he looked impatiently over his shoulder at the theater.

"See you inside," I said. I crawled out of the car and Brendan smiled at me.

"I hate feeling supervised," he said. "I was sneaking into movies with friends in fifth grade."

"Me too. Well, I paid for them. I feel bad for the guy who has to clean up all the popcorn and sticky soda pop residue. He has to get paid somehow, right?"

"Sometimes I wonder how we ended up friends, Trendon," Brendan said.

I paused. "Is that what we are? Friends?"

He took my hand. "Of course."

As my face burned with a mixture of nervousness and excitement at Brendan's fingers intertwined in mine, I tried not to focus on the fact we were just "friends" to him. Friends could become more than that, couldn't they?

"Thanks for asking me to come tonight," he said. "The movie may be really lame—okay, let's be honest, the movie *will* be really lame—but I like being here with you."

"You sure that's not just because I agreed to write your paper?"

He dropped my hand, and I immediately regretted my guilty conscience's outburst.

"I thought you'd want to help me because you like me, too."

"I do," I said. "But I thought the whole teaching you to read after school thing was helping you. You're doing really well."

He scowled. "I don't want to talk about that. Tonight's supposed to be fun."

"You're right. I'm sorry. Forget I said anything." We walked into the building in silence, but Brendan took my hand again as we waited in the lobby. He dropped it when Charity and Jacob sauntered through the doors, their hands grasped so tightly together their fingers were turning purple.

Charity smiled at me. "I expected you two to have run off by now, to get away from the 'controlling adults.'"

"Adults? Where?" I asked, glancing in all directions.

Brendan and Jacob laughed, but Charity shook her head. "I still can't believe Mom and Dad made you come along."

"I'm just too cool," I said. "The public needs to see me out and about."

Charity rolled her eyes.

"You guys get your tickets yet?" Jacob asked.

"Nope," I said.

Brendan and I paid separately, since it wasn't a "date," but Jacob paid Charity's way in. He also paid for their treats at the concession stand. I got a soda pop and Brendan got popcorn. Charity thanked Jacob each time he paid, and I watched her watch Jacob as he led us into the right theater.

I wondered if I looked as obviously doe-eyed gazing at Brendan as she did with Jacob. Part of me didn't like that; it left a bad taste in my mouth, knowing guys didn't look at me the same way. I couldn't blame them—what guy wanted to look at a girl in a back brace longer than he had to? I comforted myself with the fact Brendan would at least look at me, even if it wasn't in a complete worshipping fervor. And we were friends.

That was enough. For now.

"Sit wherever you want," Charity told me, as we filed into the rows of chairs after getting some quick snacks. "We're gonna sit toward the back."

"Keep it PG," I said.

Charity huffed. "You know I don't like sitting too close. It hurts my neck."

She followed Jacob without looking back at me. I'd made her mad.

"Did she say they're going to neck?" Brendan asked me, once we'd found our seats.

I almost shot soda pop out of my nose. "No!" I said loudly, laughing.

People around us filled the air with "shhhh" noises.

"Already getting shushed and the movie hasn't even started? Not good form, Trendon." Brendan shook his head. I threw a piece of popcorn at him.

I heard a lady behind me say, "Does she realize someone has to clean that up?"

We both laughed as the previews started. Brendan made fun of them, and I laughed, clearly making the lady behind us upset. She finally moved.

"I feel bad," I said.

"Don't," Brendan said. "We're just kids to her. We were going to make her mad no matter what."

I sighed. I was tired of being reminded of how immature I was. I lay my head back and watched as a bouncy beat began with the intro to the movie. Soon I forgot my adolescent woes and began to fall into the plot, predictable as it was. I was rooting for the cute underdog with the good heart, who wanted to get the girl. He did.

Brendan and Jacob hated the movie.

"There's no way that measly, nerdy guy would get *that* girl," Jacob said, as we walked out of the theater.

"No kidding," Brendan said. "She was a ten, and he was, like, a negative two."

"I thought he was adorable!" Charity said.

"Me too," I said.

Charity put her arm around me. We walked down the street toward the parking lot. "We girls have to stick together," she said into my ear.

I grinned, glad to be on her good side before we got home so she'd give a good report to Mom and Dad.

"He had a certain *je ne sais quoi*," I said. "Nerdy, but sophisticated. He wasn't just interested in her body."

"Yeah. Exactly," Charity said.

"That wasn't a true portrayal of men," Jacob said.

Charity's grip around my shoulders tightened. "Oh yeah? And what did they get wrong?"

Jacob scratched the back of his head, apparently regretting his word choice. "Can I retract my previous statement?"

"Only if you have a time machine," Charity said. Her voice was serious, but she was teasing him at the same time. "So if I was as hot as that girl in the movie, I could get any guy I wanted?"

"Duh," said Brendan.

I wanted to slug him so badly, but Charity had me restrained. "Huh," she said. "So, Truth, we'll go get our nails done, slather on makeup, and buy a couple of push-up bras, and we'll find us some real men."

"Sounds *great*," I said, glaring in Brendan's direction.

"According to that movie, you'll end up with a scrawny kid who can't grow a beard," Jacob said.

"I think you've already got him," I said to Charity.

Jacob laughed. "Oh yeah?"

He lunged at me, wrapped his arms around my waist, and picked me up. I was surprised, but it was a happy reminder I didn't have hard, immobile plastic wrapped around me.

"Still think I'm scrawny?" He asked as he set me back down.

"Yes," I said, "but not as scrawny as Brendan." Brendan stopped to stare at me, aghast, and then he smiled and grabbed for me. I squealed and took off at a fast sprint across the parking lot, passing cars that turned into blurs of lights and colors. I could hear Jacob chasing us, Charity laughing after him. I hadn't run this fast since I'd gotten my brace, and it was exhilarating.

I could feel my arms pumping; my feet pounding the pavement, sending shockwaves up my legs and into my back; and my heart beating as if it were going to explode at any second. It felt amazing. I didn't want to stop. Ever.

But as I heard the boys running after me and Charity yelling at me to stop, a huge light suddenly appeared in front of me, blocking my vision. I'd run out in front of a moving pickup truck.

The driver blared his horn, brakes squealing as he slammed to a stop. I leapt out of the way and skidded to a halt, slamming my foot against the tire of the nearest parked car.

I waved apologetically at the startled driver and the truck slowly continued to move past.

Brendan ran up behind me first. "Are you okay?" he asked, placing his hand on my shoulder.

"I stubbed my toe!" I said, laughing. I looked up and then I froze. Oliver sat in the passenger seat of the pickup. His large, brown eyes held my gaze. I could feel the pressure of Brendan's hand still on my shoulder, but my brain was focused on the sad eyes in front of me. I'd seen those same eyes crinkled with laughter and wide-eyed in anger, but never purely, utterly disappointed. My lips moved to speak, to apologize, to simply say hello, but the truck continued to move, and Oliver disappeared behind the reflection of a streetlight on the passenger side window.

"Are you hurt?" Charity shouted, running up to me. "That was really stupid of you!"

Physically, I was fine. But it felt like my heart had somehow been stung. I felt guilty for being there— on a date with Brendan, running without my brace, everything.

Part of me wondered what it would be like to hold Oliver's hand, or if he'd think I looked completely different without my brace on. But I knew the answer to that—he'd seen me without my brace, and it didn't matter to him. I knew Oliver was the kind of guy who wouldn't resent people for not having the same disease as him, but I wondered if he ever thought about it, deep down in the darkest of his dark thoughts. He didn't ever get the chance to hide his physical differences.

I tried to shake my mind clear. Charity helped. She slapped me across the shoulder.

"What were you doing?" she shouted.

"Running!" I said, out of breath.

"It looked like you were playing chicken with that Chevy," Jacob said.

"It's okay, Truth. You probably would have won if we hadn't stopped you," Brendan said.

I laughed, trying not to think about Oliver. "I didn't see it. It just felt good to run."

I didn't add it was the freest I'd felt in a long time. Closing my eyes, I could still hear the rush of the air in my ears and feel the burst of adrenaline and excitement. I think that's the closest humans can come to flying—sprinting as fast as we can and not caring what's going on around us.

But though I relished the adrenaline pumping through my body, my heart still hurt. I had dreamed about being seen out in public with Brendan, and what that would feel like. Every time I had imagined it, I'd pictured jealous girls at my beck and call, moaning and throwing themselves at my feet, hoping to be friends, and boys drooling with desire for me now that I was on the arm of one Brendan Matthews.

I hadn't expected to feel like I was in the wrong place, with the wrong person.

I shook my thoughts away and heaved one final sigh as a few beads of sweat formed on my forehead. I stepped back from the car in front of me. "Did I dent this car?"

"Better hope not. It's mine," Jacob said. We all laughed and climbed in.

When Jacob dropped us off, he didn't get out of the car to tell Charity goodbye like I thought he might. Brendan remained in his seat as well. I'll admit to being disappointed, but I wasn't surprised. Dad was waiting at the window, the curtain barely shifted over enough so he thought he was inconspicuous. I waved, and the curtain quickly dropped back into place.

"Thanks again," Charity said.

"Yeah, thanks Jacob," I said. "Next time I won't try to get killed."

"You make for an exciting date, Truth," Jacob said. "Maybe next time we can switch dates. You can be my arm candy."

I laughed. "I'll be a hard candy, and square looking," I said, referring to my brace.

By Jacob's confused face, I could tell he had no idea what I was talking about.

"If there is a next time," Brendan said. He was joking, but the tone of his voice, short and steely, reminded me I owed him an essay about weapons.

"Goodbye," Charity said, with a short wave, and Jacob pulled the car away.

"Doesn't Jacob know I have a back brace?" I asked Charity.

"I didn't tell him," she said.

"Why not?"

"It didn't come up."

"But he's probably noticed it, right?"

Charity sighed. "Truth, unless you've told people, they most likely can't tell. You're way more observant than most people, and way too self-conscious. Quit worrying about it."

"Okay," I said, a bit baffled.

We walked into the house where Dad stood in the middle of the living room, his arms crossed. "He should have waited to make sure you got into the house okay," he said.

Harold popped out from behind Dad's legs, where he had been hiding. "That's right!" he shouted. "You're late!"

"No, we're not," Charity retorted.

Mom laughed. "They were practicing in case you were."

"You're both grounded, young ladies!" Harold commanded.

Charity grabbed Harold's face, kissing him on the cheek. He screamed. I, however, floated on air, my mind hovering far from my family, whose muffled voices I barely heard as the reality of my life sunk in. One, I may have had to wear a brace that locked down my movements, but it didn't change the way people perceived me. Two, I had just gone on a date with the cutest guy in school, with the possibility of going on another. Three, my social status was sufficiently "neutral" and Isaac Newton could choke on an apple seed for all I cared.

If only I could shake the pang of guilt that nagged at me whenever I thought about sitting down to write a paper that wasn't mine, or of Oliver seeing me with Brendan. When I went to bed that night, I kept picturing his sad brown eyes staring back at me, so close they could have been plastered on the backs of my eyelids, and so sad I couldn't help but let the tears leak out of my own.

CHAPTER 14

The Kiss of Death

Over the weekend, I called Megan to talk about my date. She'd sounded excited on the phone, laughing at my idiotic sprint that had turned into a near Truth-to-truck crash, but when I tried to bring it up again on Monday, as we stood by our locker, she seemed annoyed with having to talk about it.

"Brendan held your hand, you want to be more than friends, and you can't wait to go on another 'date.' I heard you the first time."

"Sorry," I said. I tried not to scowl as I stacked my books onto my designated shelf.

"Well," Megan said, somewhat apologetically, "you didn't bother to ask me about my weekend."

"How was it?" I asked, my voice oozing with interest.

"Boring." She shut the locker and headed to class before I was finished getting my things.

To avoid adding another negative social interaction, I didn't meet with Oliver that morning. I wasn't

242

ready to face him. I didn't know what I'd say to him if I saw him.

At lunch, Brendan approached me while I ate with Megan. I knew he wanted his paper. I also knew I wanted to vomit in utter fear of rejection and future social excommunication. Megan saw him coming, rolled her eyes, and stood up with her tray of half-eaten Salisbury steak.

"See you later," she said.

As Megan walked away, Brendan grinned out of the corner of his mouth, leaned over my shoulder, and breathed his spectacular voice into my ear.

"Do you have it?"

I didn't. So I did what any proud American named Truth would do. I lied.

"I put it in Landers' mailbox this morning," I said, biting my tongue to keep my face serious.

"Really? Why?" Brendan scowled. "That's going to look fishy."

I was hooked instantly, caught up in the web of naughty impulsiveness I had never taken advantage of as a child. I was about to suggest something that I'd never believed I would ever do: skip school. "No, now you can fake a note from your mom, put it in his mailbox with the paper, and we can play hooky for the rest of the day."

I'd already skipped my meeting with Oliver that day. And I would miss Science, but I knew we had a review over magnetic poles that day, which I could handle reviewing on my own. If I could skip and still stay caught up, was I really missing anything?

I must have sounded convincing, because Brendan ate it up. "Trendon! You're a dirty genius!" He put his hands on my shoulders and squeezed. "I didn't know you had it in you," he whispered.

He left the cafeteria to grab a piece of paper and a pen from his locker. When he came back, he handed them to me. "Here. You write the note because you have girlier handwriting than me."

Why not? I was doomed anyway. As I wrote the note, each cursive letter flowing from my fingers like fluid magic, I thought of how the old Truth would have resolved this honestly; wouldn't have agreed to write the paper in the first place. Before-Brace Truth probably would never have been asked to write a paper for someone else because she exuded honesty and goodwill.

But the old Truth was boring. She was predictable and simple and she said weird things on her sister's dates. With my brace on, I knew Isaac Newton was there in the shadows somewhere, pushing on my spine and doing his best to ruin my life. Why wait and prolong the inevitable when I could fall on my own terms?

"Okay, Brendan," I said, folding the note in half. "Let's get you to that dentist's appointment."

"As long as you don't pull any teeth," Brendan said.

I blushed. Then he took my hand.

I was on the dark side of the law—the side I knew a good girl wasn't supposed to be on—and I didn't mind it.

We ran out of school when the bell rang and there were too many people flowing up and the down the halls for a roaming teacher to notice us. We jogged down the cement stairs outside, with Brendan chasing after me. It was awkward running in my brace, and I probably looked more like a galloping cow than a graceful gazelle, but I knew we had to hurry so we wouldn't be seen.

We ran down the sidewalk past nearby houses, hiding behind trees when cars passed by. I could feel my brace rubbing against my hip bones, which would be red and sore later. I knew my butt muscles would hate me later too. But despite this, and despite the giant knot of guilt growing in my stomach from lying to Brendan about his paper, the new version of me told myself, "It's *fine*. We'll deal with that when it comes."

And I believed me.

"I never thought you'd do this, Truth," Brendan said.

I felt my conscience-ridden organs jump inside my skin. "Lie?"

"Skip school."

We slowed our jog, and I changed my gait to a skip, pushing myself off the ground with strength I didn't realize I had, especially when confined within my detested armor. "I'm an excellent skipper!" I said.

Brendan laughed. "Where should we go?"

I stopped skipping. "I thought you knew."

"This was your idea, Truth." His voice started to lose its familiar confidence and control. "You know, my mom is going to pick me up after school. Someone could see me and wonder why I wasn't there for half the day. Maybe we should go back."

For some reason, I'd figured Brendan had played hooky before. I had, but only once when I was in first grade and craving the Velveeta cheese I knew we had in the fridge. I'd pretended to be sick, and when my mom left to take Charity to school, I'd snuck down and cut off a gigantic hunk of the processed cheese. After three huge, gluttonous mouthfuls, I actually *was* sick to my stomach. I had a feeling Brendan wouldn't think our skipping class together was worth just a piece of pasteurized cheese product.

Suddenly, I felt words coming out of my mouth that I'd never expected. "You could kiss me."

I knew my face mirrored the surprise on Brendan's (though I imagine *my* face wasn't as wonderful to look at). His eyes widened only for a second, and then he smiled, grabbed my face and pulled it closer to his.

I panicked, feeling like I was going to cry out with jubilation, explode, and blow chunks in his face all at the same time. Instead, I puckered up and wished for the best. I left my eyes open until the last moment, taking in his hair, his oily forehead, and a few dark, clogged pores on his nose. Then our lips touched, and even though I expected my brain to implode or to suddenly vibrate with the electricity of love, it was just kind of *blah*. His lips were dry, and I wasn't about to have another person's tongue in my mouth, no matter how hot I thought he was, so it was pretty quick.

"Is that what we cut class for?" Brendan said, grinning.

I didn't want to tell him I felt like I'd just kissed Harold, so I smiled back and said, "I guess."

He took my hand and we walked down the block. Apparently we were far enough away from school for him to feel comfortable walking out in the open. He was quiet for a while and then he looked at me.

"You know, you're the first girl I've ever kissed."

"Really?"

"Yeah."

"I'm surprised," I said.

He furrowed his brow. "Why?"

"Well, every girl in school likes you. You know you're good-looking." His brow furrowed with doubt, and I rolled my eyes. "You *have* to know. Look at the nerds you're up against."

"Nerds like you?"

"Yes!" I said.

He laughed when he realized I was serious. "Do you realize how fun these past few months have been for me? I was so embarrassed about not being able to read, but you've made it easy." He stopped walking. "I've read a book, Tru," he said. "Sure, it was a first grade chapter book, but do you know how long I've wanted to say that and actually mean it? I've read a book." His proud expression made my guilt dissolve into a million little pieces. I hadn't realized I'd actually helped him that much.

"So you like me because I'm teaching you how to read?" I asked, wanting again to hear him say he liked me.

"I like people I can trust," he said. He looked at me with a smile, his eyes shining from the sunlight overhead.

Oh. My guilt came rushing back. I'd never felt so terrible in all my life. Not even hearing I had scoliosis or that I had to wear a back brace had taken the wind out of my sails like those words leaving Brendan's mouth did.

"Me too," I said quietly.

We walked in silence for a while. "Maybe we should go back," I said finally.

"Now you're nervous about being caught?"

"I don't have a note from my mom to excuse me like you do," I said.

"Oh," Brendan said.

He clearly hadn't thought about the fact I would need an excuse too. It made me mad how he could seem so focused on me, and the next moment it was clear he was only thinking about himself.

He nodded his head. "Maybe you're right. We should head back."

We headed back toward the school. We walked quicker than before, and Brendan didn't make an attempt to hold my hand again. I considered reaching for *his* hand, but my braver side seemed to have shriveled up before it had even had a chance to shine.

By the time on Brendan's cell phone, we'd been gone about forty minutes. We had five minutes to spare before the next class period, so we hovered outside the side doors until the bell rang. In my heart, I felt like I'd already lost Brendan. Lost the perfect boy of my dreams forever because I hadn't helped him con his way to a good grade, and then didn't tell him I hadn't helped him cheat.

I'd cheated both of us. So I took one more chance. I stood up on my tiptoes, leaned right up to Brendan's slightly parted lips, and kissed him one more time (only the second time ever!). As far as kisses go on the Best Ever list, it probably wouldn't make the top billion; however, as far as kissing Brendan went, it was perfect. I pulled away as the bell rang and scampered through the door, leaving him standing on the stoop of the school, a bit stunned.

As I walked as calmly as I could to my locker, I couldn't quell the beaming grin plastered on my face. I never would have guessed that I, Truth Trendon, member of the scoliosis club since fifth grade and president of Boston brace wear, would have my first kiss at the age of twelve.

If I told them, I knew my parents would act calm but secretly freak out and have a big discussion about me behind my back. But I wasn't going to tell them. I probably wasn't going to tell Charity. It didn't matter. Once Brendan discovered I hadn't written his paper, he probably wouldn't come near my lips with a ten-foot pole, let alone talk to me.

"You look happy," Megan said, as she joined me at our locker.

"I am," I said.

"What's the good news, big shoes?" she said, kicking my size nine foot with her size seven one.

"Brendan kissed me," I said, unable to hold back my excitement. I thought Megan would return my delight, but instead her face fell.

"Oh," she said. "That's great."

"Well, I thought so."

Megan hugged her books and looked at the floor. "Don't you think you're a bit young?"

"Are you serious? I thought you'd be excited. All you talk about is boys—liking them, kissing them, marrying them—what's wrong with you?" I threw my hands up in the air before shoving them across my chest, in what I hoped was the haughtiest way possible.

"Nothing. Nothing is wrong with me," Megan said.

She walked away and headed for the bathroom, her head hanging low—an indication she was trying to hide the tears that were just about to exit her eyeballs. Seeing her about to cry not only made my own eyes dampen, but it also confused me beyond belief. It made no sense to me. I would have been happy for her if the roles were reversed. That's what best friends did; they got excited for each other when good things happened.

I sighed. Whatever was wrong with Megan, I hoped she'd conquer it and be my friend again soon.

"Problems in locker partner land?"

I turned around to see Jenny Henderson smiling at me.

"Kind of."

I grabbed my books and shut the locker. As I hoisted the books to balance them against my brace, Jenny linked her arm through mine and walked with me down the hallway, as if we were a pair of conjoined twins (with one of us entirely focused on keeping the perfect distance between us, so as not to let the other's elbow bump against the hard plastic of her brace).

I felt the eyes of my peers watching us; some in envy, others in shock, and others with looks of disdain.

I looked back at all of them with wide-eyed confusion. I couldn't believe it myself.

"So, did you have fun playing hooky last period?"

I almost dropped my books. "What are you talking about?"

"Brendan should have been in History last period. He wasn't. Now he's back. I heard from Megan you didn't go to Science. Now *you're* back. That's a happy coincidence, don't you think?"

"The happiest," I said, mocking her cheerful tone. She pulled her arm away from me as if I had the plague. We were near the English room, where I was headed.

"I think you and Brendan are hiding something," she said, her voice still pleasant.

I hesitated. Too long. "No," I said.

"I've seen you sneaking off with Brendan after school, and now during school. That's a lot of time for secrets between a dating couple."

"You are off your rocker," I said. "We're just friends."

"And you're a liar," Jenny said, her voice suddenly curt and harsh.

I flinched. She didn't realize how much that statement actually cut me to the core.

"Whatever. I'll pass on a ticket for the crazy train. You've obviously taken up all of the seats."

I started to walk through the doorway of the English room, when Jenny called after me, "Oh, and Coach said you can leave the football pads alone. He knows you've been sneaking into the storage room to smell them."

The entire classroom broke into laughter. I didn't mind holding the class' attention when I was trying to make a point about literature or answering a question about grammar, but when they were laughing at me, exposed at the front of the classroom and feeling like they could see me naked—or worse, see my brace under my shirt—I immediately upped my verbal retaliation game.

"Oh, thanks, *Jen*. By the way, he told *me* you can stop trying on all the jockstraps. They're never going to fit you."

The class erupted again, and I grimaced as a shadow loomed over me.

"Do you need to be excused, Miss Trendon?" Mrs. Pike asked, her usually happy and kind voice toned down to serious concern.

"No, I do not."

I stomped to my table and set my books down. Mrs. Pike said something to Jenny as the bell rang, and then she shut the door. "Enough about football. Sweaty pads and jockstraps are far from what we're talking about today."

There were a few more snickers from the class, and Mrs. Pike even grinned. "First of all, I mentioned a few days ago we would be selecting two students to speak at the next junior high assembly next month. We have now chosen the two students: one for academic excellence and the other for excelling in extracurricular activities. The committee was composed of teachers from all over the school, as well as Ms. Eastin. I'm proud and happy to announce that one of the students is among us in this class."

If Mrs. Pike hadn't been staring at me, I wouldn't have suddenly felt nervous. I'd already started sweating from my run-in with Jenny.

"Let's congratulate Truth Trendon!" Mrs. Pike said. She began to clap, and the rest of the class followed suit. "The committee wanted to honor Truth's outstanding success in her classes and in Band, and we're looking forward to an entertaining and informative presentation."

I bit my lip and turned red with embarrassment; I knew how boring assemblies always were, and I didn't want to be part of a monotonous afternoon everyone would hate and complain about for days afterward.

Out of the corner of my eye, I watched Megan, who had her hands under her desk, hidden from Mrs. Pike. I could see she wasn't clapping. The former alliance of Megan and Truth, best friends for eternity, would have made it possible for her to read my mind—*Mrs. Pike would be so disappointed to know you're not clapping*—but we were no longer comrades. I focused back on Mrs. Pike.

"Many of you were qualified to speak at the assembly," she said, "so don't feel as if you've been overlooked or forgotten. I'm proud of all of you."

"You *are* really good at the trumpet, Truth," said Eric Maloney, a trombone player.

"Thanks!" I said. "Apparently I'm also good at smelling football pads. So I'll try to work some aromatic scent descriptions into my presentation."

The class laughed. Even Megan smiled, her gaze focused on Mrs. Pike.

"Strange," said Mrs. Pike.

"Who's the other one?" asked Rebecca Kaplan, who was every teacher's pet and had probably been vying for the chance to speak at a presentation about how awesome she was since she popped out of the womb.

"Brendan Matthews," answered Mrs. Pike.

I was shocked—he'd already been caught cheating once this year! But heads nodded in agreement around the room. He excelled at sports. As far as extracurricular activities went, Brendan was clearly a good choice. I knew he'd give a great presentation, but I felt like the teachers weren't doing their job. The guy hadn't been able to read more than a few simple words before this year, and now he was reading at a first grade level. That was excellence?

For the rest of class period, we read and discussed a short story. I put in my two cents about the plot, but I was distracted, trying to think up something entertaining I could do in front of the entire junior high. The biggest things that had happened to me this year—getting a back brace and locking lips with Brendan—would be the most entertaining, but there was no way I was going to share those secrets with anyone else (although I would love to have seen Jenny's face when she heard about the kiss), especially not the whole school.

Luckily, I still had time to think about it.

My parents were proud of me. They'd gotten a call

from the school to let them know I'd be giving a presentation. Of course the school wanted my parents to be involved, but I wondered how much they expected them to manipulate my presentation—to make sure I didn't say anything against the school. Not that I would. I actually liked school; I'd enjoyed it ever since first grade when I had the alphabet down pat and got put into the top reading group. I was definitely not too cool for school—in fact, I thought school was probably too cool for *me*.

On my way to the living room, I grabbed a notebook. Maybe I could use that line—*school was always too cool for me* . . . Even as I wrote it, I knew I'd never say those words in that order in front of my peers, but it was a starting point.

That night, my family and I watched the Miss America pageant. We weren't huge pageant fans; we just liked to analyze state popularity among the somewhat-celebrity judges. Every year we worked out the statistical probabilities of who would win, based on the top states from the years before. The big, most populous states were always contenders—California, Texas, New York, Florida. The Midwestern states always seemed to be cut before the top ten. Once, South Dakota made it up to the top five, and we were beside ourselves with statistical confusion.

The judges had gone rogue that year, and it threw off our numbers for a good three pageants.

"How come they all have the same smile?" Harold asked.

"They all use teeth whitener," my dad replied.

"I like her," Harold said, marching up to the screen and pointing at Miss California, a blonde in a gorgeous flowing blue gown. "She waves at everyone."

"They all wave at everyone," Charity pointed out.

"But she really means it," Harold said, waving back.

I stayed quiet as I kept track of the states that were weeded out.

"Oklahoma's gonna be out of there," my mom said. "That dress clashes with her hair."

"I like it. She stands out," my dad said.

"So if I dyed my hair bright red and wore a hot pink dress on national television, you wouldn't mind? Hmm?"

"You'd look lovely in anything," my dad said, kissing Mom on the cheek.

"Dad has cooties!" Harold cried.

"Cut it out, you two," Charity laughed. "Hot pink is a horrible choice for pageants." She wrinkled her face at me and frowned. "What's your problem?"

"Nuffin," I muttered, pencil eraser pressed against my lips, my gaze glued to the gorgeous women walking across the stage in their evening gowns. Not one of them had scoliosis; not even a hint of one rib sticking even a millimeter out of place in any direction. I had already resigned myself years ago to not being a beauty queen, but what if that had been my dream, the one thing I had wanted to do with my life?

Nope, Brace-Wearing Truth can't do the dance number because she can't kick her legs up any higher than her ankle. Look out, Brace-Wearing Truth can't bend to see her feet with her peripheral vision when she walks, so she trips on wires, takes out the entire lighting system, and gets electrocuted. I'd be a Miss America tragedy—lying on a stretcher, strapped into my back brace, my frizzy hair fried to a crisp.

The saddest part was I wouldn't even get that far. I wouldn't qualify for the pageant because the rib-hump on my back made it clear I wasn't perfect like all of the other women. I was deformed, crooked, and ugly, and I would never be beautiful like they were. A quiet tear leaked out onto the word "Oklahoma" that I'd just crossed out in my notebook.

"What did I tell you?" my mom said. "Hot pink never makes the top ten."

Scoliosis, the physical chaos that was my life, never did either.

CHAPTER 15
The Discovery (Part 3)

Over the second week of November, I sank into a dark depression—dark in that I wore black t-shirts three days in a row and tried out eyeliner. The black makeup always ran down my face by the end of the day, leaving me with thin streaks of black on my cheeks.

"I think you should wash your face," Megan said before last period on the third day.

"Why?"

"It looks like you've been crying or you're trying to have wrinkles on your cheeks."

"Maybe I am. I'm trying to look older, wiser. Distinguished."

"It's distinguished all right," Megan said. We hadn't been talking much lately, but after a pause she grabbed my arm and asked sincerely, "Are you okay?"

My lips itched to tell her about Brendan not knowing how to read, and how he'd asked me to write a paper for him, but after I'd agreed to do it (betraying myself), I didn't (betraying him). The least I could have done was be honest with him; now he had no idea, and when Mr. Landers told him he never got his paper, Brendan would either kill me or never talk to me again. I hadn't yet decided which was worse.

On top of that, I still hadn't been back to see Oliver. I could picture him sitting there, waiting for me to show up, but I never did. After seeing him watching me from the truck that night on the double date, I felt like I didn't know what to talk about anymore. His eyes had said too much. I felt as though some invisible string that had linked us together had somehow been broken, and I hadn't the slightest idea how to repair it.

To Megan, I said, "Meh."

"I feel that way too. Do you want to come over after school? We can finish algebra and then make cookies."

I smiled, knowing "make cookies" meant her mother would make them for us while we did homework. "I would love that."

"Good." She shut our locker and we walked to History together. Brendan was just leaving the classroom with Mr. Landers.

"I put it in your mailbox. I don't know what happened," he said.

"Okay, well, get a copy of it to me by tomorrow, and I won't count it late," Mr. Landers said.

"Okay. Thanks, Mr. L."

As Megan entered the classroom, Brendan pulled me back into the hallway. "Landers didn't get my paper," he said. "Are you sure you put it in his mailbox? Can you get me another copy for tomorrow?"

I sighed. It was now or never. "I didn't write it."

"What?"

"I couldn't do it," I said, trying to make myself cry. Quietly, I added, "It's cheating."

"Why didn't you tell me? You lied to me." Brendan's voice was hardly above a whisper, but it was full and quiet and came from a harsh place in his throat.

I paused. I knew my answer was going to upset him. I could see the steam building behind his big, long-lashed eyes, feel the anger rising in his face as he involuntarily held his breath, trying not to explode. I wished he would. It would make me feel more like a victim, rather than the root of the problem.

"I'm sorry. I didn't want to upset you," I said, looking at my history book in my hands. That's what we were: *The Short Relationship of Brendan Matthews and Truth Trendon, Barely a History.*

264

"Are you kidding me?" Brendan said, exasperated. He lowered his voice even more. "I can't believe you. I would have figured something else out, Truth. I'm not an idiot."

"I know that!" I said.

"No, I don't think you do."

This time I actually started to cry. "Brendan, I'm so sorry!"

"Forget it," he said. He walked away toward the lockers, his head hung lower than I'd ever seen. Brendan Matthews—confident, strong, and cheerful student loved by all—walked through school like he'd just been told he was a loser. I felt like it was true, and I was the one who'd said it.

The bell rang.

Mr. Landers walked to the doorway and looked at me with his hand on the doorknob. "You're late."

I slowly turned my head as I wiped the tears from my eyes with my other hand. "No, I'm not," I said. I walked past him into the classroom and he just let me go.

I wanted to leap out of a window dramatically—maybe through the glass, depending on how much of a running start I had—but we were only on the first floor, and that didn't seem like it would leave the lasting impression I was aiming for. I sighed and faced forward, where Mr. Landers was in the middle of one of his rambling sprees.

"So I just wanted you kids to keep that in mind—some days are rocks, others are diamonds. Today may have been a rock, where no matter what you did, it was hard and difficult to grasp things. For some of you, it may have been a diamond—you shone on that math test or spelling test. Do you guys still have spelling tests? No? What do you study in English then? Okay, fine, no spelling tests. But keep that in mind." He looked at me, and I felt myself shift uncomfortably under his unusually sincere gaze. "Tomorrow can always be better. You can make it that way. It may seem like your parents or guardians have control over you right now, but your life is in your own hands more than you realize. School is your place to be a star, no matter what kind of star you want to be."

"Maybe he should write my speech," I muttered. *Sheesh.*

"Question, Truth?"

"Nope. Good advice, sir."

Several people snickered. *Sir?* I was really out of it.

"Thank you," Mr. Landers said slowly. "Okay. Enough serious stuff. Let's talk about the warrior and slave culture of the Sumerians."

Everyone moaned. We'd been hoping Landers would rant the entire class, but his encouraging pep talk seemed to have made him focus.

"Cause that sounds like it's full of comedy and excitement," said Tim Ackles, from across the room.

"It *is* exciting. It's history."

The class moaned again as Mr. Landers pulled down the projector screen with an evil laugh, but the rest of the class period actually zoomed by. Mr. Landers was entertaining with his lesson that day, and he didn't stray off topic even once. When the bell rang, for the first time he had to cut himself off before he was finished with his lecture—an actual history lecture, and not one of his tirades.

As I passed his desk, Mr. Landers asked to speak to me. I stopped and Megan nudged me, whispering, "I'll meet you at our locker."

I nodded. Mr. Landers kept his voice down as the rest of my classmates filtered out of the room. "First of all, Truth, I wanted to congratulate you on your selection to represent academic excellence and whatever else the description is. I recommended you myself."

I was in a hurry to go and find Brendan so I could try to smooth things over. "Thanks," I said. "I'm excited, I guess."

"So then, is everything okay?" Landers asked.

I watched his face turn to concern. "Everything's fine," I said.

"You haven't seemed yourself this past week. I just wanted to let you know you do have people you can talk to here. I mean, as long as it's not too personal. Go to the counselor for that. But if you need an extension on homework or advice about anything school related, you can ask me."

I smiled slightly, picturing Landers' reaction if I told him the truth.

"Thanks," was all I said.

"Teachers tend to know more than just the subject they're teaching. We've been through junior high ourselves."

"But you're so cool, Mr. Landers. I bet it was a breeze for you," I said, sucking up in my most sincere voice, when I really imagined he was a bit of a nerd in junior high, getting made fun of but taking it well.

"Oh, sure. I was a stud muffin," Landers said, smiling. "But everyone has their issues; no matter how 'cool' they seem to be."

"That's for sure." I thought of Brendan and how perfect I thought he had been.

Mr. Landers peered at my face. "I think you have something under your eye."

"I'm sure I do. Thanks."

"Okay, well. Have a good evening, and hopefully tomorrow will be a diamond in the rough for you."

"Yeah, hopefully."

He was really hanging on to that analogy. I figured we'd be hearing about diamonds and rocks for the rest of the year.

As I walked to my locker, I was lost in thought, trying to think of what I could say to ease Brendan's anger about my lying to him. I couldn't write his paper for him, but I could definitely help him. It could be our lesson for the afternoon. There'd be a lot of words he could learn.

I stopped in my tracks (both literally and in my brain) when I saw Brendan and Megan talking in front of our locker. She leaned with her back against the locker (something I couldn't do, because my brace would have made a noise, and it would have been totally uncomfortable), and he was leaning with one arm against the lockers, while his other hand rested on the back of his neck.

At first glance, if I hadn't known better, I would have guessed they were a couple.

I approached slowly, stalking and analyzing my prey so they wouldn't scatter and hide in an attempt to avoid my apologies (or in Megan's case, my wrath).

Brendan stood up straight as I walked up to them. I slowly turned the lock, giving myself time to think. I was thankful he waited patiently. I placed my books in the locker, taking several moments to adjust their glued paper spines so they wouldn't bend out of shape. Finally, I took a deep breath and turned around.

"Megan? May I talk to Brendan alone?"

"No," she said quickly. He laughed.

I looked at them with disdain. "Look, Brendan, I'm so sorry." I tried to turn my back to Megan, so she wouldn't hear the next part of my apology. "You have to realize I can't cheat. The genetic makeup or the fiber or whatever does not exist in my being. You have to understand. But I can *help* you work on your paper. I'd be happy to help you this afternoon. It won't take long at all."

"Megan already offered to help me, Truth. We're going to her house." Brendan sounded clinical and distant. I wanted to punch him. I wanted to punch both of them. Megan was falling into his trap; his handsome, good-looking-face trap.

"My mom's making cookies," Megan said, smiling viciously at me.

"I thought *I* was coming to your house this afternoon," I said.

"Change of plans," she said. "Something better came along. You know what that's like, don't you?" She slammed the locker, even though I wasn't finished with it yet, and stormed off. "Let's go, Brendan."

I turned to my definitely former boyfriend, my face aghast.

He shrugged his shoulders nonchalantly. "I just can't trust you anymore."

"So Megan knows your secret? You told never-lets-the-cat-have-her-tongue Borowitz? By tomorrow, the whole school's going to know."

"I figured you'd told her already, but no, I didn't tell her. I said you wouldn't help me, so she offered to help."

"I just said I'd help you!"

"Like I said, I can't trust you, Truth."

I didn't like how he said my name, like it was gross or left a bad taste in his mouth.

"Whatever." I said the meanest thing that came to mind: "I hope you get an F." Not the most mature thing to say.

"Thanks. Maybe you can add that to your presentation. I'm sure it'll be great." He started to follow Megan down the hallway.

"Well, I hope whoever you ask to write yours for you does a good job!" I yelled after him.

Brendan's shoulders jerked and he stopped walking, looking around. Seeing that no one had overheard us, he kept walking. I wanted to die when he grabbed Megan's hand and they walked down the hallway together. Part of me wished the trophy cabinet would suddenly detach from the wall and crush them both, but that would have been messy, and I didn't hate the janitor that much.

Brendan said he couldn't trust me, but a nagging voice in my head feared his rejection of me was because of my back, my crooked spine, and the brace that held me together. He'd found someone with a straight back, strong shoulder blades, and ribs in proper proportion. I didn't even blame Isaac Newton; I didn't blame anyone. I just stood in the hallway and watched the two of them disappear up the steps, their feet in matching rhythm.

I knew for sure then that I was having a rock of a day. I let my head drop against my locker as I turned the lock to get the books I needed.

"You all right, Truth?"

I looked up to see Miss Peters walking by.

"Just peachy," I said sadly.

"Okay," she said, clearly not convinced. But she kept walking.

That marked the moment I began my life as a

social outcast. I'd lost my best friend, my kind-of-boyfriend, and teachers who thought I needed cheering up, all in the same day.

Throwing my books in my backpack in the girls' locker room, I kept myself angry so I wouldn't cry. "Good-for-nothing boys and their pretty faces! Dumb jerks! Stupid Megan and her mom's cookies; delicious chocolate chip cookies I don't get to eat!"

I tried to pull on the handle of my backpack, but it was stuck. I pulled and kicked it, dropped it to the ground and slammed it against the lockers until I couldn't take it anymore. Then I dropped onto the bench in front of the lockers and cried into my open palms, knowing the eyeliner on my face would just get worse. I'd missed the bus, I didn't have a ride from a formerly nice boy's not-so-nice mother, and I didn't have a best friend who would cheer me up when I complained about my back. I was alone, entirely alone.

"Stupid Newton. Stupid scoliosis. Stupid back brace!"

I reached back, up and under my shirt, and loosened the top strap of my brace so I could breathe a bit easier.

"You wear a back brace?"

Blinking back tears, I raised my head in the direction of the voice. Immediately I wanted to throw up.

Jenny Henderson was standing in the middle of the locker room, staring at me. We looked at each other for several tense moments, until she started to smile and opened her mouth to say something.

I pulled my backpack off the floor and carried it in my arms, wheels and all. It was pretty heavy, but I managed to stumble out of the locker room without responding to Jenny.

I ran down the hallway as fast as my braced torso and tired legs could carry me, flopping back and forth from the weight of my broken backpack. I tripped up the stairs and collapsed. I heard footsteps behind me.

"Ouch!" I said, my right elbow and left knee colliding with the hard, stone steps.

Pushing myself to my feet, I ran out the door into the already dimming sunlight. It was cold out, but I didn't have a choice.

I walked home, carrying my stupid, broken backpack, cursing Isaac Newton and my back brace the whole way.

CHAPTER 16
A Rock in the Midst of Diamonds

I refused to go to school the next day. I lay in bed until my mother came up to drag me out of it. Charity had heard from her friends Brendan had dumped me, so my family assumed I was heartbroken over some boy and didn't want to face him.

In reality, I was terrified of everyone. They would all know I wore a back brace now because Jenny Henderson would tell them. She was the biggest gossip in school, even more so than Megan, and she had been trying to find out a secret about me. Now she had discovered it, and my life as a somewhat popular but socially awkward seventh grader was over—except for the socially awkward part.

Mom tugged my pillow from under my head. I nabbed it back and threw it over myself. "Ahmnagongtscoo!"

"What?" Mom asked. I felt my bed shift as she sat down on the edge of it.

I lifted my pillow, just a millimeter. "I'm not going to school," I said and slammed the pillow back over my face.

"Look, honey," Mom said, "Brendan was a nice young man, but you'll find nicer. You're too young to date anyway, so in all actuality, it doesn't matter."

I thrust the pillow onto my lap. "I don't care about Brendan!" I did, but that wasn't what I was worried about; he already knew I had a brace.

"Well, then what's wrong, Tru?"

I'd always been able to tell my parents everything. But they didn't seem to understand how much I didn't want people to know about my back brace. I knew if I said Jenny had found out and now the whole school would know, my mom would just say I was overreacting.

Mom sighed. I was making everyone late. "You know, you're going to have to go back eventually, so what does it matter if it's today?"

I thought about it. I sighed loudly and then conceded. "Good point."

"Get dressed and I'll send Charity to help you with Herman. She can pull it tighter than I can."

I rolled my eyes at her use of Harold's chosen nickname. "It's a brace, Mother. It doesn't have a name."

"Right. Sorry."

After Mom left, I found a hot pink hoodie I hadn't worn yet and pulled it on, knowing it would cover my brace entirely. With my extra-large jeans tied with my trusty shoestring and the pink hoodie hiding it all, I looked pretty decent. Charity walked in as I was posing in front of our mirror.

"Let's do this. The bus will be here in two minutes." She cinched me up and I followed her downstairs to grab a yogurt for the road.

"No eyeliner today?" she asked.

"Mr. Landers noticed it, and I figured if he's able to notice a difference, it might not be for the best."

"Hmm. Good call," she said, laughing. Then she abruptly grew serious. "I'm sorry about Brendan."

"Me too," I said.

"You just can't trust seventh-grade boys. Too immature."

I grinned, but inside I knew she was wrong. It was putting your trust in Truth you had to worry about.

Stepping onto the bus with my cursed backpack (that had been ceremoniously presented to me by Harold after Dad fixed it), I eyed Megan sitting near the back. She sat by herself, but she leaned across the entire seat, deep in conversation with an eighth grader who sat across the aisle. I could tell she had seen me because she glanced my way out of the corner of her eye.

Charity saw me pause, and pulled me down into the seat next to her. She tried to include me in her friends' conversation. They talked about turning sixteen soon and being able to drive so they wouldn't have to take public school transportation anymore.

"Saves on gas," I said. From the looks I got, I knew Charity was beginning to regret letting me sit next to her. "But you can all get your own cars!" I squealed. That put them back on track.

I had been hoping the pink color of my hoodie would brighten my mood, but I skulked toward the school building with dragging feet. It was cloudy out. The weather was copying my demeanor, and that made me even angrier. As I walked, large, cold, heavy rain drops began to fall. I looked up at the sky. *Can't you be original? Be your own person!* I thought, internally shouting at the atmosphere. Then I felt bad because of global warming—if a bully like that was picking on me, I'd need a full day to cry too.

I allowed my rolling backpack to thump loudly on the stairs, the plastic crackling piercingly against the cement. Today, I liked the sound.

"Have a good day, Tru!" Charity yelled after me.

I waved and stayed the course to the locker room, to rid myself of my satisfyingly loud bag. Then I marched back down the hallway. I was a woman betrayed, deceived, and scorned. I was on a mission to have a rare, colorful, sparkling diamond kind of day.

Down at the other end of the hallway, I could see Megan standing at our locker. As if sensing me coming, she shut the door and began walking in the opposite direction. Had I known before that Megan was acting distant because she liked Brendan, too, I wouldn't have made such a big deal over him. Talk about trust! While I told her everything, she withheld information that could have saved our friendship. Instead, she chose to keep it inside and then bash my head against the bricks when she had a chance to pounce and conquer. I couldn't find it in my heart to hold a grudge against Brendan. Indubitably, it was wrong of him to ask me to write his paper, but I'd agreed to it. I had no one to blame but myself for that.

Indubitably. *What a great word,* I thought. I rolled it in my mouth, liking the workout it gave my tongue. I bet Megan never got to that word in her stupid dictionary. Tossing my books in my locker, I headed to Band, ready to shine.

I didn't shine. I stank. I couldn't get my mouth to fit to my trumpet, or my trumpet to work with my mouth (either way, it was a mess). No one had said anything to me, but I was worried that everyone knew I was wearing a back brace. So I avoided talking to anyone, even the people beside me who I was generally friendly with, and just focused on the music. Nothing helped. I blew. Usually, I left Band with a feeling of accomplishment, but when the bell rang today, it was a relief to put my trumpet back in its case.

People pushed and shoved more than usual on the way out of class. One kid, leaping through the river of students like a gazelle, pushed me in the back to get by. When his hand connected with my brace, he shouted "Ow!" but continued to run. I was glad he didn't stop to find out what had been so hard against his knuckles.

I scooted as closely as I could to the wall, and kept my arms tight to my sides. *Keep out of my bubble. Keep out of my bubble.* I silently willed my peers to keep a safe distance. Behind me, I heard Brendan's cheerful, strident voice.

"And then my mom actually put a belt on me and made me cinch it up. She didn't want me to be a 'victim of the saggy pants syndrome.'"

Megan's annoying laugh pierced through the crowd, reminiscent of a little lap dog's yapping, and my ears rang with jealousy and fury. I clenched my fists, shoved them ruthlessly into the large front pocket of my sweatshirt, and speed-walked to my locker. I didn't want to still be there fumbling with my books and pencil bag when Megan and Brendan came up arm in arm, grinning goofily from ear to ear.

I grabbed my algebra book and scuttled off to the classroom, earlier than I'd been all year. I was one of the first few in the room, and I thumped into my seat, pinching the left side of my butt between my plastic brace and the plastic chair.

"Ouch!" I shouted involuntarily.

Miss Peters looked up from her desk. "Are you all right?"

"Yep," I said, sitting forward and discreetly trying to rub the skin. "One of those days, I guess."

She smiled. "We all suffer through those, don't we?"

I smiled back and opened my book to the chapter we were on, pretending to be reading it as the rest of the class filtered into the room.

Miss Peters started the lesson off with overhead notes. We were going to be solving equations with polynomials in them. I was excited about it (as excited as one can get about math) because I liked ending up with an answer. It was nice to have a certainty in life—even if it was a simple math problem.

"These won't be simple," Miss Peters said. "We're going to take our time with them and go through the explanation in the book in class since I'm aware none of you actually read it."

A few people giggled, but Miss Peters' stern stare shut them up.

"Now, let's see. Brendan, will you read the first section for us?"

Brendan immediately began to flip through the pages. "Sorry. What page did you say it was?" He'd had his book opened to the right page. He let the pages fall slowly as he said, "241, 243, 244."

"We don't have time for this. Sherrie, will you read from page 364?"

Miss Peters looked at her book and followed along with Sherrie, but I kept my gaze on her. When she looked up from the book, she watched Brendan. Her eyes closed slightly as she assessed him. I was worried she was going to call on him to read next, but she didn't.

We got through the two sections pretty quickly, and then Miss Peters gave us notes to take and explained them as we went through, putting the equations on one side. The equations were complicated. They took focus. There wasn't only one way to solve them; there were options. I started to see them as a metaphor for my current situation—even though I felt like my life was ruined, maybe I still had options.

By Gym, my mood had improved and I thought maybe Mr. Landers was right—maybe it could be a diamond day—but the second I loosened the last strap on my brace, I realized I didn't have someone to help me put it back on after class. Megan wasn't speaking to me. She'd rather have me suffer through the day with a loose, clanking brace than help me. My only other hope was Charity—if I went to the office and told someone I needed her help, they'd page her classroom. I hoped.

We played "hoccer" in Gym. It was exactly like soccer, only it was played inside with a giant exercise ball in lieu of a soccer ball. And we had to take our shoes off and just wear socks, so as not to pop the ball. What followed was a presentation of junior high girls' clumsiness and lack of hand-eye coordination, and the ball bounced off peoples' heads and into other peoples' faces. I wondered if Mrs. Tomjack didn't make us play this awful game for her own entertainment, or as revenge for having to put up with hormone-filled, high-tempered preteens. She was laughing her head off, and I swear I saw her wipe a jovial tear from her eye as the ball rebounded off another girl's mug.

One unfortunate girl, one of Jenny's friends, swung her leg back for what looked to be a monumental game-ending kick, but the ball bounced just as her leg went up, and she fell flat on her back, whiffing the ball completely.

"Swing and a miss!" a girl on her team said, and they all laughed. The girl who had fallen sat up and rubbed her tailbone. She wasn't laughing. I imagined that's how it would be for me soon enough. Everyone standing around me and laughing.

Hadn't Jenny told her friends about my back brace? I'd figured it would be the talk of the school by now. But I'd heard nothing about it.

As the game was winding down, I asked to be excused to go to the restroom, and ran straight to the office instead of the locker room. I asked one of the secretaries if I could have my sister called out of class—it was an emergency. She asked for my sister's name, and I told her.

"I love Charity! She sometimes stops by to say good morning to us here in the office. You're her sister?"

"Yes," I said, suddenly trying to sound more polite. "She said you're all really nice."

"What a sweetheart."

I don't know if she meant me or my sister, but she dialed the number of a classroom I assumed was Charity's, so I was happy.

Charity ran to the office–actually ran. She opened the door out of breath. "What happened? What's wrong?"

The secretary pointed at me. I smiled and waved at her as I pulled Charity into the hallway.

"I need you to help me put my brace on," I said.

"That's not an emergency!" she said.

"It is to me."

Charity sighed. "Fine. Come on."

She led the way toward the locker room. We still had a few minutes before the other girls would be excused to change clothes too.

"Isn't Megan here today?"

"Yes," I said, with a snarl.

"Why can't she do it?"

"She won't talk to me. Apparently, she and Brendan are inseparable now," I said, oozing faux cheerfulness.

"And even though study hall is Brendan-free, she still won't help out her former best friend."

"Former? Don't let a lame guy end your friendship. You two are too close to let that happen."

"Tell *her* that."

Charity just shook her head as we headed into the locker room. "Nice socks, by the way."

"Hoccer."

That was the only word she needed. Charity had undergone the bruising and bloody noses associated with the infamous game. "If only everyone didn't take it so darn seriously!"

"I know!" I said. "We were practically doing cartwheels and backflips in there, just to hit a gigantic rubber ball through a tiny net!"

"It's fun, isn't it?" Charity said.

"Probably the best day of P.E. we've had all year."

She laughed as she helped me get my brace situated on my hips. "Hopefully no one will get a black eye this year."

"Not me. Not today, anyway. I'm having a bad enough day as it is."

"It'll get better, Tru."

Charity offered to help again if I needed her and then headed up to her class to get her books before the bell rang. I sat and struggled with my tennis shoes, lifting my ankle onto the opposite leg and tying the shoelace sideways, as I waited for the rest of the girls from my Gym class to come in and change.

A locker clanged, making me jump. I thought I had been alone.

"You didn't have to run out yesterday." Jenny stood there in her jeans and a sports bra. I didn't say anything. She put her shirt on. "You know, my mom and my grandma both had surgery for scoliosis. It's kind of a miracle I don't have it."

Of course, perfect Jenny Henderson wouldn't get scoliosis when it's a hereditary disease. Her perfect genes probably murdered the one gene that carried it.

"Lucky you," I said.

"Seriously. I know all about it. It sucks to hear this, but I feel bad for you."

"Um, thank you?" That was clearly not a compliment.

"Look, I'm just saying I understand what you're going through. I'll help you if you want. I could help with your brace from now on. Then you won't have to run to the bathroom."

"You knew—"

"After I knew you wore a brace, I figured out that's what you were doing when you were leaving early all the time. I mean, football pads? Of all the lame excuses in the world. You've got to be a better liar than that."

As good of a liar as you? I thought. I still hadn't ruled out the possibility she had told her friends, or would soon—just waiting for the perfect time to pounce.

"I guess it depends on the lie," I said, thinking of Brendan's unwritten essay. I hesitated, wanting to ask the one question of which I was afraid of the answer. "Jenny, will you *please* not tell anyone I wear a brace?"

She smiled a sincere, genuine smile. "Of course not. I'm impressed by your ability to hide it."

"Thanks," I said. To me, *that* was a compliment.

I'd seen her smile in such a genuine way before, when she'd dragged my rolling backpack to the locker room for me the first day I used it. I'd always thought that Jenny would throw anyone under a bus if it would make her look better, but now I was questioning that assessment. After all, she hadn't told anyone about my brace. I didn't know if I could trust her, but for the time being, I had to.

"You know, I pretended to be sick and went home the day after I put sand in your locker." Her gaze fell to the floor when I looked up in surprise. "I felt so guilty about it I couldn't stand it. I didn't want to have to face you."

I felt my shoulders tense up and then release. "I thought you were acting fishy for a while," I said. After a pause, a knowing smile crossed her lips, and then we both laughed.

"I'd say tuna is way worse than sand," Jenny said.

"Whatever," I said, shaking my head. "Every time I grab my shoes, a few grains of sand fall out. It's like you robbed an entire beach."

We continued to laugh, and I was surprised at how great it felt to be laughing *with* Jenny.

"Well, I threw that shirt away," she said. "So let's call it even." She walked with me into the hallway. I said I had to use the bathroom, so we parted ways.

I wanted to see if Megan had actually waited for me in the third stall. She hadn't.

I don't know what made me think she'd be waiting for me, but I was still devastated to find out she wasn't there. Didn't she care about what might happen to me if I couldn't put my brace back on?

I'm not going to lie; I loved—relished, lived for— the moment I was able to ply that ugly, plastic hug from around my waist. But when I didn't wear it, I felt guilty and paranoid, worried about my back suddenly getting worse. I thought Megan might worry about that, too. Apparently not.

I stared at the ceiling in the restroom until the

bell rang, counting tiles so I wouldn't start to cry. I considered joining a convent, or venturing out into the forest to live as a hermit. Maybe someone would write a book about me. They could call it *The Hunchback of the Midwest,* or *Lonely Hunchbacked Hermit: A Tale of Travesty and Betrayal.*

I liked the second one. It would sell better based on its title alone.

I was certain it wasn't a "diamond" day when I felt Jodi, the girl who sat behind me in my next class, tap me on the shoulder. Not only was it awkward for me to strain my neck to get a glimpse of what she wanted, but also the Velcro of my brace crunched as I rotated around to face her.

"You have something on the back of your shirt," she said.

As I attempted to look, she took her fingernail and tried to scratch it off, moving the fabric of my sweatshirt against the hard plastic of my brace.

I leaned forward in a frightened spasm, saying loudly, "It's okay. It's a stain."

A few people around us looked, but I was just glad when Jodi pulled her hand away and said, "Oh. Okay."

I went to the bathroom later on in the period and looked in the mirror; the pressure of the fabric being sandwiched between my brace and chair had left a permanent mark on my perfectly good sweat-shirt. Not only that, but Jodi Phelps had copped a feel of my brace.

I felt violated. Why would she just reach out and touch my shirt? I would never do that to her.

As I walked back to class, though, I grew hon-est with myself: Before-Brace Truth *would* do that. Brace-Wearing Truth avoided all forms of physical contact. I'd literally separated myself from my peers because I was afraid they'd find out about my brace. I avoided social contact because of it. The exact thing I'd feared would happen I'd done myself, and no one even knew the truth.

To make matters worse, I passed Oliver in the hallway that afternoon. I stopped to apologize for never coming to see him anymore, but he just kept rolling right on by as if he hadn't seen me.

I had no one.

Days went by, and I couldn't pull myself out of my down-in-the-dumps funk. My world had been turned upside down: I could trust the person I used to think was pure evil (pretty, perfect Jennifer Henderson), but the person I would have given my life for in the past (Megan Borowitz, traitor to scolis everywhere) refused to even talk to me.

I also had no idea what to write for my presentation. It hadn't seemed like such a big deal at first, but then I thought about being in front of the whole junior high in the auditorium, not just in a classroom. Bright spotlights would shine down on me for all to see. And I'd be wearing my brace.

The next Wednesday, after Trendon family game night (Harold had selected Junior Monopoly—he might only be in kindergarten, but he still managed to clear me out of half my money ten minutes into the game every time we played), my mom sat me down.

"We need to talk," she said.

"We don't need to do anything," I said, slumping (as much as I could slump in my plastic posture protector) against the kitchen table.

Harold laughed maniacally, fanning colorful fake paper money in my face as he packed up the game. Mom pushed me back up, into a seated position. "Yes, we do. We all have to do things we don't like."

"I don't," Harold said, running away, the game semi–put away.

I flopped back onto the table, and looked at my mom out of the corner of my eye. She was headed somewhere—a horrifying place where good parents lead the conversation when they want their kid to realize she's being overdramatic or insufferable: the land of logic.

"I don't either," I mumbled, my face now buried in the sleeve of my extra-large sweater. I hated the fact I had to wear an extra-large. Without my brace, I could wear sizes anywhere from one to five. With my brace on, I jumped to a size thirteen. My wardrobe looked like it belonged to a yo-yo dieter.

"*Yes,* we *do.*" To my surprise, Mom flopped her arms on top of me. I had been trying to isolate myself, but she wasn't letting that happen. It made me feel connected, but also annoyed.

I slowly slid off the table. Mom looked at me, her mouth set in a sort-of-smile my dad called "the mom face."

"You will get through junior high, with or without Brendan, Megan, or a back brace. Life gives us lollipops, you know."

"I thought it was lemons."

"Nope, lollipops," she said. Harold ran back into the room and leapt onto Mom's lap, wrapping his arms around her neck. "Oof. We take our licks, and then we get to the sweet stuff."

"But a lollipop's sweet *as* you're licking it, so that metaphor doesn't work."

"Tell her, Harold," Mom said.

"Yesterday I cut my tongue on the crack of a Tootsie Pop," Harold said, sounding like he was dictating what Mom told him after it happened. "My tongue was bleeding and I wanted to cry, but Mom told me it would get better if I drank some water. So I did, and it stopped."

"Did you finish the Tootsie Pop then?" I asked.

"No! It hurt me! I don't want any more, ever!"

"See?" I said to my mom. "Faulty metaphor."

"But now I don't have to worry about him climbing on the cupboards to sneak one and then falling off the countertop."

"So you're talking about benefiting from other people's 'lollipops of life.'"

"Yes," Mom nodded.

"So if Brendan was a lollipop, now Megan is benefiting from my being hurt?"

"Exactly. Trendons are smart. We just get it."

"But," I paused, thinking it was strange my mother was telling me I had basically licked a boy. "That doesn't make Megan sound like a good person. How is that supposed to make me feel better?"

"Someday, you'll get a drink of water and the hurting part will disappear," Harold said.

My mom laughed.

"My tongue spull hurs," Harold said, pulling out his tongue to show us.

"You're so brave," I said. "Prince Harry, the courageous knight who was defeated by the sugar-coated chocolate-on-a-stick!"

"Huzzah!" Harold shouted. He thrust his hand in the air, narrowly missing Mom's face, and took off sprinting into the living room. I chased after him, glad I could still catch him while wearing my brace.

As I chased him, I thought about how little he had to worry. His biggest concern was lollipops. I'd never imagined having to go through junior high without my best friend by my side. Even with everything that had happened, I realized that until my mom had said it out loud, I hadn't thought of it as a real possibility.

I lifted Harold off the ground and he squealed as I tossed him onto the couch. I tickled him and he giggled uncontrollably for several seconds after I stopped. Then his face turned deadly serious.

"Tru?" he said.

"Yeah?"

"It was a *big* Tootsie Pop."

"I believe you, Prince Harry. I believe you."

CHAPTER 17

From the Mouths of Toads

T ime was passing quickly, and with the day of my "big presentation" (as my parents called it) almost a week away, I began to dread every minute of school life. I still hadn't decided what I would speak about. Talking about why I liked school wouldn't make for a riveting speech. No one would be listening to me anyway. No one cared about the thoughts of Truth Trendon, secret scoli. Though I small-talked with my peers and answered questions if I was called on in class, I didn't have anyone I could talk to about anything really important. Even worse, Brendan and Megan were still hanging out, growing closer than ever. I'd see them holding hands in the hallway, and Megan was always laughing when they walked by. I'd spent enough time with Brendan to know he wasn't *that* funny.

At lunch, I tried to sneak my way into several other groups of people, without success. I never felt like I was truly wanted. So I ended up taking my food to the locker room and reading a book every day. Honestly, I enjoyed this new predicament—as long as no one else came into the locker room. When they did, I hid my lunch and pretended to be getting deodorant out of my locker.

It actually happened quite a bit. That day, for instance, an eighth grader, Holly, walked in on me when I was right in the middle of one of the many devastating parts of *The Grapes of Wrath*. Just as a few tears had started to form in my eyes, the door flew open. I hid the book and tossed my egg salad into my backpack. Holly turned the corner, and as I looked up at her, a single tear slid down my cheek. Sir Newton's gravity once again leading to my demise.

Holly kind of tilted her head and looked at me. "Rough day?" she said sympathetically.

It hadn't been a horrible day, but I ran with it. "Uh-huh," I said quietly.

"I heard about Brendan and Megan. Talk about stabbing your best friend in the back, huh?"

"Yeah," I said. Her sympathy was starting to actually bring me down. I felt another tear coming on.

"You can do better. Right, Charity?"

I was taken aback for only a second, and then I laughed, knowing how angry Charity was going to be that someone thought I was her.

"I'm Truth," I said. "Charity's sister."

"Oh, that's what I meant," Holly said. "Charity's so cool. Don't tell her I messed you two up, okay?"

I wanted to say, "So I'm not cool?" But I didn't. I just smiled. Holly spritzed her already cemented ponytail with a pink bottle of hairspray and then walked back out the door. I pulled out my egg salad, not caring about the bits of it left behind in my bag—maybe they'd rot in there, and I'd be able to get a new backpack sans wheels.

Back to alone time, and back to the Joad family. I could have felt sorry for myself, but at least I wasn't a sharecropper trying to survive in 1930s California. John Steinbeck made wearing a back brace seem like eating cotton candy compared to what that family went through.

Maybe my mom was right. Other people survived many worse hardships than suffering through junior high relationships with handsome boys who broke hearts and best friends who stabbed you in the back. Maybe I'd end up okay. (Just not very cool, if Holly's reaction was any indication).

Lunch period neared to a close. I carried my book to my locker, still lost in its world in my mind, when suddenly my body stopped in its tracks before my brain registered what it was seeing: Megan standing up on her tiptoes and kissing Brendan on the lips.

Megan had just kissed Brendan in front of our locker.

How was I supposed to react to that?! My mind took off, spiraling in thousands of different directions—I imagined myself pulling the fire alarm, or calmly walking up and karate-chopping Megan's head off, or sprinting like a linebacker and plowing into the two of them. But instead, my body picked the cowardly choice and I ran back toward the locker room.

I could hardly breathe or function, and my movements were mechanical and jerky like I had turned into a robot. I almost tripped several times.

When my hand touched the locker room doorknob, the bell rang. I stood there for several seconds, my brain completely empty and bursting with thought at the same time. I'd never felt so betrayed, so violated.

"I'll have trust issues for the rest of my life," I muttered.

"Just forget them," a voice said.

I turned around. Jenny Henderson was behind me. Her sad smile told me she'd seen what I had. Then she hugged me. How was this happening?

"It'll be okay," she said. "Don't cry."

"I'm not crying," I said.

"You will later," she said. "It's okay."

"I gotta get to class," I said. I peeked around the corner to look at my locker, relieved to see Megan and Brendan were gone.

"This school needs a rule about PDA," Jenny said.

I laughed, thinking of all the times I'd seen her flirting with guys, touching their hair and leaning closer to them as she spoke. "Yeah," I agreed.

"If you need to talk to someone, you can call me," Jenny said.

I paused. Something just felt wrong. "Can I ask you something?"

"Sure."

"Why are you suddenly being so nice to me? You've been mean for years, and suddenly, after Brendan broke up with me, you've been so nice. I'm not going to break up him and Megan for you or anything."

Jenny stood there, her kind smile fading as her eyes narrowed. "I was being nice because I felt sorry for you."

"I don't want your pity."

"You need it. You're pathetic lately. Someone has to try to turn you around."

I glared back at her. Some part of my brain realized that it wasn't so bad that she was trying to be nice, and in fact, she was probably the only person I might be able to label as a friend right now. But my anger about Brendan and Megan had caught up to me, and I couldn't control it. Unfortunately, Jenny was the one to receive it.

I cleared my throat and then said slowly, "You're the pathetic one. Brendan doesn't like you. He never did. So get over him."

"*I'm* not the one who needs to get over him," she said. "Sorry for trying to be your friend. I just thought you could use one right now."

She spun around and walked away. The bell rang again. I was late for class, but I didn't care.

I'd cut class before; maybe I'd do it again now. I left the locker room and then I turned the corner and ran right into a brightly-clad body.

"Whoa there!" Miss Peters said.

"Sorry," I mumbled, looking at the floor.

"Maybe it'd be easier to walk if you looked ahead of you, instead of at the floor." Miss Peters laughed.

"Yeah," I said.

"Are you okay, Truth?"

I thought about bursting into tears and telling her everything—that Brendan couldn't read and that he and Megan had together ferociously ripped out my heart and continued to stomp on it over and over again with their large (his) and tiny (hers) feet.

Instead, I felt my eyes slowly fill with tears as I looked up at her and said, "I'm sad."

"Well, that definitely won't do." She looked at her watch. "I have about ten minutes left of my planning period. Do you want to walk with me?"

"Okay." I thought she meant that we'd walk back up to her room, but she directed me outside, around the building. I took advantage of the fact that Miss Peters didn't even ask if I was missing class.

"I like to walk during my lunch hour, but I didn't have time today. Thanks for coming with me. The colder weather always turns me off to walking alone." She paused, letting her breath catch up to her. "So, what's up?"

I liked Miss Peters. In class, she was straightforward, cracked jokes once in a while, and pursued people until they got their assignments done. But I never expected she'd actually care about what was going on in my life.

I sighed, took a deep breath, and told one more person what I'd been trying to keep secret from every living soul. "I have a back brace and I've been wearing it since July, and it sucks."

I looked at Miss Peters. Most teachers didn't like the word "sucks" because it wasn't a good descriptive word, but I found it apt for my situation.

"Really? I didn't realize that," she said. "Should I have?"

"No! I don't want people to know. But it's really hard to deal with some days." I shoved my hands in my pockets to keep the chilly pre-winter air from drying out my skin. "But please don't tell anyone. I don't want a lot of people to know. Ms. Eastin and Mr. Landers know—and Megan and Brendan and Jenny Henderson. Oh, and Oliver Nelson."

"Oliver?"

"Yeah, the counselor made us meet to talk to each other. I don't think it was the best idea."

"He's making huge progress in his physical therapy, though. Have you talked to him lately?"

I hesitated, my shoulders drooping as I admitted my guilt. "No."

"You should."

I was quiet. She kept the interrogation going.

"Have Megan and Brendan been supportive?"

"Not as supportive as this brace!" I joked. Miss Peters didn't laugh and I looked away, embarrassed. "Yeah, they have. They were. They just don't get what it's like, exactly."

"It's important to surround yourself with people who understand you for who you are. Junior high is tough because a lot of people don't know who they are yet."

"You can say that again," I said.

But I knew who I was: Truth Trendon. Believer in morals and ethics, and resister of peer pressure. Former friend. Now friendless.

"When I was in junior high, I dyed my hair bright pink, wore all black, and went through an awful black eyeliner phase. I had black streaks all the way down to my chin!"

"Me too! Well, the eyeliner only. But I wasn't very good with it, either."

"See, we would have been friends." Miss Peters grinned down at me.

Even though it was cold outside, my heart warmed me up head to toe. "Thanks, Miss Peters."

"Now, I believe you are late for class. Here's a late slip. I'll sign it. Just tell your teacher I was helping you with an assignment."

"Thank you," I said. I was glad she had the slip with her; otherwise I would have had to stay after school to make up for the time I'd missed.

"And remember, things get better. Even if they

get worse for a while, they get better eventually. They always do."

Miss Peters kept walking, her arms pumping to help propel her legs faster around the parking lot. I slipped back into school with my note, and with a feeling that my life would indeed improve at some point; brace or no brace, Brendan or no Brendan.

It was Megan who I truly missed. But I would *never* tell her that.

"Megan, I miss you!" I said. It seemed my resolve was not as strong as I'd thought. I finally caught Megan alone beside our locker before History, and bombarded her with questions and compliments.

Megan ignored me for a while, but finally, after I told her I even missed watching nightmare-creating scary movies with her, she pivoted on her foot mid-book-grab, with a smile developing on her lips. "I miss y—"

She cut herself off when a piece of paper fell out from between her books. Since her hands were full, I picked it up for her. It was crinkled, obviously a note that had once been folded. Megan reached out for it, but I pulled it back.

I saw my name, written in blocky, chunky letters—Brendan's tell-tale handwriting.

"'Kissing Truth Trendon is like kissing a dry lumpy toad,'" I read out loud.

If it had said "Megan is actually Truth's mother" I wouldn't have been more shocked. I slowly handed the note back to Megan. Then I unloaded.

"Are you kidding me, Megan? You abandon me and take the boy I liked and now you're spreading rumors about me?"

Inside I was thinking: *How could he say that? He was the crappy kisser! His lips were dry!*

She didn't say anything. She just looked up at me with big, sad eyes. "I didn't write it," she said.

"But you kept it! And you probably laughed hysterically when he gave it to you."

"I didn't! I kind of smiled, but that was just to—to—I don't know. It's mean! I'll throw it away. I'll burn it. But please don't be mad."

I felt my heart begin to melt, its stone exterior converting to ash. Then a boy whose name I didn't know walked by and ribbited at me. Actually ribbited, like a frog. I felt my frown furrow deeper into my face and then I looked at Megan. She looked like she'd just seen Medusa and was about to die.

My heart turned to stone. I slammed the locker

shut and stormed off to History, as several other people joined in with the frog-guy and his awful throaty sound bites.

As I ducked into the classroom, I heard Megan say in a disgusted voice, "Toads don't ribbit, they croak."

This just created a duet of sorts, with several kids croaking along to the ribbits. I tried to drop my head onto my desk, but there wasn't enough space for me to lean forward with my brace on, since my chair was connected to my desk with a metal bar. I wanted to scream. My legs were shaking with anger, and I'd never wanted to choke someone as much as I did Brendan Matthews.

I didn't know if I could fit my hands around Brendan's chiseled neck, but I was willing to try. What I didn't understand was why he'd do something like this. I knew his secret; I could tell *everyone* he couldn't read. Obviously he had gotten better—I mean, he did write that note—but still, he was a cheater, and I had the power to bring him down. The difference between the two of us was that I wouldn't do that to him.

By the end of the class, I was so anxious to dash out of there my desk shook as if I were the only one in an earthquake. The skin on my hands was white from my death grip on the wooden desktop. Spreading a rumor that I was a bad kisser—or actually, that I was ugly and had a gargantuan mouth, humongous eyes, and protruding skin bumps, so it was a trial to have to kiss me—was one thing, but I worried Brendan had prepared to save the best for last, and tell everyone what a hunchbacked, brace-wearing loser I was.

When the bell rang, I sprinted to my locker, tossed in my books, and ran to the locker room in record time.

Rumors spread quickly, especially in a small Midwest school. People call us the "Bread Basket" (hearth and homey) or the "Heart of America" (then where's the brain?), but people are just as mean here as anywhere else.

Charity did her best to quash all the "Prince Charming" and wart jokes over at the high school, calling Brendan and Megan immature and lame—and for the most part, none of the high schoolers cared anyway. But in junior high, "the Kiss of Truth" became known as the equivalent of the kiss of death in a matter of days.

Apparently, so did talking to me. Even girls stared at me, worried that if they approached, they too would be branded as inadequate kissers.

I still did my best to appear happy. At first, I figured everyone would see that their teasing and taunting didn't bother me in the least; however, the more I smiled and cheerfully said "Hello!" after a hateful croak, the more they responded with additional amphibious sounds. Some of them became almost fluent in a combination of English and toad-speak; creating a messy, throaty Toad-lish that made teachers angry. It had become an epidemic.

"Can we *ra*-get extra *ra*-credit?" Jimmy Wyate, his voice croaking like crazy, asked Mr. Landers about an upcoming test.

"Everyone else can, but since you asked in that voice, you may not. And that goes for anyone else should they decide to talk like an imbecile." I thought I saw Landers look in my direction, but I probably just imagined it. I assumed most teachers had heard about my toadish smooching, but they acted unaware.

Things really got out of hand in Algebra. Since Brendan and Megan were in the class with me, everyone else seemed to think their frog impressions suddenly had more significance. Miss Peters, however, didn't put up with their bullfroggy-ness. "Anyone who imitates a frog or toad, or makes any type of noise unrelated to common human decency, will be sent to reside on a lily pad for the afternoon. It's a lovely lily pad, with all kinds of time to work on assignments; you know it better as detention."

Several people raised their hands.

"Accidental burps are unwelcome but acceptable," Miss Peters said. All the hands except one dropped. "And whether or not it is an accident will be up to me." She smiled as the last hand dropped. "Now, let's get down and dirty with decimals, shall we?"

I swore someone whispered a ribbit under his breath, but I let Miss Peters stare down the culprit. If I'd gotten that stare, I think I would have willed myself to completely disappear.

After working by myself for most of class, I heaved a sigh of relief when the bell finally rang.

"Brendan, could I talk to you for a second?" Miss Peters said.

I piled my books up slowly, to see what she wanted to talk to him about. Megan did the same. I was a bit disappointed when I saw Miss Peters point to her math book. I exited the room quickly, glad to no longer be sitting next to the two lovebirds. I felt like a creepy vulture, sitting on the edge of the same branch, waiting for their love to die so I could sweep in and scavenge the remains, or at least wallow in their devastation for a while instead of my own.

That day, during study hall, I perked up my courage. It had been nearly three weeks since I'd talked to Oliver, and I missed him. Though he'd probably think I was stupid and silly, I knew he'd still listen to my problems. What he thought about me and Brendan didn't matter now. And if he didn't want to talk to me, what did I have to lose? No one else would talk to me either.

Though, if I were being completely honest, I feared that his rejection on top of everyone else's would actually break my heart for good, crushing it into tiny, irreparable pieces.

I walked into the Resource Room and began to say "I'm sorry," but then I closed my mouth. There was Oliver, standing between two newly installed rails, his arms holding his body up and his feet flat on the ground. Then he lifted his hands off the bars.

I had to sit down. "Am I witnessing a miracle?" I asked.

Oliver grinned. "I just wanted some relief," he said, tilting his head at his wheelchair. I nodded, knowing he was quoting me. He needed to get out of the chair. "I know that someday I probably won't have any leg-strength left. But until that happens, I'm going to keep trying to get a break from sitting all day. This is what I wanted your help with before, but I found out I could do it on my own."

I started trying to come up with the words to even begin to apologize, but he smiled. "Sometimes, it feels good to work things out by ourselves, doesn't it?"

I nodded, and he smiled again, and I knew he forgave me. By the end of his therapy, my face hurt from smiling so much.

Oliver took twenty small steps that day, and I almost tackled him as I threw my arms around his neck in a hug at the end of the period. The physical therapist who was there watching chastised me, but I didn't care, and Oliver was laughing. I was so proud of my friend.

It was only after Oliver was back in his chair and the physical therapist had left for the day that I was able to actually apologize. "I really needed to see you," I said. I looked at the ground and slowly met his gaze when I spoke again. "My life gradually got worse without you in it. I'm so sorry I avoided you."

"Why did you?" Oliver asked. His voice was softer than normal, and his eyes looked the same as they had that night weeks before.

My face warmed, and I worried I might cry. "I saw you outside the movie theater that night, in the pickup, and you looked so sad. I couldn't shake the thought that you were mad at me—that you resented me. I couldn't come to see you knowing you might hate me."

"Hate you? Are you crazy? I'll admit, when I saw you running—without your brace on—and then that football flounder grabbed you, I couldn't help but feel jealous."

I sat up at this admission.

"You just looked so happy," he said. "And then I thought about it: if there was one thing I wished I could do that would make me as happy as that, what would it be? I wanted to walk. And I realized there was something I could do about it." He paused. "You and I are alike, you know. We both need to get away from the things that are keeping us upright."

"I know. But—" I stopped.

"But what if I can't stand up tomorrow?" I looked at the floor as he continued. "Then at least I tried today, Truth."

I nodded. We were trying, both of us. Maybe it was true that my spine would always be crooked. But I was doing something about it, and putting up a good fight (if I do say so myself, Sir Isaac).

Then Oliver leaned forward and grinned crookedly. "Is it true if I kiss you I'll turn to stone?" he asked.

I laughed because I knew he was joking, but it made me wonder if people actually said that.

"Yep. Then I eat your firstborn."

"And that's how rumors get started."

We laughed. It felt good to laugh with someone.

The bell rang, but I barely noticed it.

I looked at Oliver. He was smiling so wide. I leaned forward and gave him a tight hug, and when I let go, he held my gaze.

Suddenly, the door opened and I leaped back. Mrs. Werth walked in. "About time you two got to class, isn't it?" she asked.

I stood up, too embarrassed to make eye contact with Oliver. "Bye," I said quickly, and I left the room before either of us could say another word.

For the next few days, I rallied against my classmates' continuous croaking. After seeing what Oliver could do after only a few weeks of therapy, I realized that I had worn my brace for five months. I had survived five months of battling Isaac Newton, and I was still here. Still fighting. Brace-Wearing Truth was just as strong and resilient as Before-Brace Truth—maybe more so—and I could get through another five months, a whole year even, as long as I pushed myself.

Thanks to Oliver, with a renewed spirit and new-found confidence, I finally began to prepare for my upcoming presentation. I would allow enough time for people to ribbit and croak all they wanted and still hit my eight-minute time limit. I planned to play a short song on my trumpet and then talk about what it meant to me and why. It was the first solo song I'd learned to play, and the song itself wasn't very long or difficult, but I thought I'd be more comfortable playing it than having to talk the entire time. It also came parent-approved, and Charity said I'd be less likely to say something stupid if I didn't have as much time to talk. Harold told me that instead I should put Hairy the guinea pig in the end of my trumpet and try to shoot him to the moon. There's nothing like the undying support of my siblings.

Megan's dad, life coach extraordinaire, was hosting the production, and would be giving a talk about living life to its fullest. Forget that—if I'd learned anything so far in junior high, it was that everyone was just trying to get by without getting thrown under the social bus. I'd basically been thrown between the wheels a few times already, shattering my world into what felt like a billion microscopic pieces. Lucky for me, I was patient enough to pick them all up and put them back together, even if the glue took forever to hold.

CHAPTER 18
The Final Discovery

The day before the big presentation, my nerves were roiling inside my belly, and I was certain I was going to spill my lunch, dinner, or breakfast at some point. However, on my way out of school, I ran into Oliver; or rather, he almost ran over me. He rolled toward the door wearing a dark corduroy coat, his head down as he stared at his cell phone, and his brow furrowed in consternation.

"Heads up!" I shouted, jumping out of the way at the last minute.

"Hey, Frog-face," Oliver said, without any semblance of apology.

"Oh, so you *can* see me!" I said. I playfully swatted at his phone. "No texting and driving. It's dangerous."

"I could drive better than you with my eyes closed."

I stepped back and raised my eyebrows. "Is that a challenge?"

He grinned. I grinned back. "Yep," he said.

"Well then, we just have to find someone stupid enough to lend us their car."

Oliver laughed and pushed himself out the door. I followed.

"My mom's going to be late," he said. "I hate having to wait for her."

"We could walk," I said. I was supposed to ride the bus, but I didn't feel like dealing with all my ribbiting peers, especially without adult supervision to control them. It was a farther walk than I preferred to make in my brace, but the pain in my butt from my brace was less annoying than the constant croaking in my ears.

He thought about it for a minute, and then he nodded. "All right."

We took to the sidewalk. I told him about my grumbling gut of nerves, and he told me about a math test he'd aced. I had yet to hear Oliver complain about his daily life like I did. I told him that and he shrugged.

"Seems pointless," he said.

"But that's all I talk about with you. My lame, day-to-day battles that are about as important as a fart."

He laughed so hard I could see all his straight white teeth. No cavities from what I could see (I wasn't an expert dentist, but I'd pulled teeth; I got the gist of it). "I like hearing about your day. It makes my life seem way less tragic."

I sighed. "Glad to be a martyr for your ego."

About a block away from my house, we approached the top of a rather steep downhill; it was so steep that I had always been afraid to roller-skate down because I thought I would lose control at the bottom and go sailing into a curb or, worse, a passing car. Oliver hesitated.

"We can go a different way. The sidewalk is less steep two blocks down." I pointed and began to turn in that direction, but Oliver grabbed my arm.

"No," he said. He gripped both wheels and stared straight ahead. "Can you run in that thing?"

My hands went instinctively to my brace. "I don't know—"

Before I could answer, he had taken off, whooping at the top of his lungs. I flung my backpack down and chased after him, wondering how I was going to stop him. I ran, my legs pumping and my butt skin pinching with every plastic jab. My chest ached where my brace bit into my rib cage, my stride was ungainly, and my coat flopped open with each step. But I chased after Oliver, watching his dark curls lift from the breeze, and as he slowed and I got closer,

I could hear him laughing. There was enough side-walk that he was able to slow to a stop before the street.

I shoved him gently when I caught up. "You—you could have—" It was hard to catch my breath after running with my brace on.

"Is that what you felt that night in the parking lot? When you were running?"

I straightened up, feeling my lungs expand in their constricted plastic lining. "No. You were faster."

He laughed at my fatigue. "That was fun. I don't usually get to do that."

I was about to chastise him—I remembered that story he'd told me about his mother sitting on his lap after he was almost hit by a car. But then he smiled up at me.

"Well, I left my backpack at the top," I said, "So . . . wanna do it again?"

He beamed, and began to wheel himself back up the hill. "You read my mind."

We raced up and down the hill again and again, Oliver in his chair and me in my brace. The third time, Oliver's mother showed up and yelled out the window of her car at him to stop, and met us at the bottom. Once she saw how happy he was, her worried expression lifted.

"Hop in, Truth," Mrs. Nelson said. "We'll give you a ride home."

"Thanks, but it's just a block. I'm almost there."

"You need running practice, Frog-face. I won every time," Oliver said, taking my hand and squeezing it. I was surprised, but my heart warmed at his touch. I smiled at him.

"I know," I said, squeezing his hand back. "What do you say, Mrs. Nelson? One more rematch?"

Instead of racing, Oliver pulled me onto his lap and we rolled down the hill together. I was both surprised and terrified. That wheelchair went fast! The rush of cold air bit at my skin. *Did this physical contact* mean *anything? Was my brace hurting Oliver?* I didn't have time to think about it as we sped downhill. I screamed, and Oliver laughed. Mrs. Nelson bit her fingernails at the end of the sidewalk, ready to throw herself in front of us should a car come.

"You know, your brace is actually really soft," Oliver said, as I climbed out of his chair.

"And you're actually not funny at all."

"No, really, you hit my arm a few times and I don't think it's even broken." He waggled his arm at me.

I laughed and followed him to his mother's car.

"No more races. It's cold out and *I'm* exhausted from them," Mrs. Nelson said.

"Don't worry, Mom," Oliver said, as she helped him into the car. "I was declared the winner already. You can contain your motherly pride until Truth leaves."

He put on his seatbelt, then rolled down his window to talk to me. "Whatever happens tomorrow, run," he said.

"Yeah, I'll just run out the door before the presentation even starts."

"No. Be you. Be Truth. Run like only you know you can."

Oliver's mother drove away and I waved goodbye. I was still too exhilarated to feel nervous about tomorrow. Instead, I ran the rest of the way home, as fast as I could in my brace.

The next day, Mr. B wanted to make sure Brendan and I weren't afraid of the mic. It wasn't the microphone the scared me; it was the crowd of my peers staring up at me, and only me, for several minutes.

On my way to the auditorium, I saw Jenny approaching from the other end of the empty hallway.

"Hey," she said.

"Hey, Jenny," I said. I'd been avoiding her ever since I'd blown up at her in the locker room. "Look, I'm sorry about last week—"

She waved her perfectly manicured hand. "Don't sweat it. I know you had a lot going on."

"You were right, though. You were the only person trying to be my friend, and I acted terribly. I'd love to call you my friend."

Jenny hesitated, but then she smiled.

I smiled back. If Isaac Newton had wanted to destroy my social life, he surely hadn't counted on Jenny and me becoming friends. But honestly, I hadn't counted on it either.

"Good luck today," she said. "I'm looking forward to your speech more than Brendan's, FYI."

She was probably the only one. Still, with Jenny's encouragement, I walked through the doors of the auditorium with my head and shoulders high, hoping that if Isaac Newton were standing on my shoulders today, he would whack his head on the doorframe.

Take that, gravity guru!

Thirty minutes later, students filed into the auditorium like ants following each other to the mother of all anthills (though I imagine ants complain a lot less than twelve- and thirteen-year-olds). I stood there clutching my trumpet like a shield in the extra-large business wear my mom had bought me from the department store over the weekend. I had on black dress pants (tied with my trusty shoelace, of course) and a huge, not-at-all-body-hugging sweater Charity had found in the women's department. I knew I didn't look professional, and I'm certain my parents knew it too, but they'd sent me out for the day in my oversized outfit with two hugs and a piece of toast. I was still finding crumbs in the folds of my sweater, and it was after lunch.

Mom and Dad were going to be at my presentation ("in the back" they said), so I'd have their full support.

"Two more reasons not to picture the people in the audience in their underwear," Charity had said.

"Already ruled that out," I'd replied, shaking my head with a grimace.

Now, waiting backstage for the principal to intro-duce Mr. Borowitz, who would start his talk and then introduce us, I was already pitting out in my sweater that was almost large enough to serve as a chair cover. Mr. B would love that idea. *This sweater could go places—do great things.* I could picture him saying it.

Voices echoed past the ugly brown velvet curtains and up onto the stage. Voices buzzing like bees and sirens and music all rolled together; I shut my eyes and felt myself begin to sway back and forth to the erratic rhythm.

Bumping into someone with my right shoulder, I opened my eyes. I pulled away when I saw Brendan.

"Hey," he said.

"Hi," I squeaked.

We stared at each other, silent.

He was wearing a navy suit. I looked like a sloppy, chaotic mess compared to him. Hair gelled, cologned, he was a debonair young man. In comparison, I was a twelve-year-old *child*. I suddenly really didn't want to go on stage.

Instead of panicking, I took a deep breath. If I could stand up to a hundred or so bored tweenagers, I could stand up to one attractive, charismatic one. "You know, that was a really mean thing you said about me."

He looked confused. "What?"

"Don't act naïve. The toad thing. I get an occasional zit, but lumpy? Come on, that's just a horrendous hyperbole."

"First of all, I didn't start that, and secondly, I don't know what hyperbole means."

"Exaggeration. And you did start it. I saw the note you gave Megan. Then that kid ribbited at me and the whole thing took off."

Brendan looked at the floor. "Megan wrote that. She was mad I hadn't kissed her since I kissed you, and she thought that meant I still liked you. It was a joke—her way of apologizing for making a big deal out of it—but some people saw the note in class. I guess she didn't want to throw it away in case someone else found it."

"You're a liar," I said.

He looked up. "No, I'm not."

"Yes, you are. You couldn't even look at me when you were telling that story. And Megan would never say that about me, anyway."

Brendan blushed bright red. He kept his gaze low, but he sighed. "I'm sorry. I didn't mean for anyone besides her to see that. I was . . . showing off, I guess. It was stupid."

"Yes," I agreed. "It was."

"I only came over here because I wanted to tell you good luck."

"Thanks," I said. "You too." *Jerk-face. Pretty, pretty jerk-face.*

He walked away, and I stood alone with my trumpet, wondering how I'd ever trusted him at all. If he had really liked me, he wouldn't have gone after my best friend seconds after letting go of my hand.

Finally, Ms. Eastin sauntered up to the podium

and introduced Mr. Borowitz. When she called Mr. B's name, she began to clap respectfully. Quite a few people joined in, but from my hiding place behind the curtain, I could see a lot of them were already considering Mr. Sandman and his land of dreams. Mr. B ran out, swinging his arms and legs further than a runner naturally would. He grabbed the mic, and shouted, "Good afternoon, West River Junior High! How's everybody doin'?"

Some clapping again, but not very loud.

"I can't hear you! How are you doing?"

Even fewer people clapped.

"That's wonderful!" Mr. B undid the button on his suit jacket so it hung open, and he placed his left fist on his hip. "How many of you are bored and tired with the same old day-to-day routine of junior high life?"

I knew Megan would be writhing in her seat. This was the same speech her dad gave for many other organizations; he just substituted their age group in instead of "junior high." Dozens of senior centers and business management training workshops had already heard this same schmaltzy speech.

"Let's welcome the two people you came here to see: the talented Brendan Matthews and the lovely Truth Trendon!"

327

I followed Brendan onto the stage to the two chairs set out for us. The audience clapped wildly along with a few throaty croaks, but nothing too out of hand. I sat, frowning, because Mr. B had called me "lovely" instead of "talented" like Brendan. For one thing, did Mr. B not think I had talent? And for another, I was definitely *not* lovely in my sweater-robe.

"We're going to hear from these two in a few minutes, but first, I want you all to consider this: have you really lived?"

"Duh," a voice said.

Several people laughed, but Mr. B was unfazed. He smiled. "Seriously, think about it. I know you're hardly even teenagers, but that's not too young to make an impact in the world. It's never too early or too late to make a change."

He went on a motivational rampage for a while, and I zoned out, trying to pick out faces of people through the glare of the bright stage lights. When I realized several people were staring at me, I focused back on Mr. B. Someone needed to pay attention to him.

"Our goals for this assembly are to remember that we need to strive to have L.I.V.E.D. What do those letters stand for again?" Mr. B leaned forward with his hand behind his ear. The junior high student body started to repeat the words, and I could kind of pick out "Learn," but that was it. The rest of it was just voices jumbled together into a garbled, un-enunciated mess.

"Good!" Mr. B threw up his arm in victory. "Learn, Investigate, Value, Execute, and Develop. L.I.V.E.D.! Together, we can help each other live to our fullest extent."

I saw a girl yawn. She didn't even bother trying to hide it; her elbows were resting on her knees, her head was in her hands, and her mouth opened in a huge stretch of her jaw muscles, her teeth showing all the way up to her gums.

Staring at her made *me* yawn, but I covered my mouth, pretending I was going to sneeze. It wasn't a great attempt, but at least I'd put in the effort. According to Mr. B, I'd probably L.I.V.E.D. more than she had.

"Next up, we have a very talented seventh grader. He's already been recognized for his talent in football, basketball, and track, and he has been on the honor roll the past two semesters. Let's welcome one of your very own Junior High Bucks, Brendan Matthews!"

The crowd of students erupted into applause, jolting awake the bored ones, including me. I knew

I wouldn't receive applause that loud; I wouldn't even kid myself by dreaming about it. Mr. B would announce my name and we wouldn't even hear crickets—not even bugs wanted to cheer for Truth Trendon, the toad monster. Maybe Harold had been right all along; maybe I did have cooties and they were finally rubbing off on people.

While Brendan began his presentation (it was memorized—no speech written, no cue cards, nada), I pictured myself turning into a giant amphibious cootie mass. Eventually, I'd be eating children instead of passing off my contagious inept social skills; swallowing them whole, homework and all. I'd hide in the school broom closet, and I'd survive by eating the paper towels in the wee morning hours (everyone knows cooties don't sleep). Pulling myself back to reality, glad to find my hands weren't the lumpy green appendages I'd just been envisioning, I heard Brendan's voice.

"My success as an athlete has taught me dedication. Without that, I wouldn't have the means to be responsible to this school or to myself. I have always believed I can do anything I put my mind to."

Not everything, I thought bitterly.

"I believe he's right. If you all dedicate yourselves to your goals, you'll accomplish them too," Mr. B summarized.

My butt was falling asleep in my chair, so I shifted my weight, then sighed and mentally shook myself; I had to speak soon.

Brendan said a few more words and then stepped back from the microphone. Everyone applauded, though a little less exuberantly than before. The charismatic charmer, *the* Brendan Matthews, had bored his peers.

I scowled; that was bad news for me. *You better get ready, fellow Bucks. Truth's gonna put you to sleep.*

Mr. B leapt back into the middle of the stage. "That's awesome, Brendan! Thanks for sharing that with us! Let's hear it for Brendan one more time."

He started clapping, but very few people joined in. Mr. B was no idiot; he could tell he'd lost us. People were fanning themselves, yawning, and burying their faces in their hands. I was squirming in my seat on stage. Even Megan, sitting a few rows up, looked bored, not really caring if her father sank or sailed in front of her peers.

So Mr. B asked for Brendan's help. Brendan slowly walked back up to the mic.

"Help lead us through the five stages of L.I.V.E.D., Brendan!"

Mr. B pulled out a sign with the words listed vertically down it in white letters. "Repeat after Brendan!"

It may not have been apparent to everyone in the audience, because of the bright lights already washing him out, but Brendan suddenly turned absolutely stark white. He clenched and unclenched his hands, and I saw beads of sweat on his forehead.

I couldn't remember all five words, even though Mr. B had just gone through them five minutes ago, so I would have been glad for that sign if I'd had to do the same thing. As I watched Brendan stand there in fear, a small part of me (maybe larger than I wanted to admit) began to rejoice. He'd broken my heart and tried to get me to cheat. If the universe was providing vengeance, who was I to intervene? But the rest of me began to panic for him. He'd know some of those words just from seeing them around school, but I wasn't sure if he'd be able to pronounce them on the spot like this. I knew this was his fear: reading in front of other people. And this was not just a classroom full of his peers, but an entire lecture hall.

"Okay," Brendan said.

A few students repeated "okay," their laughter dancing up to the stage. Brendan laughed nervously.

"Learn," he said.

Mr. B pointed at the crowd and they shouted back, more enthusiastically than I had expected, "Learn!"

"In—investigate."

"Investigate!" Mr. B was on cloud nine, happily bouncing between Brendan and the crowd. He'd gained their attention back.

"Value."

"Value!"

Brendan paused. My heart went out to him. He laughed nervously again. Whispered voices began filtering throughout the crowd. I saw Miss Peters look at Ms. Eastin, who was watching the presentation with an unpleasant look on her face. I bit my lip. Then I saw Oliver. He could tell something was wrong, and when he turned his gaze to me, I felt an idea boiling in my gut.

This was Brendan's back brace moment—knowing he was different from everyone else and fearing everyone was going to find out. Some people need to hide things about themselves, to keep their secrets until they feel ready and comfortable to disclose them. At one time, that was me.

Now, I knew I had to do something stupid enough to shock everyone and big enough to cover the mess Brendan was about to be in. Every self-conscious cell in my body was crying "Don't you dare!" but I knew what I was going to do—what I had to do—in the next ten seconds. I set my trumpet carefully on the floor next to me.

From my close proximity on the stage, I could see Brendan's eyes were welling up with tears.

They were pleading, *someone save me.*

I felt myself leaning forward. Oliver smiled.

I thought: *Truth will set you free!*

And then I did what any self-conscious seventh-grade girl would do: I bounded out of my chair and tore off my tent-sized sweater (it didn't even get stuck on my head like my shirts usually did). I hadn't meant to shout "free," but I did, and I think that threw people off more than my stripping, because it clearly was *not* one of Mr. B's steps. But I was caught up in the moment and I couldn't help myself.

Now, with all of the glaring and judgmental eyes on me instead of my former-crush-turned-enemy, I began to regret my rash decision. In front of the entire seventh- and eighth-grade student body, I stood there in my brace and surprisingly breathable white cotton undershirt for all to see. Mouths were agape, and after the utterly complete and horrifying silence, everyone began to whisper to one another. No one was sure what was wrong with me.

I took the microphone from Brendan, whose mouth was also agape, but I imagine he was more shocked by the fact I had saved him from definite social annihilation than he was by me exposing my secret to the world. I was Brendan's hero, for once. Sure, people might find out he couldn't read very well, but not if I could help it.

I took a deep breath, lifted the microphone to my lips, and looked out at the now-very-wide-awake crowd.

"My name is Truth Trendon, and I have scoliosis," I said.

The mic squealed a bit when I said "scoliosis" but I didn't stop. "Scoliosis is a deformity of the spine. My spine curves to the right and shoves my ribs all cattywampus, so I've worn this brace since July. I was afraid to tell anyone because I thought everyone would think I was gross or weird."

I felt their gazes burning holes in me. I kept talking and didn't make eye contact, for fear I'd burst into tears or hysterical laughter.

"But now you all know, and I guess I don't care anymore. I'm not gross; I just have to wear this thing."

I tapped my fist against my brace. All was quiet again, except for a few hushed voices. I began to set the mic down in its stand, but then I pulled it back up to my mouth. "Oh, and I'm an okay kisser. Not stupendous, but not horrible. And nothing like a toad or a frog. Okay, thanks for listening."

I found my gaze drifting toward Oliver again. I

thought about giving my prepared speech, but this seemed to be enough. Just like Oliver had said, I'd run with it. So I shrugged my shoulders and stepped back from the podium.

Megan's dad couldn't contain his excitement. I could already hear him in my head: "*You accepted yourself! You can now go on with your life without fear!*" I thrust the mic at him and he took it.

"Don't you see?" His eyes seemed to light up the entire room as he thrust his left arm out toward me and tilted his head back. "Truth has L.I.V.E.D.!"

"Except for the developed part," some kid called out.

Giggles wafted throughout the room. I crossed my arms protectively over my chest.

Brendan moved closer to me. He lifted his hands and slowly began to clap. It was quiet. No one clapped along with him. Finally, he stepped up to the mic at the podium. Some people clapped for *him* as he pulled the microphone a little higher.

"Truth Trendon is the bravest person I know," he said. "You should all be grateful she goes to our school. I know I am."

He looked at me, and even though I knew I'd never feel the same way about him as I had a few weeks before, my heart fluttered one last time at that smile. One more smile just for me.

"I'm grateful for Truth!" a familiar voice hollered. I looked up and saw Megan leaning forward in her seat in the middle of the rows of chairs.

"So am I!" Jenny Henderson stood up and smiled at me. It was still shocking that we were friends now. I smiled back.

"Me too!"

Near the end of the row, Miss Peters stood up. She started clapping; and whether or not people were just excited because the boring, motivational talk was nearly over or because Miss Peters was their favorite teacher, they started clapping too. They were clapping for me.

I looked at Oliver again, who had a look of disbelief on his face. I knew he was thinking this was the corniest thing he'd ever seen. I agreed, but it was for me, so it was hard to dislike it. I liked it even more when he finally gave in and joined in the ovation.

I smiled and took a goofy bow. They clapped harder. I waved like I was a beauty queen in a pageant; they cheered wildly. Caught up in the growing anticipation in the room, I grabbed the mic, reeled my sweater above my head like a helicopter, and shouted, "YOU CAN'T HANDLE THE TRUTH!"

I was a rock star—the Lady Gaga of my junior high—wearing something ridiculous and new that they'd never seen before. They loved it. The principal did not. Ms. Eastin grabbed my arm and pulled me off the stage.

I exited the gym with a newfound respect for Megan's dad, for Miss Peters, and also for myself. I'd beaten him—Isaac Newton, the villain of my story, who'd done his best to bring me down but still failed. I was finally free. Everyone knew my secret (except for the five or so kids who were sick from school that day), and most important, I realized it wasn't as big a deal as I'd thought.

In fact, keeping the secret had been way worse than having to tell it. The truth of it all was that if I'd just been willing to not judge myself so much, the first semester of my seventh-grade year would have been a whole lot easier.

Happily Ever After (For Now)

"I hate to say I told you so," my dad said. My parents had decided they would run into more parents of junior high students in the grocery store than they would at the nicest diner in town (and would have more explaining to do about their daughter de-clothing during a student assembly), so we'd gone out to eat to celebrate my newfound freedom.

"That's right," my mom agreed. "We knew no one would care that much. Everyone's too busy worrying about themselves at that age."

"Hey! I'm at that age!" I said.

"And you were worried about yourself, weren't you?" Charity said.

"Thanks, Miss 'I can't be seen without makeup because Jacob will think I'm ugly.'"

"Whatever." She rolled her eyes.

"You got in trouble," Harold said, before licking mashed potatoes off his spoon.

"No," I said, shaking my head so my nose was right next to his. "I didn't. I just got a little carried away. Ms. Eastin didn't want a riot on her hands."

"It's Herman's fault," Harold said.

"Oh yeah? An inanimate object?" I said.

"Yes!"

Harold threw his spoon at my stomach, which left a few potatoes on my awful sweater as it bounced to the floor.

"Harold!" my mother said, surprised.

"I'm starting a riot!" Harold said.

"Well, I guess we all deserve a chance to have L.I.V.E.D." My dad raised his eyebrows, and we all laughed.

When I went back to school the next day, not one person croaked at me. In fact, life was pretty similar to the way it was before I'd dated Brendan—except people were more helpful this time around. If I dropped a pencil, there were three people who would stoop to pick it up for me. It was rather nice. I'd suddenly become the princess, rather than the toad nobody wanted to kiss. Eventually though, that wore off too, and I was back to being the same old somewhat-well-liked seventh grader.

Brendan was back to being nice to me, as a friend, though his gravitational pull no longer existed as far as I was concerned. Miss Peters had discovered his inability to read, and he was set to stay after school for lessons and attend summer school until he caught up. Unlike mine, his secret never reached the student populace. I encouraged him to come to me for help, but he didn't seem all that interested in my help anymore.

I no longer had to sneak around before and after Gym class, because Jenny Henderson helped me with my brace. With her family history, she was fascinated with the deformity and my brace and kept asking me which parts of it pressed against which bones in my body. I had no idea, other than where my skin hurt, but it was refreshing to have someone interested in it. She even said I'd inspired her to consider becoming an orthopedic surgeon. That sounded just fine, as long as she wasn't operating on me.

Overall, though, I felt silly for thinking people would find me gross. Telling my secret had made Jenny and me friends, and with each passing day and every secured strap of Velcro, I realized she wasn't the mean girl I'd thought she was at all. I had more friends now than ever before. I wouldn't say Before-Brace Truth had been friendless, but now I was certainly less worried about myself and more interested in those around me, and that made junior high much more enjoyable.

The best (and most predictable) part of my story was that Megan and I were best friends again. She'd broken up with Brendan after I'd told her Brendan had claimed *she* wrote the note. Apparently she felt horrible enough already, and something hadn't felt right when she was with him—she'd felt like she was always trying to impress him. I understood, but I didn't tell Megan that.

I decided to let her feel a *little* bit of remorse for betraying me.

I went to Megan's house for a sleepover not long after that fateful day in the auditorium. We watched an old horror movie, something about a werewolf that wasn't especially scary, and Megan kept apologizing for dating Brendan.

"I'm such an idiot," she said.

"Shut up already!" I said, throwing a pillow at her. Popcorn sailed everywhere.

"He told me he spray-tans abs onto his stomach." She wrinkled her face. "I mean, he has abs already, but he wants them to 'stand out more.'"

We laughed. It was nice to have Megan back by my side. My life finally felt somewhat back to normal; words couldn't describe how nice it was to not keep secrets. Not even gravity—or anything else related to Isaac Newton—was going to bring me down.

Oliver and I continued to meet during study hall, even though I didn't need his secret support anymore, and we also started meeting outside of our scheduled time. He'd come over and hang out with Megan and me, or just me, and we'd just sit and talk like we did at school—only we talked about things other than me complaining about my brace. He was becoming a real family friend, mine most of all.

One afternoon, Charity and I were rolling on the floor laughing after Oliver had Harold convinced aliens had abducted the two of them and returned them that same day. Harold went to bed that night assuring my parents that even though he now had extraterrestrial powers, he still loved them and would make sure they had a powerful position when he and Oliver planned their overthrow of Planet Earth.

On one particularly sunny winter's day during the holiday break, when Oliver was leaving for the afternoon, I knew there was something I had to do.

I was just about to close the door and go back

inside when I leaned down, and before he could stop me, I kissed Oliver on the cheek.

"Ribbit," I said, and I went back inside, glancing over my shoulder only once.

Oliver's laughter chased me through the door.

So much for toads.

On my third check-up with my orthopedist, he wanted two x-rays: one with my brace on and one without. I didn't understand the need to zap me with extra radiation, but when he put the two films up against the examination light, I understood.

"Truth Trendon, age twelve. Curve holding at eighteen degrees when braced. Thirty-five degrees when freestanding," Dr. Clarkson said into his recorder.

He left the room and the nurses packed up the films. I sat for a few moments while my mom followed the doctor out of the room, to ask questions he hadn't hung around long enough to hear.

As I sat there, waiting for my mom to come back, I thought about how strange it was that my body was able to convert itself that quickly—with and without my brace. My body was so *malleable*. My bones, my whole spine for goodness' sake, could be moved. Physically, I could be changed so easily to fit what I was supposed to be. Why had it been so difficult to conform to what Brendan had wanted me to be? Apparently I didn't have the genetic makeup for that. Ol' Truth Trendon, with or without a brace, would stick to her guns, no matter what. Plus, when the brace came off, Isaac Newton would pull my spine right down again. Maybe my body was just stubborn.

As I pondered what it would be like to store water (or even something else?) in my rib-hump, like a camel, my mom returned to the room. "I managed to sneak in a few questions," she said, "but I think they're on the recorder, and I think he's mad."

"Do you think he ever listens to it?" I said. "Do you think he goes home at night and listens to hours of his own talking, going 'Yes, yes. Truth's back is holding. Excellent,' as he evilly taps his fingers together?"

"I think that's exactly what he does," my mom said.

She ruffled my hair and we left the hospital.

We stopped by Christopher's Orthotic Design to have him tighten up my brace. He also had new under-brace shirts, with V-necks. I was excited, because now my big over-brace shirts could dip down and let in more air. I suggested Christopher create some kind of ventilation or even a self-air-condition-ing brace, but he just laughed. I sighed as he cinched me up. I hadn't been joking.

Mom bragged about my presentation at school, and Christopher became animated. He was sincerely excited for me. His enthusiasm was contagious. That's one thing I can say about Christopher; no matter what mood I'm in when I see him, I always leave feeling somewhat better about my situation.

With every visit, I am reminded I won't wear my brace forever. And no matter what happens with my back, I'll still be Truth—not Truth who wears a back brace, or Truth who kind of dated Brendan Matthews, or even Charity's little sister. Just Truth Trendon: friend, sister, daughter, and, yes, scoli-extraordinaire.

I still don't like it, but my spine is a part of me, crooked or not.

And I can accept that.

How do you like them apples, Mr. Newton?

Acknowledgments

I would like to acknowledge that any disease or deformity is unique to the individual. I wore a back brace for two years (and later had corrective surgery), and though some of my experiences were similar to Truth's—such as not wanting people to know I had a back brace—my experience was different than what occurs in this novel. With that in mind, I would like to thank my twin sister, Sarah, for going through the brace process with me with a much more confident attitude and joyful outlook, and my brother John, whose jokes made those two years more tolerable. Without them, life would not be life. Unwavering gratitude also goes to my parents, Dennis and Monica, who always have supported me, not just in terms of the scoliosis running rampant in our family, but also for encouraging me to write. Love you.

Thank you to my editor Becky Herrick for her guidance and expertise, and to the whole team at Sky Pony, including Alison Weiss, Emma Dubin,

Joshua Barnaby, and Annie Lubinsky for their help in this exciting publishing process. A special thank you to my agent and second brain, Lisa Jane Weller, who has given me hope and served as a lighthouse when my thoughts have been lost at sea. And a huge shout out to the Nebraska Spine + Pain Center for their medical expertise and to Dr. John McClellan for providing a much more personable and pleasant experience than Truth has with her doctor.

Finally, thank you to my great love, Timothy Hruza, for always being at my side and never making me second guess my dreams. If gravity wasn't keeping my feet on the ground, your love and our dog would.

About the Author

Rachel Hruza has always loved everything related to books. She received an MA in creative writing from the University of Nebraska-Lincoln, and her short stories have been published in Scintilla and ScissorTale Review. This is her first novel, and was inspired by her own experience: Rachel was diagnosed with scoliosis at age eleven, she and her twin sister wore back braces through all of junior high, and Rachel had corrective surgery while in college. Rachel hails from the middle of the United States, where she teaches English at the local college, plays piano and guitar, and spends much of her spare time with her husband and their snaggle-toothed peeka-poo. Visit her online at www.rachelhruza.com.